I've Got You, Babe

Vanessa braced her hands against Crash's chest and pushed him away. "Oh my God," she said. "I can't do this!"

He sat back on his heels, took one of her hands in his, and asked the most simple of questions. "Why not?"

"Because . . . because you're a student! This could mean my job, could destroy my reputation. And I don't know you all that well, and you're related to Miss Eugenie, and . . ." She looked at him desperately.

He stood up, brushed off his knees, and looked down at her. "I scare you."

"Yes, you do."

"You want to keep me at a distance."

"Yes, I do."

"You still want me, but you don't want to take the risk."

"Yes, I—no, I don't. This is not a good idea."

"Oh, but I think it's the best idea to come around in a long time . . . "

ATTENTION: ORGANIZATIONS AND CORPORATIONS
Most Avon Books paperbacks are available at special quantity
discounts for bulk purchases for sales promotions, premiums, or
fund-raising. For information, please call or write:

Special Markets Department, HarperCollins Publishers, Inc.,
10 East 53rd Street, New York, N.Y. 10022–5299.
Telephone: (212) 207–7528. Fax: (212) 207-7222.

KAREN KENDALL

I've Got You, Babe

AVON BOOKS

An Imprint of HarperCollinsPublishers

**With special thanks to
skydiver Heather Caristo,
who is braver than I am**

AVON BOOKS
An Imprint of HarperCollins*Publishers*
10 East 53rd Street
New York, New York 10022-5299

Copyright © 2002 by Karen Moser
ISBN: 0-06-050232-0
www.avonromance.com

First Avon Books paperback printing: November 2002

Avon Trademark Reg. U.S. Pat. Off. and in Other Countries, Marca Registrada, Hecho en U.S.A.
HarperCollins ® is a registered trademark of HarperCollins Publishers Inc.

Printed in the U.S.A.

10 9 8 7 6 5 4 3 2 1

Chapter One

VANESSA TOWER jammed hard on the clutch of her PT Cruiser and shifted down into second gear. The machinery groaned and complained, even though it was only a year old.

Fitting that the car wanted to be here as little as she did. Yet here they were, inching up the side of a mountain at what was surely an eighty-five-degree angle. Worse, the top of the mountain—for she was determined to get to the top—promised no relief from stress.

No, at the top of the mountain was a person who didn't have the decency to respond to repeated requests by telephone, U.S. mail, or e-mail.

This man promised to be a louse extraordinaire. Vanessa frowned. *Brain*, she said to her brain, *nobody uses the word "louse" anymore.* "Louses," not to be confused with lice, went out with the what—

fifties? Her friend Shelly would laugh at her. Shelly teased her affectionately about how unhip she was, how her mind remained mired in the nineteenth century instead of acknowledging the fact that it lived in the twenty-first. But then Shel had a belly ring, and Vanessa had a Ph.D. in art history. She'd written her dissertation on Rodin, to whom her friend referred as "that rodent guy."

Brain! You're wandering again. Must get back to the business at hand. Namely what she was going to say to Christopher Dunmoor, the man on top of the bloody mountain she was scaling. "Mr. Dunmoor," she'd say, "the faces of the unforgiving look remarkably like sphincters as they age."

No, no, no! That was not an opening calculated to persuade the louse to do what his grandmother wanted. And she had to persuade him, for Miss Eugenie's sake.

Vanessa wrapped the Cruiser around another curve, keeping so close to the side of the mountain that she almost scraped the paint off. If she arrived at the top with deep gouges in the gorgeous shimmer of green, she'd sue the louse for criminal elusiveness. It sounded good, anyway.

She inhaled the crisp scents of pine and heather, and the danker smells of moss and loam. Though it was August, the temperature in Massachusetts for the past week had been balmy; in the lower-to-mid seventies. The higher she went up the mountain, the cooler the air became, raising slight goose bumps on her bare arms.

With a last corkscrew turn and groan from her usually purring car, Vanessa emerged from the rough trail and pulled into a clearing. In front of her sprawled a rustic cabin with a shingled roof, and upon the roof was a . . . dear God. Upon the roof was a . . . well. Upon the roof was the louse.

But what a glorious, glorious louse. Booted, denimed, and shirtless, he stood tall on the apex of the little house, swinging a hammer and glistening copper in the sun.

Vanessa pushed her wire-framed glasses up her nose and closed the mouth she hadn't been aware was open. She got out of the car, still staring.

The louse set his hammer down and ran a big hand through his mane of dirty gold hair. He picked up a large insulated cup, took several gulps, then sluiced a good amount of water from it down his back and chest.

Vanessa swallowed hard as the rivulets rushed, without foreplay, between his shoulder blades and down his spine into the waistband of his jeans, where they dampened the whole seat. The fabric molded instantly to his buttocks and thighs.

Oh, yes, he was a glorious louse. He had the arms of Atlas, with shoulders like . . . uh, boulders, and those buns were of truly mythical quality. He seemed to sense eyes upon him, if not salacious drool, and he turned on his heel to face her.

Dunmoor's eyes were a piercing green even from the roof. They were also cool, critical, and downright crotchety. "Whoever you are," he said, "go away."

His attitude was enough to dry her drool on the spot. Vanessa gaped at him, caught off guard. Then she put her hands on her hips, and said, "No."

He shot her an annoyed look. "Why not?"

The man had a nerve! "Because, Mr. Dunmoor, I've gone to great lengths to talk to you, and I'm not leaving until I've done so."

He shrugged. "Mr. Dunmoor was my grandfather."

Yes, he was. And that was the reason she'd inched her way up his antisocial mountain. They stared at each other for a long moment, during which she didn't move a muscle. She felt like an idiot in her pale green linen suit and stockings, and she glanced down to find a wayward ant scaling her leg much as she'd scaled the mountain.

She broke the mutual glare first, to flick the insect gently back into the grass, where it hightailed away from her cream sandals and the panty hose she'd hatched fresh from the package that morning.

"If you're not leaving"—he sighed—"then call me Crash."

Crash? *Crash?* What kind of ridiculous name was that? "As a matter of fact, Mr. D—uh, Crash, it's your grandfather I've come to discuss."

His green eyes flashed from cool to frozen. "I don't discuss my family with anyone."

Well, wasn't Miss Eugenie's Little Christopher an affable guy. But the old lady's troubled face swam into her memory, reminding Vanessa that she was here with a serious purpose. She sighed, and tried for a smile. "I'm Vanessa Tower. I teach at Seymour College, about half an hour southeast of here."

Crash Dunmoor eyed her quizzically and folded his delicious arms across his scrumptious chest. "And you came to see me on your way home from church?"

She flushed, feeling even sillier that she'd worn a suit. She'd donned it like armor, to protect her and help her feel professional. In the face of the louse and his cabin, the suit was ridiculous, like wearing pearls into a reggae bar.

"I've been doing research on your late grandfather's paintings for the past eight months, and in the process have become friends with your grandmother. I'm here at her request, and I'd like to talk with you."

"No." Crash turned away and reached for a roll of tar paper, dismissing her.

Louse. No, think 2001—butt-head. "Look, I've driven a long way. I've tried to contact you by mail and phone—"

He pivoted on one heel, holding the roll of tar paper at an angle. She could see through the long, dark tunnel of it to a small circle of blue sky. "Which part of 'no' did you not understand?"

Vanessa clamped her mouth shut and thought about snarling. This guy was not only arrogant, but rude. She counted to three and decided she wasn't going to let him run her off. But she had to get up to eye level with him. As it was, she felt like a pale green grasshopper at the feet of Zeus. She spied his ladder on the left side of the cabin, and prayed that he was fresh out of thunderbolts. She'd come up a mountain, so why not a ladder? It was a vertical kind of day.

"Fine," she said, and walked to the ladder. "However, I need to have a frank discourse with you, and I don't suppose you can work effectively with your fingers in your ears, so I regret that you may actually hear what I'm going to say. And it does, unfortunately, concern your family."

He'd turned away again. She set the ball of one sandaled foot on the lowest rung of the ladder, and found that in order to make it up to the next rung with her other foot, she was going to have to hike up her skirt. She slid the lousy thing over her knees and scrambled up.

As she got to the top rung and teetered out onto the roof on all fours, Crash was on his knees. He needed to assume that position more often.

She watched him slice through the tar paper with a utility knife and anchor the far side of it to the roof with a staple gun. Then he turned his head and stared incredulously at her. "What in the hell are you doing?"

She tilted her chin at him. Any minute now they were going to circle each other like strange dogs squaring off over a lawn. She figured they'd get straight to the growling, without any preliminary butt-sniffing.

"What are you doing?" he repeated.

"I told you. You may not want to listen, but I'm going to talk anyway." She gingerly straddled the roof's apex, keeping her knees bent.

"You're more likely to fall off the roof."

This was true, but she didn't feel like admitting it.

"Take off those shoes. They're slick on the bottom."

That was true also, but her panty hose were fresh from the package.

As if he'd read her mind, he told her, "Your life is worth more than four bucks at the supermarket. Take 'em off."

She sighed and did so. She'd probably have ripped them anyway, and it only brought her total lifelong expenditure on stockings from $8,233.00 to $8,237.00 and change. "I could help you hold that paper stuff down while you staple it."

He shook his head at her. "Stubborn wench." An unexpected flash of humor appeared for an instant in those startling eyes. "I hope you brought up a cold beer."

Wench? Beer? "Excuuuuuse me? Just who do you think you are?"

"You've informed me that I'm Crash Dunmoor. If it's up for debate, and I can assume some other identity, then I don't have to listen to what you're determined to tell me." A ray of hope crossed his face, and it gave him away.

True butt-heads didn't express hope; they blocked it out like the sun. The guy would listen to her, not push her off the roof. "Dunmoor," she began.

"Smith," he corrected. "Bob Smith."

"Try again," Vanessa said.

"Jones, Bridget?"

"Not falling for it."

"Damn." He accompanied the epithet with a wry grin.

So there was a sense of humor buried under the avalanche of attitude and muscle. Vanessa took a couple of wobbly steps onto the roof, which was hot under her feet, and he put out a long, lean hand to steady her. *Hmmm. Maybe he's even partially human.*

"Sit there," he ordered, pointing at a spot near the chimney.

She narrowed her eyes. *Maybe not.*

"It's the safest place. You can lean back against the chimney."

Okay, borderline human. She made her way there and released his hand, which was wired with bad-boy arrows that fired at all her neurons. Her hormones clucked like a gaggle of hysterical hens, which was humiliating. Good thing he didn't know.

She took a moment to slam the door to the chicken coop, only to look up at those damned green eyes of his and sense a fox sniffing around the blasted birds. This was bad, very bad. Badder than LeRoy Brown. *Speak, Vanessa. And not about Shelly's favorite retro song.*

"So . . ." prompted Crash, his mane of hair wild in the rooftop wind.

"So!" *Tell him why you're here, you lunatic.* Her smile was too bright. She opened her mouth only to have it filled immediately with her own hair. She pulled it out and twisted it back into a knot at the nape of her neck, then squashed the mass between her neck and the rough brick of the chimney. She pushed her wire-framed glasses to the top of her nose.

"Even if you only read the first lines of the letter you ignored, you know that your grandmother Eugenie is drawing up her will."

Crash rocked back on his heels. Impressive, given the fact that he was squatting. "I think my silence has indicated that I'm not interested in it."

"Point made. But Miss Eugenie wants you to know exactly what you're turning up your nose at. Your grandfather's paintings, as a collection, are now worth upwards of 2.6 million dollars."

Crash rocked forward again and whistled. "So the old coot turned his yellow ocher to green." Next came a careless shrug. "It still has nothing to do with me."

Vanessa, still choking at hearing the great Thomas Dunmoor called an "old coot," said, "It has *everything* to do with you. You're the last of the Dunmoor line. You'll ultimately decide whether or not the paintings stay together as a collection or are sold piece by piece. You have an obligation to educate yourself about them, and a duty to pass on that education to the public." *Aaaack*. Now didn't *that* sound stuffy and righteous.

Crash let out a short, unamused bark of laughter. "Obligation and duty aren't concepts I entertain much, Vanessa. And I don't feel the faintest desire to carry on either my grandfather's legacy or his seed. He was a stubborn old bastard who had some talent with a brush. So what?"

"Have some respect! Have some heart, for heaven's sake." The words flew out of her mouth before Vanessa could recall them. Her skills as a negotiator had shredded faster than her stockings. What was wrong with her?

Crash leaned forward and grabbed her arm, his eyes dangerous. "Careful, Miz Tower." His fingers dug into her flesh, and she pulled away. "You really don't know what you're dealing with here. Have some respect, you say? Have some respect for a man who didn't bother to respect the truth?

Have some *heart*? Thomas Dunmoor pulled it barehanded right out of my chest twelve years ago. Then he stomped on it in a pair of Timberland boots just like the ones I'm wearing."

He took a long, measured lungful of mountain air. "So you see, Miz Tower, I don't give a rat's ass for the great Thomas Dunmoor or his heritage."

She blinked.

"And I don't give a damn about what it's worth, either."

You're nuts, but I think I might respect that about you.

"You're wasting your time." He bent over the tar paper again and added punctuation to his words with the stapler. *Kathunk. Kathunk. Kathunk.*

Good, Nessa. Now how are you going to change his mind? She needed to go buy a copy of *How to Win Friends and Influence People.* And read it fast. Miss Eugenie was expecting better than this.

She thought of the old lady, clutching her multicolored sweater around her bony shoulders. "I want to see him," she'd said wistfully. "But that may be too much to hope for. Thomas—we both—hurt him so badly. And now it's been so long. So many wasted years."

Miss Eugenie hadn't seemed to want to talk about it, and Nessa didn't like to pry, so she still didn't know what had happened. All she knew was that twelve years was a long time to hold a grudge against a sweet little old lady.

She looked for some kind of family resemblance

between Crash and his grandmother, but could find none. Miss Eugenie was tiny—birdlike—with a cloud of perfectly white hair that had once been dark, like her eyes. Her nose was straight except for the very tip, which age and gravity had pulled down a bit. And one of the most endearing things about Eugenie Dunmoor was that her small ears flared from the sides of her head. Instead of trying to pull her hair forward to hide them, she wore dangling silver earrings that only accentuated them.

Crash was at least six-foot-four-inches, and sported a crooked, tapering nose that on anyone else might have been ugly. His ears were barely visible under all that hair. He looked like a Viking on a raid. She was picturing him in a horned cap when she realized that he was speaking to her.

"Pardon?"

"I asked if you'd pass me that box of staples."

She did so. "You don't look like either of your grandparents." From pictures, she'd seen that Thomas Dunmoor had also been dark-haired, though he'd had blue eyes.

"Nope. They used to call me the Throwback." His mouth twisted slightly.

"The Throwback?"

"Nordic ancestors. On the Dunmoor side, actually. I'm the only one in the family who got the recessive genes."

They don't look at all recessive on you.

"Not my father, not Ste—" he shut his mouth,

jamming staples into the gun with more force than necessary.

Ste—? Steven? His uncle? His brother? One glance at the jumping muscle in his jaw told her it would be useless to ask. There was quite a mystery behind the rift in this family.

But anyway, the horned cap wasn't too far off the mark. Come to think of it, Crash would look very fine in the horned cap and his Timberlands and absolutely nothing else. *Oh no. Shelly is having way too much influence over me these days . . .*

"Crash," she said, focusing again on the task at hand. "You may not care about the money, and you may have hated your grandfather, but—"

"I didn't hate him." Crash put the stapler aside. "I loved that old bastard."

"All right." She absorbed this. "The fact is that your grandmother loves *you*. And she'd like to see you."

"That's not going to happen. She made her choice twelve years ago."

"What do you mean? A choice between you and her husband? That's awful. She wouldn't have been able to win either way."

Crash shrugged.

"She'd like to discuss the will in person."

"No. End of discussion. Tell her to leave the damn paintings to someone else."

"She's considering that, but she'd rather leave them to you."

Crash shook his head. Then he turned his back on her and reached for the roll of tar paper again.

"She's very ill," Vanessa said quietly. "Colon cancer."

His arm froze in midair, then fell to his side. He faced her again, and the hollows under his eyes suddenly looked pronounced. He was silent for a long moment. "What's the prognosis?"

"I don't know the specifics, except that they're taking immediate action. After that, it's a question mark. As her next of kin, you'd be entitled to the results and further details."

The pupils at the centers of his remarkable eyes widened, then contracted to pinpoints. The green of his irises deepened. And Vanessa decided that Christopher Dunmoor was, indeed human—just trying hard not to be.

She put her hand on his arm. "Why don't you drive down with me? I'll take you to the hospital."

"Thanks," Crash said. "But when I go, I'll go alone."

Chapter Two

HE COULD SEE only the top of her auburn
head, the part slightly crooked, as she descended
his ladder with her sandals hooked over one
thumb. Well, he could also see the slim, creamy
expanse of half of each thigh, punctuated by very
cute knees, since she had to ruck up her skirt
slightly to reach each rung. And if he weren't a
gentleman, he could peer out beyond her head
and that intriguing part line to the roundness of
her sweet little ass.

It was that ass, and the crooked side part, and
the wire-framed glasses that saved Ms. Vanessa
Tower from looking like a tall, thin, slightly awkward stick of celery. Even the timbre of her voice
indicated that she was made of rigid, stringy stuff.
He wondered if she'd be crunchy spread with

peanut butter, and cast the image aside before it got too interesting.

He'd just been accosted by strong moral fiber on his own roof. Strong moral fiber with disturbing news and unwelcome opinions.

She got to the bottom of the ladder and pulled her skirt down over her knees, which was a damned shame. Miss Celery had nice stems. She held on to the ladder with one hand while she slipped her sandals back on with the other, and picked her way through the grass to the old-fashioned-looking Cruiser.

Straighten that part and pull it right down the center of her head, add some length to her skirt and a white ruffle to her collar, and she could step into a cameo pin. One with a jade background. The vintage lines of the car suited her.

Her suit was fussy, her glasses were prim, but the ever-so-slight zigzag on top of her head indicated that perhaps Miss Tower wasn't as precise and rigid as she seemed.

Her sales skills were nonexistent, but she certainly seemed to care about his grandmother. At the thought of Eugenie, he frowned. Slowly he collected the miscellaneous tools from the roof and made his own way down the ladder as Vanessa Tower's vehicle disappeared from view.

Crash tossed his tools into the small shed behind the cabin, wiped his face on the T-shirt he'd discarded, and went inside.

The little house was musty, as usual, and he left the door wide open to let the fresh air in. He knew he'd regret it later because of the mosquitoes and flies, but the moldy, stuffy air had to be chased away, like unpleasant memories.

He went to the little porcelain sink and filled a mason jar with water before flopping on the daybed he'd spread with a Navajo blanket. He drank half the water while staring at the ridiculous chair the previous occupant had left behind. It had once been a rocker, but one of the runners had been replaced by two Shaker legs, so that the chair neither rocked nor sat entirely steady. It was the most peculiar repair job Crash had ever seen, but it was barely functional, like the rest of the cabin.

The place had been built in defiance of any construction code. Neither a beam nor a rafter was level; not a single cabinet door hung straight; the rough-hewn mantel was six inches wider on the left side than the right. Everything was off-kilter, but the cabin possessed an odd charm.

Granted, the charm did little to replace the stove burner (one of two) that didn't work, or the freezer (part of a dorm-sized refrigerator) that ran a steady temperature of thirty-eight degrees Fahrenheit, but Crash didn't much care. It kept four beers at a time reasonably chilled. He'd owned the place for two months now, and hadn't gotten around to buying new equipment. All of his time and cash went into his latest venture.

Crash was in the business of encouraging people to defy their mortality. It didn't sit well with him to contemplate terminal illness, just as it didn't sit well with him to relive the past.

He spent his days teaching witless thrill-seekers to sky-dive. There was nothing like jumping out of a perfectly good airplane to remind you that your life was your own. You were free as a bird, reminded of your humanity only by the skin of your face flapping and the tiny kernel of uncertainty that this time you might not make it.

The earth spread out below you like a funky patchwork quilt, and it was yours. You might be flying by the seat of your pants, but you were King of the Wind, Emperor of the Air. And you were free-falling, and the rush was enormous . . . and then you pulled the cord that sent your 'chute billowing out behind. You knew an instant of exultation that you were going to make it, and rode that high for a few moments longer. Then that bitch, gravity, pulled you back to earth.

The birds, damn it all, still had it better. A bird could escape the clutches of gravity simply by dipping and lifting its wings. A bird could float on the currents, drifting for hours, not simply minutes. And a bird could skim close to the ground, dropping ammunition on the hapless without guilt.

Human beings will always be bound by gravity and

guilt, Crash thought. The two inescapable forces. Funny how guilt functioned as mental gravity.

Here he was, twelve years later, still bound by guilt. For he didn't like to think of Grandmother Eugenie frail and helpless in the grip of some terminal disease. He wasn't sure he wanted to see her—hell, he knew he didn't want to see her like that. How could you maintain hurt and anger in the face of helplessness? How useless, how small, emotion seemed beside the permanence of looming death.

She wants to see you. Vanessa Tower's voice echoed in his mind.

Does she? What does she expect to see? The face of the boy who ran? The bitterness of twelve years ago? Grief? Or impassivity. Or greed?

Perhaps she thinks I'll visit her out of sheer greed. Crash's mouth twisted.

He wasn't sure why Vanessa Tower had chosen to get involved in all of this. She claimed to have become friends with Eugenie during the past eight months. But why would his grandmother have sent *her* out here? Surely a courier could have delivered the same message. What was her story?

He drained most of the water from the mason jar and gripped the cool glass in both hands, hanging it between his knees. He stared at his own fingers, brown from the sun and callused from both work and play. They were magnified through the glass of the jar, as his grandfather's brushes had been. Yellow ocher, cadmium blue, vermilion red. The smell of turpentine. The black nail of the second finger on the old man's left hand, where he'd hit it with a claw hammer.

Crash had raised the jar to gulp down the rest of the water when his arm froze. Thomas Dunmoor had kept his artist's brushes in mason jars. "Hell and damnation!"

He threw the jar and its contents into the fireplace.

"You look like a human scoop of pistachio ice cream," Shelly said, as she slid a calorie-laden iced café mocha in front of Vanessa.

"Thanks."

Shel wiped her hands on the seat of her jeans and leaned on the bar of her coffee shop. "Or an upside-down carrot."

"Stop it with the compliments already," Vanessa told her.

"It's just so . . . *Talbot's*. Yeesh."

"I know you're secretly conniving to borrow it."

"Yeah, that's it."

Shelly had long dark hair cut in a hip, sexy, uneven shag. She knew exactly how to wear a short, tight T-shirt so that it showed off her silver belly ring to perfection.

Vanessa didn't envy her the belly ring; just the blasé attitude it required to sport such a thing.

Shel took a gulp of her own iced coffee, and left

a screaming red lip print on her tall paper cup. Lip print number seven thousand four hundred and thirty-nine.

Vanessa had once witnessed a man *pay* for one of Shel's empty, lip-printed cups. He had actually forked over five dollars for it, since the print in question was so perfect and luscious. He was a complete fool, but Shel had that effect on men.

"So," her friend asked, "how did your trek up the mountain go?"

"I'm not sure. He's . . . quite something."

"What do you mean by that? Is the jerk going to visit his poor grandmother?"

"Yes, I think he will. He's not a jerk, exactly. But he's not *not* one, either."

Shelly stared at her. "Either he is or he isn't."

"Okay, then. He's not."

"So he's just a really, really nice guy who won't return phone calls or answer letters or e-mail."

"There's some mysterious family rift," Vanessa told her. "Something terrible happened twelve years ago that he hasn't gotten over."

"Ah. A really, really nice guy *who holds a grudge* and won't return phone calls or answer letters or e-mail. And you're defending him, so . . ."

"I'm not defending him—"

". . . he must be incredibly hot."

"Shelly! I—he—"

"Yes or no?"

"He's not hard to look at."

"I knew it!"

"But that wouldn't change my opinion of him."

"Oh, of course not."

Vanessa glared at Shelly as she excused herself to take a customer's order for a large no-fat vanilla cappuccino. The woman was a trip. And an amazingly quick study of people.

She'd met her while coming here to get her nightly caffeine fixes, necessary for preparing her lectures and grading painfully boring student papers and exams. They had nothing in common besides a certain cynicism and a love of coffee, which freed them up to talk about anything and everything. Neither could imagine living her life as the other did, but Shel was fascinated by what she thought of as the highfalutin' intellectual life.

Vanessa, on the other hand, sometimes thought wistfully of what it would be like to live unencumbered by academia and its inherent infrastructure of criticism. No pressure, no publish-or-perish mania, no endless committees on this or that. What heaven!

"The people-watching is great," Shelly had admitted. "But the financial pressure is hell. Gotta make your rent, gotta pay your employees, gotta meet the electric bill. There've been months where I lived on Top Ramen and peanut butter and jelly. Didn't seem totally fair, given that my customers were getting real cream and imported Sri Lankan cinnamon . . . but hey, you do what you have to."

Vanessa sipped her iced mocha and thought about the comfort of a regular paycheck. The problem was that for an assistant professor without tenure, the regular paycheck wasn't guaranteed to last. And tenure was dependent upon publishing a book and passing the gauntlet of the promotions and tenure committee.

The good news was that Princeton University Press had shown interest in her Thomas Dunmoor book. The bad news was—

"Why, Dr. Tower, what a pleasant surprise."

The bad news was suddenly standing in front of her: Creighton Conch, chair of the Fine Arts Department. Vanessa dredged up a smile. "Dr. Conch. How are you?"

"Fine, fine. Preparing for the fall semester, as I'm sure you are." He spoke imperiously to Shelly—"A double latte"—as if she were no-account help.

Vanessa resisted the urge to add "please," for him, and murmured that she was indeed busy.

"I notice that your Rodin seminar is short two members. I don't know if we'll be able to offer it, my dear."

Your pre-Raphaelite course only has six students signed up. But you wouldn't dream of canceling that, you old windbag. "Oh, well, I'll just have to keep my fingers crossed that we get two more signed up in the next few days," she chirped.

"Always a good attitude. Thatta girl."

Why, you patronizing s.o.b. She half expected him to pat her head.

"So, Vanessa, have you had a chance to broach that little matter I spoke to you about?"

"Mrs. Dunmoor has been in the hospital for the past six weeks, Dr. Conch. It didn't seem appropriate . . ."

"Yes, yes, very sad. Not to be unfeeling, but time may be of the essence in this case."

She opened her mouth, then shut it again, before she said anything too pithy and honest.

"I realize your feelings are delicate in regard to this matter, so perhaps it would be best if I were to accompany you in a friendly visit to Mrs. Dunmoor, whereupon I could plant the seed of generosity in her mind."

"I—I—"

"Is tomorrow convenient for you, Dr. Tower? Shall we say elevenish?"

You unspeakable slime. You testament to beastliness. You grasping, grunting warthog. "Eleven," Vanessa agreed, faintly. He was the chair, and she was an assistant professor.

"Wonderful. I'll pick you up outside the slide library." Dr. Conch accepted his latte from Shelly with a supercilious nod and no tip, and departed the shop.

"Asshole," Shel muttered. "Gee, I wonder how that laxative tablet got in his coffee?"

"Shelly, you didn't!"

"I damn sure thought about it. So the scumbag wants your old lady to donate those paintings to the college?"

Vanessa nodded, miserable.

"And he's going to use your relationship with her, then take the credit. I see why you climbed the mountain today."

"Yes. And if the louse doesn't come down soon, I'll climb it again."

Chapter Three

"Mrs. Dunmoor, may I introduce Dr. Creighton Conch, chair of Fine Arts at Seymour College." Vanessa got the words out in polite tones.

"Dr. Conch. How nice of you to visit." Eugenie extended a thin hand, which looked as if it had been covered in wrinkled parchment paper.

"Enchanted to meet you." Creepy Creighton lifted it to his lips. "Our dear Dr. Tower has spoken nonstop of you around the department."

What a whopper. She'd done nothing of the sort.

Miss Eugenie assessed him instantly and lowered her sparse lashes over a coy smile. "Has she?"

"Yes, indeed. You've been so helpful with the research for her book."

True. Okay, he was one for one now.

"She's a lovely person. How could I not help?"

Eugenie Dunmoor's skin might be as pale as the hospital sheets, but her personality made up for it. Vanessa repressed a chuckle when she saw that the cheesy mallard print of two days ago now had a caricature taped over it. It was rapidly drawn on computer paper, and depicted a doctor hanging from a noose. The noose was formed by his own stethoscope, and he hung from a peg on the door of his office. A patient looked at him with revenge in her eye, and the caption read, "say 'ah.'"

Eugenie had also had someone supply her with a portable CD system, which was playing big band tunes from the forties. She lay propped against at least five pillows, and in her lap was a large basket with knitting spilling out of it.

As she and Creepy Creighton exchanged small talk, Vanessa eyed the basket with curiosity. In the eight months she'd known Mrs. Dunmoor, she'd never once seen her knit. Come to think of it, she hadn't once seen even an afghan lying over a sofa in her home, and the multicolored sweater she was so fond of had been made for her as a gift by a friend.

"Your late husband's work is marvelous, both as a monument to American painting itself and as an inspiration to the young artists and students of art history today . . ."

Dr. Conch wound up for his preliminary pitch.

Miss Eugenie's face reflected serenity as she placed her hands on her knitting. She took the long needles into her right hand and twiddled them like a pair of chopsticks, while her left hand dug under the wool.

Vanessa had never seen a true knitter handle the needles like that. Something was just a little "off" here.

". . . his skill with not only the brush, but the palette knife . . ." Conch droned, and then said a hasty "Excuse me!" before he let out a bellow of a sneeze.

"Bless you, dear," exclaimed Miss Eugenie. And then her basket sprouted a couple of whiskers.

Nessa covered her mouth with her hand and tried to repress the sudden shake of her shoulders.

The old lady shot her a glance positively dewy with innocence.

Dr. Conch scrubbed rather violently at his schnoz. "As I said, these paintings are quite a legacy—" Haaah—Choooo! "—to American painting—" HaChoo . . .

Vanessa squashed her laughter, but then Miss Eugenie's knitting basket sprouted the tip of a tail, and she had to fake a coughing fit.

How had the old lady managed to smuggle her cat into the hospital? The nurses would have a coronary if they found out. Not that Vanessa would tell. First of all, she understood the need for Eugenie to see her pet. And second, Creepy

Creighton richly deserved to be punished this way.

His adenoids obviously inflamed, he forged on in his quest for the collection, doing his dishonorable best to be subtle. "Bissus Dudsmoor, have you thought about the future of the paintings?"

Cat dander notwithstanding, she was going to make him sweat. "Why, what do you mean, Dr. Conch?"

"Ahhh—chooo. Beg pardon. Er, we all know that saying about art imitating life. It does! And for the most part, it's a poor second. Yet art does have one advantage over fleeting existence . . ."

"And that would be—?" Miss Eugenie continued to play dumb.

"Well, you know." Creepy Creighton laughed uneasily.

She simply cocked her head and looked at him askance.

"Its uh, *permanence*. Its ability to commudicate to later generations the transient dature of a moment, caught in tibe."

"I see. You mean that my late husband's paintings aren't subject to mortality, as I am. That they can't be eaten up by . . . shall we just say it? Cancer. As I am."

"Oh, no! I wasn't—haaa—choo—"

"Yes, you were." Miss Eugenie smiled gently, but her eyes had turned flat, like a shark's. "And I imagine you have some sort of eloquent recommendation to make concerning my husband's work. Out with it, then."

Vanessa almost felt sorry for Dr. Conch, who'd turned the exact shade of the petunias in her window box.

"Why, I merely thought—that is, you might wish to consider—" He interrupted himself with another violent sneeze.

The old lady regarded him sweet-faced, while her hand moved furiously under the knitting, sending a fresh batch of cat dander into the air.

"Seymour College, as I'b sure you know, has a very fine art museub. In the light of the work Biss Tower has dud on your husbad, what better institution to leave the collegtion to?"

Vanessa wanted to die of shame. She sent a silent look of apology toward Miss Eugenie, and strode to the window, mentally propelling herself out of it.

"I *do* have a grandson, Dr. Conch."

"Blahchooo! Ub, you do?"

"Yes, she does." A deep, grim voice came from the doorway.

Vanessa whirled to find Crash Dunmoor leaning against the wall, eyeing her as if she were cockroach dung. Judging by his expression, he didn't find Creepy Creighton even that valuable.

Oh God. Oh, no. Now he'll think I'm part of this.

He wore dry jeans today, with a blue polo shirt that did little to disguise his solid torso. She could see each ridge of muscle along his flat stomach, and though he wore no cologne, he simply reeked of machismo.

Your average male with a shaggy blond mane would look like an overgrown Beach Boy, but Crash Dunmoor looked like a wild, testosterone-driven legend. The legend of her fall.

Her hormones clucked again, nervously flapping their wings. Why did they have to do the Funky Chicken every time this guy showed up?

His expression softened when he turned his gaze to Miss Eugenie. "Hi, Grandmother. It's been a while, hasn't it?"

Her mouth trembled. "Oh, Christopher, yes it has."

He stood a bit awkwardly in the doorway for a moment, then moved to her bedside. He covered her hand with his own and bent to kiss her cheek. "What's a nice girl like you doing in a place like this? Too much dancing?"

"Always, my dear. I'll never learn to behave." Two tears rolled down her papery cheeks.

Vanessa forgot her own mortification as tangible emotion arced between the two: love dipped and wheeled there like a gull on the shoreline, yet it remained a silhouette on the horizon. Waves of regret pounded the sand, yet couldn't wash away every particle of anger and misunderstanding.

What was this whole rift about? Why hadn't they just sat down and talked it through? She didn't understand the concept of a twelve-year silence between two people who had obvious love and respect for each other.

Miss Eugenie had closed her eyes, but more tears squeezed past her lids and rolled down her cheeks. Crash kept her hand in his and sat next to her on the white hospital blankets. He took a tissue from a box on the nightstand and dabbed at her face.

After twelve years, they deserved some privacy, especially from the likes of Creepy Creighton, who looked as if he were about to introduce himself. "Blaaachooo!" he said instead.

"We were just on our way out!" Vanessa grabbed him by the elbow and dragged him to the door.

"Yeah. I'll bet you were," said Crash, not turning his head.

His grandmother opened her eyes. "Oh, dear, I'm forgetting myself. Christopher, meet Dr. Creighton Conch, chair of Fine Arts at Seymour College. And I believe you met Dr. Tower yesterday."

Dean Conch raised his brows at her. Great. Now she was going to have to explain her actions to him, as well as to Dunmoor. The day was shaping up even better than she'd originally thought.

Crash raked his eyes over Dr. Conch—and his absurd pocket handkerchief—with an almost imperceptible nod, then skewered Vanessa in his next glance. Any humor or tolerance from the day before had vanished, leaving his green eyes cool, suspicious, and protective of his grandmother. "Yes, we've met. And believe me, we're going to meet again."

Chapter Four

"GRANDMA EUGENIE, why does your knitting basket have a tail?" Crash asked with a chuckle.

"Why, all the better to wag at you, to show you how glad I am that you've come." His grandmother stuffed the telltale tail back inside.

"Uh-huh. And why does it have a paw poking out of the far left corner?"

She tilted her chin. "Why, all the better to greet you with." She poked gently at the paw, and it disappeared.

"Right. Grandma, why did your basket just meow?"

She raised her liquid brown eyes to his in a silent plea. "Why, that will just have to be our secret, won't it?"

He sighed. "Your secret's not exactly hygienic, you know."

"Pooh. Who cares?"

"This is a hospital."

"It's a horror shop where they do beastly things to one. Allow me my small pleasures."

"How did your small pleasure get here?"

"With my friend Mabel. She's gone to the library to get me the latest saucy romances, but she'll be back soon, and then my knitting will depart with her."

"Does your knitting have a name?"

"Lancelot."

Crash's lips twitched. "Does he hang out on a round table?"

"No," said Eugenie. "He lances me a lot."

Crash laughed. He'd forgotten how entertaining his grandmother could be. "You could have him declawed."

"Absolutely not. Then he wouldn't be able to frighten the maid with half-eaten birds. He'd lose all sense of purpose and identity, and go into a terrible depression." She plucked at the white cotton blankets covering her ribs and absently tossed a tuft of fuzz to the floor.

Crash had a feeling she wasn't talking about her cat any longer. He cursed himself for a bastard. How could he not have visited for so long?

"Grandma," he said, "you haven't lost your claws. Not by a long shot."

Her head jerked. "Keep your observations to yourself, Christopher." But she smiled anyhow. "Or you'd better be wary of what I bring home to scare *you* with."

He grinned. "I don't scare easily."

Her eyes danced. "Is that so? Let's see . . . what could I hunt down that would frazzle you?" She thought a moment. "Oh, yes. I believe I have it."

Crash raised his eyebrows at her.

"I'm thinking of a very dangerous animal, one that pretends to be domesticated, but actually functions mostly on instinct and sheer intelligence. She's sleek, with long legs, smooth hair, and polished claws. She only bites occasionally, but when she does—watch out."

"I don't know," he said. "I give up."

"A woman! Ha—when you snap your brows together like that, you look like an angry lion."

"Thank you. But I'm definitely not on the hunt for a woman."

"Told you it would horrify you." Eugenie grinned.

Crash knew that all this lighthearted banter flowed between them to disguise deeper currents. The ones with an ugly undertow that might pull them down into painful topics. But it was no use avoiding them forever.

"Grandma," he murmured, taking her hand again, "I'm sorry I stayed away so long. I'm so sorry."

Her lips flattened, but in regret, not anger. "I thought you'd at least come for your grandfather's funeral."

"I had moved, and your letter didn't get forwarded for weeks. By the time I got it, a month had passed. Then I left the country."

"I got your damned flowers and tried to trace you through them. But you'd paid cash." She removed her hand from his and raked it through her hair.

"Then I hired a detective, but fired him just as fast. I told myself that you had every right to your privacy, that you'd show up when you were good and ready." Her mouth trembled again. "That was the hardest thing I've had to do since Tom died."

He closed his eyes. *Damn it, Grandma.* "I always thought it'd be easy for you to locate me if you wanted to. And took it as a sign when no guy in a trench coat ever showed up on my various doorsteps. I knew you had the money to hire someone . . ." He met her gaze levelly. "I just thought it was lack of interest."

Eugenie balled her hand into a weak fist and brought it down on his jeans-clad knee. For the first time, she looked angry. "You were a stupid, stupid boy! I was a silly old bat, but that doesn't excuse you. I've loved you ever since your pointed head emerged into this world, and you were a *homely* little critter."

He choked on an unexpected laugh. "Grandma, are you saying I was an ugly baby?"

She nodded. "Like a red, squalling human raisin. I fell in love with you immediately. Your mother took one look at you and said you obviously weren't done cooking yet. She told them to put you back in."

Crash stared at her, his mouth working.

"She was kidding, of course," Eugenie reassured him. "Never lost her sense of humor, that woman."

At least not until she and his father had died together in a tribal uprising in Mali. Crash and his brother Steven had been too young to understand where Mali was, much less what their parents were doing there or why they'd been involved in the Peace Corps. Their grandparents had raised them ever since.

"Don't worry," Eugenie reassured him. "Steven was an ugly baby, too."

Mr. Chiseled? No way.

"He was just as raisinlike, but not as loud as you were. I remember him blowing a lot of silent spit bubbles. You howled."

Crash shook his head. "Grandma—"

"At least you boys began to get cute after a week or so. Your father, bless him, looked like an enraged shar-pei for the first six months of his life."

"Grandma, people tend to be a little sensitive about babies. I hope you don't go around describing other people's children like this?"

"It's far too late in life for me to learn tact, Christopher. Don't even bother."

On that note, a nurse came in to check his grandmother's vitals. Crash paced the room, uncomfortable with the fact that they needed to be checked. Once she'd left, Eugenie patted the edge of the bed again. "Makes you antsy, eh? Dials and needles and hoses. Disease, mortality. That's why you came, isn't it? You didn't want to read about my funeral in a forwarded letter. You're not here because of any damn will, are you, Christopher?"

He shook his head.

"Eloquent, like your grandfather, I see. Except that you're stronger in some ways. You've got the same stiff neck, but you're capable of bending yours. I never heard him apologize to anyone his entire life. It simply wasn't in him. It's not really in you, either, yet you told me you were sorry." Her bony chest rose and fell.

"Tom would have apologized, my dear. He searched the whole rest of his life for the ability to do it, but the thoughts and words stuck in his craw. The only way he could express himself was through the brush. You'll find his message to you in those paintings, Christopher. He said what he could, in the single solitary way he could say it. I know you don't care about the money, my dear. But please study the work."

The neck Crash had bent just for her stiffened again. "Grandma Eugenie, I don't know the first thing about squiggles on canvas, and I don't want to. How can you say his apology lies in the paintings?"

"Because I knew him. We were married for forty-seven years, and after that amount of time I could read him like the morning paper. I knew his secret visual alphabet like nobody else."

"That doesn't mean I know it—or want to know it."

"He mourned you both, my dear. I don't know how to make you believe that. Both of you. Not just Steven. Oh, he could always *talk* to Steven more easily, since they had the art in common. But he didn't love you any less. Just didn't know quite what to do with you . . .

"You were larger than life, and full of adventures you hadn't yet undertaken. You challenged him instead of worshiping him, and he didn't know what to do with that. He'd been worshiped for so damned long!"

Crash shook his head. "I don't think—"

His grandmother cut him off, as desperate to say these words as she was to continue breathing. She'd probably had them stored up for years. "There you were, four inches taller and with every bit as much heart and soul, but in his eyes you were *misusing* them. He didn't understand that your version of painting was to make marks in God's landscape, that your version of music was the libretto of a mountain stream. I tried to explain it to him . . ." She wiped her eyes. "But then the accident occurred, and he said those things, and you were gone. Gone for good."

Crash rolled his stiff neck around his shoulders. It was getting stiffer by the second, and he didn't know what to say to her.

For some reason, he found himself thinking about Vanessa Tower.

"Christopher," his grandmother said, "if Tom could have shot those words clean out of the air before they reached your ears, he would have. He didn't mean them. They were said in shock and anger and pain. You have to believe that. You have to look at the paintings. Study them as a series. Please."

He rolled his shoulders, since he didn't think he could move his neck another millimeter. It ached, sending shooting pains to the back of his cortex.

He walked to Grandma Eugenie's bed again, took her hand, and kissed it. "I'll think about it, okay?"

Chapter Five

VANESSA KEPT her hands clenched in her lap so that she wouldn't pluck Creepy Creighton's spotted hankie from his breast pocket and stuff it down his pompous throat.

They glided up Main Street in his navy Cadillac, and she stared out the passenger-side window, tuning out the purplish drone of his voice. They passed the Ambrose Apothecary, the First Methodist Church of Ambrose, the small branch of Fleet Bank, and Shelly's coffee shop, Joe to Go.

Seymour College was nestled in a valley at the west end of town and populated by female students only. It was one of the last of the dying tradition of women's colleges, and could afford to remain single sex only by virtue of its massive endowment.

The college had a somewhat odd relationship

with the rest of Ambrose. On the one hand, it kept the town alive economically: three thousand students and a staff of around four hundred supplied a great deal of business.

On the other hand, the townspeople resented what they saw as the elitism of the school, whether intellectual, social, or financial.

Creepy Creighton was a staff member who didn't help this image. ". . . ergo," he puffed at her, "I perceive a conflict of interest."

Ergo? For God's sake, she might not be exactly hip, but at least she didn't use the word "ergo."

"Dr. Conch," she said, "Mrs. Dunmoor asked me, as a special favor, to persuade her grandson to visit her. How could I refuse? Especially in light of all the help she's given me on the book?"

"I simply don't understand how you failed to mention the grandson to me."

"I . . . didn't see the point. They hadn't even spoken for twelve years, until yesterday."

"He's very inconvenient."

Oh, well, don't let a human life get in your way. She said nothing aloud.

"If we were living a dramatic novel," Conch said, "this would be the precise chapter in which he'd be bumped off."

Her mouth fell open.

"Only joking, of course."

Of course. Mwahh ha ha ha. She shivered, even more appalled than usual at Creepy Creighton.

"What I need to know, my dear Vanessa, is where your loyalty lies."

"My loyalty?"

He nodded and stroked his chin. "Mrs. Dunmoor was very helpful with your book. Naturally you wish to repay the favor. But Seymour College is your employer, and would greatly benefit from acquiring the Dunmoor Collection."

Unbelievable. He might as well drag her into a dark alley with a switchblade and scrape the message across her throat. If she didn't know so many Ph.D.s who were waiting tables, she'd quit there and then.

Aloud she said, "Dr. Conch, the decision rests entirely with Mrs. Dunmoor, and though we've become friends, I have no influence over her. What I *can* tell you is that her grandson has no interest in even seeing the paintings. He's made that clear."

She dug her nails into her palms and kept her thumbs firmly locked over her fingers, which were itching to rip off his navy blue glasses and smack his well-fed face. *Yeesh.* She was going to have to attend an anger management class.

"Excellent. Looks like an unreliable runabout, doesn't he? With all that unkempt hair."

Depends what you want to rely on him for. "Umm," she said. Thank God they were approaching the Fine Arts Building, where she could escape into the slide library.

The chair pulled the fat Caddy into his designated parking spot and cut the engine. "We'll need to meet again over the next few days to discuss tactics," he told her.

Tactics. Oh, nice. "I'm going to be awfully busy with course preparation and all . . ."

"Classes don't start for two weeks. I'm sure you can spare an hour here and there."

Sigh. "Of course." She hitched her tan nylon bag over her shoulder and walked crisply away from the baddy and his Caddy. The sinus headache from hell was settling in behind her eyeballs, squeezing them with a vengeance. She'd dump her bag in her office, grab a couple of ibuprofen, and retreat to the blessed darkness of one of the viewing rooms in the slide library.

She arrived at the smoked glass door of the Fine Arts Building, tugged it open, and stepped onto the mint green tiles of the hallway. She bent her head and opened the flap of her nylon bag, fishing for her keys. Retrieving them, she pulled her head out just in time to miss colliding with a solid chest in a sky-blue knit shirt. The chest belonged to Crash Dunmoor, and he was blocking her office door.

She backed up a step, but not before inhaling his scent. A potent mix of warm skin, laundry detergent, and eau de muscle, it knocked her off-balance. *Oh, God. What is he doing here?*

"Hello, Ms. Tower."

Frozen courtesy didn't sit well on him. She preferred his blatant rudeness of the day before. "If I have to call you Crash, you can call me Vanessa."

"Vanessa. I'd like to know exactly what kind of game you're playing."

"Ibuprofen," she said, as she unlocked the door.

"Excuse me?"

She beckoned him in, dumped her bag on a chair, and went straight to the desk drawer she kept medications in. She grabbed the white plastic bottle, tapped three tablets into her hand, and swallowed them with a few gulps of the bottled water she always kept in her office.

She set the bottle down, leaned against her desk, and folded her arms. "I'm not playing any game."

Crash loomed over her, his mouth set in a straight line. He towered over her bookcases, and could probably tell that the plants sitting in the dust on top were fake. Great. He'd never trust a woman with fake plants, but she couldn't keep real ones alive, just as she couldn't make a dessert that didn't end in disaster.

What did these things say about her? Probably that she'd done the right thing by becoming a scholar.

"Then explain to me," demanded Crash, "why one day you're up at my cabin urging me to take responsibility for my heritage, and the next you're trying to brainwash my grandmother into leaving the collection to your college."

Maybe it was his tone of voice, or the headache, or the fact that she'd just been badgered by

Creighton. But for some reason, she got angry.

"I resent the implications of that statement! And if you think your grandmother can be brainwashed into anything, you sorely underestimate her."

"My grandmother is vulnerable at this point in her life, and I don't want her taken advantage of."

"Well, then," said Vanessa before she could stop herself, "maybe you should visit her a little more often to ensure that doesn't happen."

Crash looked as if she'd struck him. His green eyes blazed with resentment, a muscle jumped in his jaw, and though he didn't move at all, he seemed to harden into marble. "I plan to."

They glared at each other for a long moment, and heat bloomed on her skin. She told herself it was because she hated confrontations. The truth was that he made her itchy.

"I want to know what you think you're up to."

It infuriated her that he thought she was playing some kind of double game. That he thought she would have any part of manipulating a little old lady. She dodged the niggling fear that by not telling Creepy Creighton to go to hell, she was doing just that. "I don't have to explain myself or my actions to you."

"It would be quite a feather in your cap, wouldn't it, to acquire the Thomas Dunmoor Collection for Seymour College. The perfect follow-up to your book. You might even get a nice promotion out of it. Are you tenured yet, Vanessa?"

She looked daggers at him.

"I didn't think so. Yes, I'm beginning to understand." His lip curled.

"You understand nothing," she told him. "If all this were true, why would I have gone to find you? Why would I have tried to get you interested?"

"Well, now, I've been asking myself that same question. And finally it came to me why you had such bad sales skills. You took one look at me and knew I'd run like hell from words like 'duty' and 'responsibility' and 'legacy.' So you used them, every single one, sure of how I'd respond. Am I right, Vanessa?"

She stared at him, horrified. "No!"

"Uh-huh."

This was worse than anything she'd expected. How could she reveal that her pitch had been so rotten because he'd unnerved her? That she'd been focusing on his pecs, his chest, his *buns*—instead of her own words?

How could she admit that she'd been picturing him in a horned cap and boots and nothing in between?

"Look," she said, "I really had nothing to do with Dr. Conch's position this morning."

If anything, his sneer became more pronounced. "You brought him. You can't deny that you'd benefit from the acquisition."

"I brought him because he pretty much commanded me to. He's my boss."

"Oh, so now you're the victim here."

Her temper flared again. "I'm not claiming to be a victim! I'm trying to be straight with you. But since you're not going to believe a single word I say, why don't we just end this conversation?"

"Then you'll agree to stay away from my grandmother."

"*What?* She's my *friend*."

The look on the Louse's face said it all.

"She's my friend, and she's in the hospital, and she needs all the cheering up she can get. No, I'm not going to stay away from her. You're outrageous!"

"Mighty convenient friendship."

Vanessa felt as if the breath had been knocked out of her. "How dare you!"

"How dare *you?*"

Their faces were inches from each other, and she could see each angry pore of his skin. Pugilistic bristles emerged in rough patches like platoons, and the nostrils at the end of his crooked nose were flared. The pupils of his eyes moved over her face like searchlights.

She refused to back up, even when his eyes dilated even more, and he looked as if he were going to kiss her.

Kiss her? Who was she kidding? The guy would sooner bite her. She'd been studying art in the dark for way too long, and her imagination was running away with her.

Chapter Six

THE ROOM was full. Miss Eugenie and her hospital bed occupied the whole of one end, and the rest of them sat in an awkward half square around her, in miserably uncomfortable metal folding chairs. Three lawyers formed a clump on the left side, Creighton and Vanessa sat on the right side, and Crash Dunmoor sat in the middle, looking once again as if he were armed with thunderbolts.

He'd dressed for the occasion in a pair of khakis and a deep green shirt, and His Manliness actually sported a belt today, though no socks.

Vanessa found herself unaccountably fascinated with the way a light sprinkling of golden hair curled at his ankles.

Miss Eugenie's precious wallaby eyes were bright, and though her knitting basket was conspicuously absent this morning, she twirled her

IV cord in her right hand. This made Nessa nervous; she kept expecting it to fly out of the old lady's arm and thwack somebody in the face.

Miss Eugenie had come to some mysterious decision and called them all here with her attorneys, the youngest of whom had just passed out Styrofoam cups of coffee from Joe to Go.

Nessa hid a smile as he dunked the end of his yellow silk tie in his own java while reaching for a packet of sugar. He wrung it out under the disapproving gaze of the senior suits.

She took a sip of her own coffee as Miss Eugenie got down to business. "Thank you all for coming here this morning. I've reached a decision over the past few days regarding my late husband's collection of paintings. As you all know, they are now worth a great deal of money, and I don't take their disposition lightly."

Creepy Creighton folded his hands across his paunch and pursed his smug lips.

"These gentlemen," Miss Eugenie indicated the clump of attorneys, "are from the law firm I retain, Smith and Smiley."

They nodded. "Robert Smith," said the most senior of them, a man with a gaunt face and bushy gray eyebrows.

"Andrew Gillespie," the middle one stated. He possessed square, forgettable features and sported gold mallard cuff links.

"Giff Smiley," said the youngest one, he of the caffeinated tie. His blue eyes held a twinkle to which Vanessa couldn't help but respond.

"The Third," added Smith. "Gifford Smiley III."

Smiley shrugged and sipped his coffee.

Eugenie turned her head in Crash's direction, and he introduced himself. He didn't go out of his way to avoid eye contact with Vanessa, but when he glanced her way his expression was cool and dismissive.

Creighton was next. "Honored to be in attendance," he declared, in a voice like plum jam.

"I'm sure," the old lady murmured. "Gentlemen," she turned toward the lawyers, "why don't we begin."

Robert Smith retrieved a sheaf of papers from his briefcase, stood, and buttoned his jacket.

"It is Mrs. Dunmoor's fondest wish that the collection of paintings by her late husband, Thomas Dunmoor, be cared for properly and not simply sold at auction to the highest bidder. The collection has great historical and educational value, and she wishes it to remain intact." Smith cleared his throat and took a sip of his coffee before continuing.

"Mrs. Dunmoor's logical direct heir is her grandson, Mr. Christopher Dunmoor, and it was her original intention to leave the paintings to him. However"—he looked up with a puzzled frown at

Crash—"Mr. Christopher Dunmoor has indicated a lack of interest in this inheritance, which causes her concern."

Crash met the attorney's gaze with one of supreme indifference, and it was Smith who looked away first.

"Mrs. Dunmoor recognizes that her grandson has every right to dismiss her wishes . . ."

Now it was Crash's turn to frown, and the lawyer's to look bland.

". . . but does ask that he educate himself about the collection before he makes his final decision. To this end, since representatives of Seymour College have indicated great interest in acquiring the Dunmoor paintings, our client asks that all parties present consider the following proposal."

He took another sip of coffee and looked at Vanessa, now. "Professor Vanessa Tower is in the process of completing a definitive treatise on the life and work of the late Thomas Dunmoor. She is, in Mrs. Dunmoor's opinion, an expert on his paintings."

A feeling of foreboding stole over Vanessa, and a sidelong glance at Crash found his eyes narrowed and greener than an angry panther's.

"Professor Tower is offering a seminar on the work of Thomas Dunmoor this semester at Seymour College. It is Mrs. Dunmoor's suggestion that her grandson be given special dispensation by the college to enroll in this course."

Crash made a strangled sound, and Vanessa opened her mouth to protest, but the lawyer held up his hand. "Please allow me to finish before voicing any objections."

"If Christopher Dunmoor applies himself to his studies, and makes an 'A' in the course, then he will still inherit. If he does not choose to take the course seriously, and makes a 'B' or below, then the collection will be turned over to the Seymour College Museum of Fine Arts, along with a stipend for its care."

Smith cleared his throat. "The reasoning behind Mrs. Dunmoor's plan is simple. Christopher will be exposed to the full body of the work in form and content, but it will be his decision and his alone as to whether or not he works hard enough to keep it. If he does not, at least he will know what it is he's giving away.

"Mrs. Dunmoor has worked with Professor Tower extensively over the past few months, and judges her to be a young woman of integrity and fairness. She trusts her not to allow the college's interests to sway her objectivity in grading."

Smith straightened his papers and his lips, and sat down again. For a long moment, nobody said a word.

Vanessa searched for a tactful approach to express her shock and discomfort with the entire situation.

Crash, take her seminar? *Crash* and his invisible

friend, machismo, unnerving her every other day in the classroom? Miss Eugenie had to be kidding. But one look at the old lady's sweetly determined face told Nessa she wasn't. In fact, she looked pretty pleased with herself.

Vanessa glanced at Creepy Creighton, whose formerly pursed lips had widened into a delighted smirk. *Uh-oh.*

She started to open her mouth to say something, *anything* to put a stop to this gruesome proposition, but hadn't even gotten a word out when Crash began to laugh.

Rich, hearty, and completely unamused echoes of his mirth filled the room.

She herself was leaning more toward tears, but she couldn't really blame him. This was a situation so unbelievable, and so somehow *gothic*, that extreme reactions were warranted.

Yet his laughter also seemed disrespectful, not only to his grandmother and her wishes, but to Vanessa herself. He obviously doubted her ability to be objective, and found the idea of taking her class ridiculous.

Well, when she thought about the oversize Crash and his attitude, squished into one of those chairs with the mini desktops attached, it *was* funny. Especially since he'd be surrounded by twenty-year-old college girls—oh, heaven help her. She'd have to teach on an ark to survive the buckets of drool. No, it was out of the question!

"Christopher," said Miss Eugenie in sweet tones, "you find my proposal amusing?"

He looked her in the eye. "Yes, ma'am, I do."

"And why is that?"

"First of all, Grandma, it's fiendish."

She grinned. "Why, thank you."

"Second, I have serious doubts about Professor Tower's objectivity, and third, I have no desire to take her course."

Vanessa stood. "I resent your comment on my objectivity!"

"You're wrong, Christopher," said his grandmother. "I've been around many more years than you, and I'm an excellent judge of character. As for your desire to study . . . I know you've never been bookish, my dear. But"—and she seemed to shrink and pull helplessness over her like a quilt— "I'm asking you please, to do this as a favor to me. Look at it as . . . my last request."

"Grandma!" Crash exploded. He cast a glance of sheer frustration at her.

But in his eyes, Vanessa saw love and regret—and guilt. Oh, this was bad. If Crash folded, there was no way she'd get out of it gracefully.

She had to wave a red flag in front of the bull *now*, or she'd be stuck facing his horns every day. And she'd rather teach hara-kiri with a rusty razor blade than art history to Crash Dunmoor.

Ignoring Creepy Creighton's kick at her ankle, she said, "I don't feel comfortable with this situa-

tion, Miss Eugenie. The teacher-student relationship can be adversarial enough. Starting it with
reluctance and suspicion is just not a good idea."

"Nonsense," Dr. Conch broke in. "That doesn't
have to be the case. And Dr. Tower is a fine, up-
standing young woman. I, too, object to any as-
persions being cast on her character . . ."

*Well, that's certainly ironic, since you're a walking
aspersion yourself.* Vanessa wanted to kick him
right back, but maintained her dignity.

The chair looked smug and that bothered her.
What was the old warthog up to now?

Crash remained silent, so it was time to get
back to the flag-waving. "The problem, as I see it,
lies more in Christopher Dunmoor's attitude toward me and my class."

He turned those green eyes on her, and she
raised her chin. "I don't need or want to contend
with hostility and disinterest from a student on a
daily basis."

"I understand your concern, dear," said Miss
Eugenie. "But my Christopher will behave himself, won't he?" She cast a sharp glance at him.

"Vanessa," added Dr. Conch, "surely you're not
calling your own excellent teaching skills into
question?" He folded his hands over his paunch
again. "Besides, the boy looks fairly harmless under all that hair. Not as if he's going to bite, after
all."

"The boy" slowly turned his head toward the chair and bared his teeth.

An alarmed look crossed Conch's face, and he sat up a little straighter in his chair.

"Looks as if we're boxed in, doesn't it, Miz Tower?" said Crash.

She folded her arms and met his wicked gaze. "I suppose so." *But what will remain of the box when we're finished?*

Chapter Seven

GIFFORD SMILEY III managed to ditch his senior partners, Smith and Gillespie, by telling them
he had a meeting in Amherst with an old college
buddy. The college buddy was conveniently going to pick him up right here on Main Street in
Ambrose.

It was an outright lie, but he had no intention of
riding back to Boston with them in the firm's
black Lincoln Continental. Smith and Gillespie
gave him the hives. In his nightmares, he looked
into a mirror and found himself wearing plaid
boxer shorts, one of Smith's club ties, and Gillespie's mallard cuff links.

Giff dropped the last three letters of his name
because they each stood for several million dollars, which embarrassed him. His surname, Smiley, he pretty much had to live with, but he

shunned the "III" because he felt that those three numerals stood for pomposity, not simple birth order.

Giff just wanted to be a regular guy, which was hard when your name was so dopey and your family owned a third of Boston. He'd really rather have been born a member of Aerosmith than a member of the Blue Book, and it seriously got in his way when it came to women.

Giff had been chased by herds of coltish debutantes all his life, and found this frustrating in the extreme, since they usually had all the sex appeal of a hitching post.

He was completely unembarrassed to admit that he was a big fan of the Sleazy Nasty Babe. But your average Sleazy Nasty Babe took one look at his Gucci loafers and careful side part and laughed her ass off before running in the opposite direction.

It wasn't Giff's fault that he hadn't owned a pair of blue jeans until he was a sophomore in college. Like most guys, he just wore what he found in his closet, and he'd never found such an item there.

Like most guys, he stripped in front of the shower and threw his clothes on the floor. He had no concept of what happened to them next—they just disappeared into that mysterious ether populated by the laundry fairies, who returned the clothes to his closet once they were clean.

It wasn't Giff's fault that he'd only just learned to fill his own car with gas. The tank just always got magically topped off, so there had been no need for him to learn.

Giff was a regular guy who just happened to have grown up in irregular circumstances, but nobody else would acknowledge that. He hated being called "sir" by men twice his age. It made him feel like a phony. He hated being fawned over because of his surname. Most of all, he hated working for his father's law firm, but it was a family responsibility, and Smileys didn't shirk those.

Since Giff had worked thirty-six hours on Saturday and Sunday, he decided that he was taking the rest of this sunny Monday off. He wanted to enjoy the scenery of beautiful downtown Ambrose, Massachusetts. He'd just amble down Main Street and sniff around the flora, since the foxy fauna in Joe to Go had already caught his eye.

The foxy fauna had a belly ring that triggered the most feverish and unholy thoughts in him. It had glinted behind the Danishes, winking and teasing, beckoning to him across the cinnamon-swirl coffee cake. Above the belly ring was a tiny cotton T-shirt, black as sin, that holstered two magnificent mouthfuls of lovin'.

Below the belly ring was a delicious expanse of creamy skin snugged into low-riding boot-cut jeans. And when he'd found an excuse to go to the trash can on the far wall, he saw those inky dominatrix-heeled boots. Those had him throwing away his sugar packets and dumping only the torn top edges into his coffee. He'd had to fish them out, and during the process had burned his finger while staring at her mouth.

Those red, plump lips were curved into a mocking grin, and it took him a moment more of finger-sucking to realize that she was laughing at him. Even *before* he told her his name was Giff Smiley.

This was bad. This indicated that his chances of a date with her were about as likely as the survival of an ice sculpture at Satan's wedding.

He kept on looking at her anyway, during the process of getting replacement packets of sugar and putting them into his coffee.

She had huge dark eyes that turned down slightly at the outside corners, and a perfectly sculpted nose. Milky white skin and sexy, wispy shoulder-length hair provided a further study in contrasts.

"Did you want anything else?" She'd asked the question with no inflection.

Giff blinked. *Why, yes. You, bent over the Danish case.* "Um . . . no, thank you." He'd taken the tray of six Styrofoam cups out to the car, and they'd gone to Miss Eugenie's meeting. But he thought about her the whole way, while Smith and Gillespie were chastising him for not making the chauffeur go in for the coffee.

Now he walked down Main Street, hands in his pockets, and thought about how to get his chosen Sleazy Nasty Babe to talk to him. God, was she hot!

He wanted more than ever to be just a regular guy, and wished he had a fairy godmother to give him a pair of glass loafers for the ball. Truth be told, they sounded damned uncomfortable, not to mention dangerous, but if they'd get him a date, he'd risk 'em.

Since he'd scoped out the fauna already, he turned into the Rose of Ambrose, Main Street's florist shop. There he took his time hand-selecting a dozen different exotic flowers and having them arranged in a crystal vase.

When it came time to fill out the delivery information, he asked for help.

"I don't know her name," he said to the plump man with glasses behind the counter. "But she works across the street, in—"

"Joe to Go," the guy finished for him.

Giff stared at him. "How did you know?"

"Buddy, you ain't the first to fall for Shelly, and you won't be the last. We get at least a couple of poor slobs in here every week with the same idea."

Giff didn't know whether he was more irritated at being called a "poor slob," or at not being original. "I see," he said. He supposed it was too late to cancel his order, since it was staring him in the face, tied with a huge red bow. He'd signed the card simply, "An Admirer."

If Shelly—he brightened, since he now knew her name—got flowers at least twice a week, he wondered what she did with them. He decided to hang out and watch.

"Would you mind delivering them for me now?" he asked politely.

"Sure. And I bet you wanna stay right here in the shop so you can see her inhale the scent of them and clasp them to her chest, then read your romantic card and dance around her shop. Ain't gonna happen, I'm tellin' you. But okay. I'll go schlep them to her now."

"Thank you." Giff watched as the man crossed the street with his offering and pulled open the door to the coffee shop.

He went up to the counter, exchanged a few words with Shelly, and handed her the flowers.

The first thing she did was untie the bow and give it back to him. Interesting. Then she yelled something into the back of the shop, and whipped the whole bouquet out of the vase. She laid it on the counter, poured the water out of the crystal, and gave it back to the florist as well.

They chatted for a few moments while she dismantled the arrangement, pulling the flowers apart and putting one each into separate glass bud vases an employee brought her.

Shelly placed one of these on top of each of her

twelve café tables, tossed the greenery, and that was that.

The florist waved good-bye and walked back across the street with the vase and the bow. "She always gives me back the vases and bows for reuse," he said cheerfully, as he came back into his store. "A real sweetheart."

"Yeah," said Giff. *A real sweetheart.* "Well, I appreciate it."

"No problem. See ya."

Giff thought about demanding the vase, since he'd just paid 120 dollars to decorate Shelly's tabletops, but what would he do with it anyway?

Disconsolate, he left the shop. He'd have to come up with an entirely different plan. Where the hell was your fairy godmother when you needed one?

Vanessa burst through the door of Joe to Go, glasses slipping down her nose and her hair on fire.

"Hoo boy," Shelly said. "What's the matter?"

Nessa's hands shook as she put them on the counter. "I need protein to stave off an attack of hypoglycemia, and then anything decaffeinated with lots of chocolate in it. I've had what you could call a really bad day."

"I'm sorry. Sit down and tell me all about it." Shelly put a ham-and-cheese croissant on a plate for her and passed it over. Then she pumped chocolate syrup into a tall cup, started the espresso machine, and got some crushed ice ready in another tall cup.

"I'm going to be stuck with the Louse in my class! I got steamrolled this morning by one old lady, three lawyers, and Conch. Miss Eugenie drew up a diabolical proposal . . ."

"Lawyers," muttered Shelly. "That's where the suit with the hangdog eyes came from."

"What?"

"Sorry. I had another psycho guy send me flowers from the Rose today."

Vanessa sighed. "You know, if I didn't adore you, I'd have to detest you. At least you don't walk around with a fake Swedish accent, saying. 'Don't hate me because I'm bee-yu-ti-ful.'"

Shelly made a face at her. "I'm not going to dress in a potato sack and wear a bag over my head because of wacko men."

"Of course not. And hey, look on the bright side: Your tables have never been lovelier. Is that a bird of paradise?" Vanessa gasped. "And look at those orchids. This guy spent a fortune."

"Yep, and it gave me the creeps immediately. They all do—that's why I dismember the arrangements. Sending flowers to someone you don't know is just weird."

"Some women would describe it as charming, Shelly."

"Nope. It's an entirely unoriginal way of saying 'Hey, baby, I wanna get in your pants.'"

Vanessa blew out her breath. "You personify the word cynical."

"Come on! What else could it mean?"

"Maybe that the gentleman would like to get to know you better."

"Yeah. Meaning take me to dinner, liquor me up, and then get into my pants. My pants are size four for a reason: I don't want anyone in them but me."

"Shelly, there's a seven-letter word missing from your vocabulary, and I think you should look it up in the dictionary. It's r-o-m-a-n-c-e."

"Haven't you heard? Romance was invented to fool women into a lifetime of slavery."

Vanessa stared at her. "Whoever got to you sure did a job of messing you up."

Shelly finished blending the iced mocha she'd created for her friend, poured it into a plastic cup, and snapped a lid on it. She pushed it across the counter. "I am not," she said, "messed up. I'm practical, and I call it like I see it. That's all. So tell me why you're stuck with the jerk in your class."

Nessa pushed a straw through the lid of the cup and took a long, grateful swallow of mocha. She slid her wire-framed glasses to the top of her nose and smoothed her hair. Then she explained just how neatly Eugenie Dunmoor had boxed them in.

"Ha!" said Shelly. "So she's having a great time pulling all your strings. She's a helluva puppeteer."

"I can't teach with that Louse in my classroom," Vanessa wailed.

"Sure you can. All you need is a few tips from me. Cruelty to Men 101—it's my specialty." Shelly wiped down the counter for the fiftieth time that day. "Where'd this 'louse' word come from? My great-aunt doesn't even say that."

Nessa grimaced. "Louse," she repeated. "you know, like cad, or heel, or scoundrel—but worse, because it's a pestilent insect."

Affectionate laughter bubbled up in Shelly's throat. "You're something else. Like you're stuck in an eighteenth-century novel. Repeat after me: *jerk, dickhead, asshole,* or *bastard.*"

Her friend made a face at her. "Louse," she said again. "What's so outdated about it? They still exist."

"I know. My brother caught 'em at school. But nobody uses that as an insult these days. Trust me. I'm up on the hip insults. So repeat after me: *dickhead.* Come on, you can do it."

Vanessa shuddered. "Now there's an image. I'm not saying that! *Jerk* or *bastard* I can handle, but that's it."

Shelly nodded. "It's a start."

"Are you done improving me for the day? Is it

my turn? I'll bet anything that velvet Elvis is still on your wall."

"Hey! That's a classic."

"And the 'seventies platform waterbed? Is that a classic, too?"

"It's comfortable. I like sloshing to sleep every night."

"Enough said. I'll update my speech patterns when you update your tacky décor."

Shelly laughed. "Deal."

Vanessa fell silent while she sucked down the confection of caffeine, sugar, and fat. Shelly frowned at each of the exotic blooms on her café tables. Every single flower was different, and had been carefully chosen. Their fragrance had melded with the overriding aromas of fresh-ground coffee beans, steamed milk, and the dizzying array of baked goods.

She stared, bellicose, at a lovely hibiscus the shade of new love, tinged with joyous yellow. The petals were generous, open and vulnerable, glowing in the afternoon sunlight. The golden-tipped stamens extended foolishly, tiny hopeful male stalks for which Shelly had little patience.

Yet the sheer beauty of these particular flowers seemed to get to her. Vanessa suppressed a smile. "What planet are you on?" She asked.

"Huh?" Shelly blinked. "Oh—just spacing out. Long day."

"Hmm. Well, I think you should give the Flower Man a chance."

Shelly rolled her eyes. "I don't go out with men who wear suits. Or fancy loafers with miniature horses' bits attached to them. Where would you even go with a person like that? The opera? I'm not about to listen to some cat-strangling diva vibrate my belly ring right out of its hole."

Vanessa had to laugh, but she eyed Shelly with concern. She hadn't dated anyone since she'd met her. Why not? Vanessa sensed a well of pain behind Shelly's blasé attitude, but her friend had never confided in her.

Chapter Eight

IT WAS the first day of the fall semester, and Vanessa rolled, with trepidation, out of what felt like the wrong side of bed. She'd slept with her arms over her head, embracing her pillow as if it contained all her knowledge and competence, and it might sneak away in the dark of night.

The pillow was still there when she woke, though squashed into impossible bumps and bulges. Her protective arms—and hands—were asleep. They buzzed with what felt like ten thousand ants apiece, and she could barely control her fingers.

She stood in front of the window doing circles with her arms, then flapped them like some ungainly bird. It was a gray, sticky day beyond the curtains of her bedroom.

Crash Dunmoor would be invading her classroom today, laying siege to her nerves and hormones. She pictured him approaching the Fine Arts Building stealthily in a longboat, all horned cap, fierce green eyes, and leather weskit.

Vanessa blinked at her fanciful imagination and wanted to smack herself. She stumbled blearily into the bathroom, snatched her toothbrush from the ceramic cup where she kept it, and squeezed toothpaste onto the bristles. She spied a robin in the branches of the pear tree outside her window, and his tiny beak, bright eyes, and quick movements reminded her of Miss Eugenie.

Nessa stuck the toothbrush into her mouth. A bitter, nasty chemical flavor spread across her tongue. Blek! It most definitely was not toothpaste she'd spread on her brush.

She gagged, spit into the sink, and pawed water into her mouth with both hands, dropping the brush into the basin. Eeeuuuuwwwww—nasty. She recognized the smell as hair gel.

Crash Dunmoor had her brushing her teeth with hair gel, curse him, and class hadn't even begun. This didn't bode well for the coming week—not to mention the rest of the semester.

She climbed into the shower with a scowl, soaped her silly self, and shampooed her hair. While she waited the couple of minutes required for her conditioner to soak in, she let the hot water drum over her shoulders and neck, welcoming the rhythm and pressure. Ignoring the rest of her body, which always made her uncomfortable, she looked down the length of her legs, frowning at the hundreds of despicable freckles. She noticed that her toenails were scraggly and wore only half of the polish she'd applied a couple of weeks ago.

It was going to be too hot for closed shoes, so she'd have to do something about it. For some unknown reason, the idea of facing Crash Dunmoor with scruffy toes was intolerable.

Vanessa emerged from the shower, wrapped her hair in a towel, and stuck one foot up on the side of the tub. She'd painted three toes with Persimmon Pleasure when the phone rang. Trying not to growl, she hopped to her bedside table and answered it.

"Hallo, Pumpkin."

She smiled in spite of the inconvenience. "Hi, Papa. How are you?"

"Fine, fine. Just called to wish you luck with the semester."

Shemester. Her father had the sweetest, gruffest case of Long Island Lockjaw. "Thanks, Papa." *You have no idea how badly I need that luck.* "I hope you have a good group of students yourself." He'd taught architecture at Boston University for as long as she could remember.

"Yesh, well, sho do I. Had wonderful classes lasht spring." He paused, but stayed on the phone. She could hear him stirring sugar into his coffee. "Okay, then, m'dear. Shuppose you've got to run."

Vanessa could tell he was lonely, but as usual, he had a hard time dredging up conversation. "Oh, no," she lied. "I have plenty of time." She didn't tell him that she was shivering under the vent in her bedroom. Always uncomfortable in the buff, she foraged for underwear and a big T-shirt. She felt odd without panties . . . vulnerable, exposed, almost dirty.

"Ah. Well, okay then," he rumbled. And then stalled once more.

"Papa? What's on your mind?"

"Aahhhhggg." She heard him gulp down some coffee. "Haaaarrr. Ummmmmm."

"Just say it."

"Well, you shee . . . there's a new assistant in the department."

"Okay," Nessa said, puzzled. "Is this a problem? Is she a bad typist? Can she not spell?"

"Noooooooooo," replied her father. "That's not it."

She waited.

"She's grammatically irreproachable . . ."

"Do you need to speak to her about something in particular?"

"Aaaaahhhhhggg. Haaarrr. Ummmmmm."

Vanessa waited some more, utterly in the dark.

"She's got terrific legs."

"Terrific legs," Vanessa repeated, stunned. "Oh. I see. Papa, are you trying to tell me you're dating somebody?"

"Ummmmm. I shuppose you could say that."

She struggled for words. "Well, that's . . . wonderful." *She'd better be nice. If she hurts him, I'll kill her.* "Do I get to meet her?"

"Yes, I think you will. Shoon."

"Okay. I . . . look forward to that. Thanks for telling me. And good for you, Papa." Vanessa hung up the phone, bemused.

Papa, after all these years of solitude, was poking his head out of his shell to risk dating again? It was so out of character for a man who'd destroyed or hidden away every last picture of her mother and told Vanessa silly stories about how he'd had to lasso the stork that brought her to him.

She sat down on her bed, pulling the covers around her. How old had she been? Five? Six? One Christmas years ago, full of hot, cinnamon-spiced apple cider, and candy canes and truth. She'd learned the words to "Oh, Tannenbaum" in German, the significance of mistletoe, and the meaning of shame.

Aunt Gertie and Aunt Tabitha, believing her asleep, had discussed a mysterious packet that she'd seen arrive in the mail. The envelope displayed a foreign return address, strange stamps, and unfamiliar handwriting. It upset everyone in the household, her father most of all. He'd left the house to walk alone in the darkness, and no one would tell her what was going on. The evil packet disappeared.

"Shameless hussy!" Aunt Gertie spat. "How dare she?"

"Devious slut!" said Aunt Tabitha. "How could she?"

They'd showered Vanessa with hugs and kisses and cookies, as if somebody had died, and tucked her into bed with not one but two bedtime stories.

She lay awake in bed and worried about Papa, trudging around in the dark and snow, while her aunts hissed and squawked downstairs in the kitchen. If no one would tell her what was going on, she'd have to find out herself.

She slid out of bed and tiptoed to the top of the stairs, where she sat, drawing her knees up and pulling her nightgown over them. She then tucked it under her cold toes and cocked her head.

Her aunts' voices were audible from the kitchen, just around the corner.

"I knew no good would come of it," Tabitha declared.

"She was bad news from the start," said Gertie. "Shaking her bosom, twitching those hips, flipping that hippie hair around. She thought she was something special, all right."

"So did Henry. He'd never seen anything like her before, poor boy."

Henry was Papa, Vanessa knew that. But who was the shameless hussy?

"She sucked the life out of him and moved on, leaving him like some poor dead insect in her web." Aunt Gertie slammed something—a mug?—onto the table.

"Women like that should be sterilized," Aunt Tabitha snapped. "How could she leave him with a two-year-old? How could she leave her own child?"

Vanessa hugged her knees to her chin. The shameless hussy was her *mother*? A chill shot through her, and her stomach roiled. She wasn't even sure what a hussy was, but it had to be bad, from the sound of things.

"And now," continued Aunt Gertie, "she has the unmitigated gall to send pictures after all these years. Pictures of herself and that Latin Lover of hers. As if we'd show our poor darling . . ."

Vanessa hadn't found the packet for years afterward, but she'd disentangled her knees from her nightgown that evening and gone upstairs immediately to look up the word "hussy" in her father's dictionary. "A lewd or brazen woman," it told her. "Lewd" proved to mean evil or wicked, but the first entry for "brazen" simply meant "made of brass."

So her mother was a shameless evil woman made of brass . . . the discovery confused her. Did that mean she, Vanessa, was shameless and evil, too? If she tried really really hard to be good instead, would it work?

Since Santa didn't put coal in her stocking that year, her efforts must have meant something, and she'd try even harder next year . . .

Vanessa pulled herself out of the past and shrieked as she looked at the clock. She'd forgotten that she needed to run off the course syllabus before class.

She pulled off the T-shirt and twined a bra around her torso, trying to fasten it and apply deodorant at the same time. She dived into linen slacks and a top, shoved her feet into sandals, and grabbed a short-sleeved linen jacket.

Next she ran into the bathroom, ripped the towel off her head, and aimed the hair dryer, full blast, at her head for a couple of minutes. Then she twisted the mass of her hair into a knot and secured it with a pair of Japanese hair-sticks.

A quick slash of lipstick completed her toilette, and she ran down the hallway to her office to gather the papers and notes she'd need for today. Stuffing these into her nylon satchel, she leapt down the stairs and out the door, only to rush back in again when she realized she'd forgotten her keys.

Then she burned rubber to the college and the art building, squealing the Cruiser into a parking place that she suspected wasn't entirely legal.

She dashed into the department office and pulled the syllabus from her bag, eyeing the copy machine warily. It was her nemesis. If something could go wrong with it while under her hands, it would.

"Nice copier," Vanessa said, patting the dirty beige plastic lid. "Good boy." It loomed, menacing, in its corner, and certainly didn't wag its power cord. Well, what did she expect?

She flipped open the lid and placed the first page of the syllabus inside, not trusting the machine enough to load it from the top and let it collate for her. She set her teeth and pushed "start."

Amazing! The technology gods were with her, and the thing began to slide, flash, and whir. She closed the lid thankfully. Twenty copies emerged obediently into the output slot.

She opened the lid and exchanged the first page for the second page of her syllabus, programmed the machine for a second twenty copies, and pressed "start" once again. One, two, three . . . Vanessa looked at her watch, just as the copier emitted a thwack and a groan. *No!*

The thing glowed evilly at her, igniting the "paper jam" button. *No, no, no!*

She opened it and managed to tear out a piece of paper stuck in its hidden roller. She closed it. She pressed the "start" button again.

Whirr, kathunk, kathunk. It reset itself and spit out all of two more pages before thwacking and groaning again. This time, she swore she heard fiendish laughter emanating from its bowels.

"You piece of—" She opened it again, wondering savagely why the department secretary wasn't there. Kate would know what to do. Kate and technology had no problems, since Kate lived in the twenty-first century, unlike Vanessa.

She ripped out the jammed paper once again, and slammed the machine closed. This time, three copies emerged before the diabolical thing sputtered and died.

Vanessa took a long, slow breath and counted to three. Her gaze fastened on the fire extinguisher to the left of the copier. She had a vision of seizing it and beating the Xerox machine into shards of plastic wreckage.

But if she did that, then she'd not only have to explain to her class—and Crash Dunmoor—why she was late, but also why her next lecture would be videotaped from a psycho ward.

She began again, and only had to unjam the machine six more times before she had all twenty copies. Kate tripped in blithely as Vanessa removed the last two.

"Good morning!" she trilled. "Oh, sorry I wasn't here to run those for you . . ."

"Not a problem," Vanessa said, trying to wipe the serial killer expression off her face. The machine's hiccups really weren't Kate's fault. And she should have run the copies on her printer the previous day . . . "Must fly! Late!"

She waved good-bye to Kate as she dodged into the hallway.

Run, run, run! She popped frenetically in and out of the slide library, grabbing the slide carousels she'd need for her lecture. Then it was run, run, run again to her seminar room.

She blew in two minutes late, puffing like a first-day freshman, and painted what was surely an insane grin on her face. Fourteen junior and senior young women stared at her, analyzing her inch by inch while she unloaded her materials and caught her breath.

Crash Dunmoor was nowhere to be seen. Vanessa didn't know whether to be relieved or irritated. Mostly she was just on edge. What was wrong with her? She was normally prepared to a fault, but just the thought of Crash in her classroom had her completely askew. She needed to get her act together, *now*, before walking on stage.

After her bout with the copier, she eyed the slide projectors even more warily than usual. She knew her carousels were in order, and that she'd put in each slide correctly. But that didn't mean that the projectors were easy to position, or that a bulb wouldn't burn out midlecture, or that some mechanism wouldn't malfunction, popping a slide into the air like a tiny pictorial piece of toast.

She pulled down the large screen in the front of the seminar room, then walked back to fiddle with the projectors to get them elevated to the right height and positioned at the correct distance and focus.

She'd clicked the first sequence of slides into place and was making minor adjustments when a hulking shadow appeared across the screen, blocking the light. The twin barrels suddenly illuminated Crash Dunmoor's fab abs, the best of his chest, and his impeccable pecs.

A collective, appreciative murmur rippled through the ranks of young women, and Vanessa groaned silently.

Back to school. Crash had never felt more ridiculous in his life. He shielded his eyes from the projector lights and made his way beyond them, looking for a seat. Christ Almighty, was he going to have to sit in one of those tiny chairs with the miniscule writing desks attached?

Appalled, he searched the room for any other viable option, and found none. A pert brunette scrambled to pull her backpack off the seat next to hers and all but leered at him.

Reluctantly, he walked to the seat and nodded at her briefly before squeezing into it. The freakin' thing was like a medieval torture device: far too low and narrow, so that it was impossible for him to bend his knees and sit comfortably. Instead, he had to extend his legs straight out ahead of him, his feet straddling another student's seat.

The back of the chair hit him at an agonizing place along his spine, so that he had to straighten and arch to avoid it, throwing out his chest like an angry ape. No way in hell was he going to sit in one of these all semester. He'd be lucky to make it through the next hour.

Miz Tower walked to the light switch and illuminated the room—and the barely disguised lust of his fellow classmates. Every single one of them seemed to be eyeing him covertly or overtly, and it took a superhuman effort on his part not to blush.

He sighed in relief as he spotted one girl with a crew cut and a silver ring through her nose, glaring at him with open hostility. Hatred was preferable to salacious stud fantasies. He smiled and nodded at her. Her brows drew together, and she looked as if she'd gladly put his most precious part through a salad shooter.

"Good morning, everyone," said Miz Tower in that cultured voice of hers. "I'm Dr. Vanessa Tower, and this is History of Art 367, Thomas Dunmoor and the American Scene. Is everyone in the right place?"

No, thought Crash. *I'm in an alternate universe.*

She looked at him severely, as if he'd said the words aloud.

He met her eyes with a bland stare, then let his gaze run over the rest of her. She'd covered up her legs entirely today, to his regret. He had to fill those in from memory: svelte, creamy, with dozens of tiny little freckles to punctuate their shapeliness. Trim, tailored ankles, disciplined long, supple calves, and those knees! Suffice it to say that those knees had been made to be nudged apart.

He'd better stop there, he thought, trying without much luck to x-ray through her pale linen slacks. So he began again at her neck, where he detected an uneasy flush, and found himself speculating about her breasts. They'd been far too well disguised the other times he'd met her, but he had a feeling they were small, high, and proud under that sexless little jacket.

Her waist nipped in so neatly—it really did—and he found himself approaching that forbidden zone again and had to distract himself.

Up, eyes, up! Up to that gorgeous knot of flaming hair, and those prim, intellectual, wire-framed glasses that straddled her nose and teased her high cheekbones. The flush at her neck rose until her face was bright pink, and the gray eyes she narrowed at him from behind the spectacles were deliciously stormy.

Miz Tower broke eye contact with him, and he realized he'd been giving her quite the randy once-over. She strode to a corner of the room and retrieved a long wooden pointer, which she held

like a weapon now in front of her. *Oh, spank me!*
Crash thought, and grinned.

His grin triggered a new expression on her face:
Her nostrils flared, and she pursed her mouth until it resembled an insulted prune.

Aw, don't do that, Professor. Let those pretty lips
spread wide, now. Show us those lovely, even teeth, and
the mysterious depths of your mouth . . .

He knew he was making her uncomfortable
and didn't much care.

Play a double game with my grandmother, will you,
darlin'? Then you'll deal with me on the offensive line.

Her hands tightened on the pointer and went
white-knuckled. Maybe she'd raise it aloft like a
spear and skewer him right here in her classroom.
Hey, now there was a nice new image: Miz Tower,
clad only in a scrap of animal skin and maybe
some blue paint, running after him with a spear.

Her voice interrupted this pleasing fantasy.
"We'll go through the attendance sheet, and then
we'll start with an overview of the work of
Thomas Dunmoor, whose paintings and prints
are a fascinating study of American city life before
and after World War II. We'll look at how his work
changes over the years, and analyze why."

Miz Tower's voice was smooth, professional,
and calm. But her fierce grip on the pointer, that
telltale flush, and other signals belied her crisp
enunciation. He noticed when she turned her

head that her hair was still damp. She wore no eye makeup, and her lipstick was slightly askew. She'd gotten ready in a hurry this morning.

"We're very . . . lucky . . . to be joined by Thomas Dunmoor's grandson this semester," she said.

Crash felt sixteen pairs of female eyes upon him and resisted the urge to squirm. Instead he pulled his mouth into a grin and continued to take inventory of Vanessa Tower.

His gaze swept down to her toes, clad in brown sandals. His grin widened: only three toes on her left foot sported polish. The remaining seven were bare.

Her glance followed his, and he choked back laughter as the flush at her neck rose again up her cheeks to suffuse her whole face. It remained as she finished calling the roll. ". . . Jennifer Schmidt, Tanya Ullman, and Deirdre Weinberg."

She put down her pencil and the class roster, took a deep breath, and eyed the slide projectors warily, as if they were raptors escaped from Jurassic Park. Then his professor turned off the lights and flashed two images on a wide white screen.

Crash looked up at them and froze. On the left side, his grandfather's craggy face stared out at him from under a beetled brow. On the right side was the old Victorian house in which Miss Eugenie still lived.

His throat closed, and he was unable to breathe for several seconds. It was one thing to remember the old man's face, and another to be confronted with a two-foot-by-three-foot mug shot. Six square feet of unforgiving judgment. Six square feet of hard-bitten reproach. Six square feet that were six feet under, yet jarred him with the force of a blow.

Meanwhile, the mellow Victorian, once a childhood haven, mocked him on the right. The sight of its cheerful gingerbread trim caused bile to rise in his throat.

Crash knew the urge to bolt, to throw his ridiculous chair right through the screen and smash the twin projectors to the floor.

He did none of those things. Instead he turned and narrowed his eyes at Vanessa Tower, who returned his gaze evenly. Without a word, and in the space of perhaps five minutes, they'd gone a silent round in the ring. And the damnedest thing was that though he'd had her breathless against the ropes, off-balance, and on the defensive, she'd won with a single gesture.

Chapter Nine

VANESSA SAT in her office, her mouth on her knuckles, elbows planted on her desk. She stared at her wall calendar, seeing not the photo of the French countryside, but Crash Dunmoor's neck stiffening as she'd flashed the first set of slides onto the projector screen.

Yes, the back of his neck had stiffened, and when she'd gone to the front of the room to get her notes from her desk, she'd noticed more. His jaw jutted pugnaciously toward the older Dunmoor's image, and the tendons under that stern jawline had corded. His lips flattened, instead of curving in their normal mocking sensuality.

Projecting his grandfather's image on that screen had definitely either provoked or upset him, and she wasn't sure she was interested in awakening any sleeping demons in Crash Dunmoor's past.

Yet somehow Miss Eugenie had outfitted her for the job, and it was all the more disturbing that Crash was one hot, sexy guy. However, he'd better keep his libido to himself.

He'd used his disturbing sexuality to harass her silently until the slides went up. She was still furious about it, but curious about that turning point. Those first two slides had disarmed Crash, made him forget about squaring off with her, and focus on . . . what? Some long-ago rift with his grandfather. Crash was not only fighting her, fighting the situation, but fighting the past.

She thought about it some more. For heaven's sake, the man taught *sky-diving* for a living. He had a battle going on with gravity itself. While eventually the laws of nature won, bringing him down to earth, he still defied them on a daily basis.

The only person who'd made him lay down his weapons was Miss Eugenie: He wasn't savage enough to disregard her. But even she was throwing him back into a wrestling match with his grandfather.

Vanessa recalled what had happened after the first set of slides. When she'd launched into a presentation of Dunmoor's work, Crash's posture relaxed and his eyes hooded with deliberate boredom. He crossed one ankle over the other.

So he wasn't intimidated by his grandfather's

creativity or talent. He was just angry at the man himself. That was an important distinction. But by blocking out the elder Dunmoor's raison d'etre, he was refusing to engage with him. He was rejecting the man's form of communication with the world.

How was she, as a teacher, going to reach him? Vanessa continued to consider the problem, while trying desperately not to consider him naked.

Crash entered her classroom the next Tuesday carrying a folding lawn chair and an insulated quart-sized cup that rattled with ice.

She put her hands on her hips as he slid a couple of desks aside to make room for his lounger. As he bent at the waist to do so, three of her female students shamelessly glued their eyes to his glutes.

Vanessa herself couldn't help noticing the muscular, tanned forearms emerging from the rolled sleeves of his flannel shirt. Golden hair dusted those arms, glinting under the fluorescent lighting, and she had an uncomfortable flashback to his naked chest gleaming sweaty in the sunlight.

A spark of heat ignited in her belly, and she grabbed for the Diet Coke on her desk. She'd drown the embers before they could flare up. What was wrong with her?

Irritated, she said to Crash, "This isn't a beach, you know."

Green eyes challenged hers as he settled into the chair, leaning back with his knees spread.

Classic gorilla-man mode.

"What a shame," he said, quirking an eyebrow. "And here I was, hoping you'd teach today in a bikini." Ignoring the gasps of her other students, the horrid man looked her up and down. He didn't miss anything, not even her toes. Doubtless he was checking to see if she'd painted the other seven yet. She had.

She gritted her teeth. So Crash Dunmoor liked to jump out of planes voluntarily? She was beginning to have fantasies of *pushing* him out.

Unconcerned and unaware that his professor's mind was straying to homicide, Crash scooped his quart-sized cup from the floor. The ice rattled noisily, and he drank.

The liquid poured down his sexy gullet, and she watched his throat master each swallow. In some insane corner of her mind, she wanted to *be* that liquid, wanted Crash to suck *her* through a straw.

The spark in her belly licked into a bona fide flame now, and she told herself it was anger.

She was positive it was anger when his even white teeth grinned at her around the straw. He released it, but then flicked at the tip with his tongue. Horrid, horrid man!

Vanessa turned on her heel, marched to the door, and flipped off the lights without even calling roll. The blessed darkness hid her mortification.

How dare he? Had she somehow inherited her mother's shameless hussy genes? Was she sending the bastard siren signals? Surely not. She didn't wear shrink-wrapped clothing, or bare provocative body parts. She hadn't even let a drop of drool escape her.

If he didn't keep that lizard tongue between his teeth, she'd poke it right back into his mouth with her pointer, by God she would.

For the rest of the class, she was hyperconscious of his presence, lousy with testosterone.

She could feel her own heartbeat in her throat and had difficulty coming up with adjectives to describe the images projected on the screen.

She knew she was losing her mind when she used the word "compelling" for the fourth time. And what the blazes did that mean? It was one of the most useless modifiers she'd ever encountered.

Crash creaked every so often in his lawn chair and rattled his ice or cracked his knuckles.

The sixteen young women in her class all sat in various pretzel-like contortions to make sure they had a good view of him. She tried not to take it personally, but it was hard.

Chopped liver. I am chopped liver in my own classroom, while that man is filet mignon.

The whole atmosphere of the class had changed

because of Crash. On the first day she'd been in command of a small battalion of earnest, studious, young female achievers. They were dressed conservatively, in baggy unisex clothing, and half of them wore glasses.

By the second class, bare legs and short skirts were in abundance, as were spandex and small T-shirts. The young women had swapped their eyeglasses for mascara, and it was simply amazing how much their posture had improved. Sixteen pairs of breasts now followed Crash's every movement. Disgusting.

Seymour College women had the reputation of being intelligent, articulate, and self-possessed. Tanya Ullman, for example, was the senior class president and had spent her junior year in Hamburg studying economics. But when Vanessa asked her a simple question about Thomas Dunmoor's educational background, Tanya looked blank, then *giggled*.

"I really couldn't say, Miss Tower."

"Maybe Crash knows the answer to that question," offered Jennifer Schmidt, turning toward him and actually batting her eyelashes.

Crash returned her eager smile with bone-melting ease, and she looked as if she wanted to throw herself naked on his chest. Vanessa blanched.

"My grandfather attended the Ecole des Beaux-Arts, I believe, from 1923 to 1925. He traveled for a few months after that, and then returned to the States in early 1926."

"When did he meet your grandmother?" Deirdre Weinberg cooed the question, almost falling out of her scoop-necked top.

Vanessa was horrified. She'd never seen Deirdre in anything but oversize turtlenecks, and she was attending Seymour on a chemistry scholarship. Yet another Brain was metamorphosing into a Bimbo under her eyes.

"They met in 1929," Crash told her, "and married two years later. He got jobs with the WPA, the Works Progress Administration, and she taught piano lessons to help make ends meet until he was more established."

His voice mesmerized them all, while Vanessa's did not. Of course, her voice didn't resound with masterful gravel. It didn't ooze masculinity, or echo with the timbre of testosterone. Her voice didn't purr like a jungle cat's, edgy and dangerous and sexy as hell . . . Vanessa blinked.

Please God! Just smack me. Just deliver me from the force of this awful attraction to the Louse. This Pied Piper and his peter-power are driving us all insane.

Chapter Ten

AFTER CLASS Vanessa retreated, miserable and ruffled, to the student union for a greasy burger. Nothing like chomping on something high-calorie to put you in a happier frame of mind. Even if you knew each mouthful bypassed your stomach entirely and zipped right down to your thighs. There you could feel it making an evil "splat," and leaving another dimpled crater. She waved the disconcerting thoughts away: A greasy burger she would have.

She pulled open the heavy doors and clicked in her heels down the hall that led to the food service area. She could taste the burger already, made just the way she liked it, with no lettuce, no mayo, and no giggles.

Giggles weren't dignified, weren't appropriate,

weren't characteristic of Seymour College. So why could she still hear them?

She rounded the corner and stopped short at the sight of Crash Dunmoor ensconced in a booth, sharing platters of french fries with Tanya, Jennifer, and Deirdre. Not content with rendering her students brainless in class, he was teasing and flirting with them outside of class!

She glowered at him. Louse.

What kind of thirty-five-year-old man flirted with nineteen-year-old girls? This didn't say much for his character.

He relaxed against the vinyl padding of the booth. She knew it was only her imagination, but even the damned cushion seemed to gasp with pleasure at having his masculine thighs pressed into it. Aaarrggh.

The gaggle of formerly brilliant and accomplished Seymour girls hung all over him, practically crawling into his lap. If she didn't block her throat with that burger soon, she was going to throw up.

And if she didn't establish her authority over the situation immediately, she'd never gain control over her seminar again.

"Crash," she said, thinking of hot beef, "when you're finished, I need to talk to you."

He raised a tawny eyebrow at her. "Why, Dr. Tower, are you holding me after class?"

No, I'm holding you in contempt. "Something like that." She flashed a crisp smile at the group.

The girls straightened self-consciously and picked at their fries. Crash continued to lounge, the picture of virile indolence.

She walked past them to order her burger from Tracy, a former student who worked this shift.

"Hey, Miss Tower. How're you?"

"Fine, thanks. How was your summer?"

Tracy shrugged. "Okay, I guess. What can I get for you?"

Peace of mind. A steady pulse. An exterminator who specializes in large, blond bugs. "A cheeseburger, please. Ketchup, mustard, pickle—but hold the lettuce and the mayo." *Not to mention the giggles.*

"No problem. Fries?"

Vanessa shook her head. "Thanks."

"Drink?"

Yes, I could use one. "Diet Coke."

"So who's that guy over there?" Tracy asked as she took her ten-dollar bill.

Vanessa didn't have to ask which one. "Thomas Dunmoor's grandson. He's taking my seminar."

"Cool," said Tracy. "I might have to come audit."

Crash joined her as Tracy forked over her bag of sin. "Why don't you walk back to my office with me?"

"That sounds like more of a command than a request." But he fell into step with her.

Jennifer, Tanya, and Deirdre gazed longingly at him as they passed the booth. Ugh.

They followed the narrow walkway from the student union back to the art building. Lined with trees and flower beds, the path pulsed with the beginnings of autumn color: riots of gold, pumpkin, scarlet, and bronze.

Vanessa was tempted to shove her face into the paper burger sack, like a horse with a feed bag, so she wouldn't have to say anything to Crash.

What *was* it she was going to say? How could she phrase things so that she didn't come off as a sour old biddy? *Was* she a sour old biddy? The thought made her want to pull the entire burger bag over her head.

Nonsense! She wasn't a biddy. She had the right not to be visually stripped in her own classroom.

But would bringing it up and confronting him with it only worsen the situation? Shouldn't she just rise above it? Or was that cowardice talking?

Crash hadn't said a word as they walked along the path. His hair gleamed in the sunlight, and she noticed strands of red and mahogany underlying the dark gold. He turned his head, saw her studying him, and raised an eyebrow.

"I wasn't flirting with those girls. It's important that you know that. We happened to meet up again at the student union, and they invaded my booth with military precision."

She didn't reply.

"Understand? I don't hit on teenage girls."

Vanessa nodded. She'd seen them in action in her seminar.

"It's not the most comfortable situation for me, either. Is that what you wanted to talk to me about?" His green eyes held rueful amusement.

She looked quickly away, put the straw of her cup to her lips, and took a long swallow of Diet Coke. Then she thought of him back in her classroom, teasing his own straw with his tongue.

She choked on the sexual image, sending cold liquid down her windpipe. Her lungs protested, sending it right back up, and suddenly she was spitting Diet Coke onto the autumn leaves by the path. It dribbled onto her chin, and her pale linen jacket. Her humiliation was complete.

Crash thumped her between the shoulder blades. "Are you okay?"

"Fine," she wheezed. She looked up, sure his Viking face would be suffused with laughter, but saw none.

His green eyes searched her own, and only when he seemed certain she was okay did they crinkle at the corners. "If just plain soda did that to you, I'd hate to see what a shot of tequila does."

"You'll never have the chance," she assured him.

He looked speculative.

They reached the art building, then her office, where the first thing she did was grab a tissue, wet it with bottled water, and dab at her jacket.

He watched her for a moment and folded his arms. "So what was it, then, that you wanted to talk to me about?"

Okay. Time to stop procrastinating and bring up the subject. She cleared her throat and threw the tissue in the wastebasket. Then she tossed her dignity after it.

"I can't have you . . . doing what you're doing to me in the seminar."

He folded his arms, and the green in his eyes intensified. He filled the whole office with his presence, and the walls seemed to close in on her.

"Doing what I'm doing," he repeated. The corner of his mouth quirked upward. "And what exactly is that?"

"You know very well."

"No, I don't. Tell me." He moved closer to her.

She wanted to step back, but held her ground. Her damned hormones started fussing and clucking again, hopping nervously and bobbing their heads.

"Don't play games, Crash."

He took another step toward her. "What if I'm very, very good at certain games, Miz Tower?"

His voice was low and husky, and her blood began to pound. Her palms heated. *Bok! Bok!* said the hormone-chickens.

"What if I could teach you a whole new set of rules?" Crash continued.

Oh, that voice. Deep and musical and full of the promise of tangled sheets. Her whole body vibrated in response to it.

"Rules that don't have anything to do with boxy jackets, or slide projectors, or academics?"

Cluck. Squawk. Shut up, hormones! Tyson, she thought. *Butterball. Campbell's.* I'm a professional, here. This man is all but harassing me. So why is my blood pounding? Why is my stomach doing backflips? Why does my conscience seem to have passed out, like a bum on the street? She kicked it, hoping to revive it.

"I don't want to learn your game," Vanessa said. "And I think you make up the rules as you go along."

His white teeth flashed at her, then disappeared again. Two steps closer, and he was inches away from her body.

She inhaled his scent—the detergent of his shirt, the faint traces of deodorant, and the more primal, indescribable machismo to which language couldn't do justice. How could bad news smell this good?

And Crash was most definitely bad news, a male headline in 120-point type that screamed, "Run for your life!"

The problem was, she had little room for running at the moment, and even less inclination for it. When Crash reached one of his large, beautifully shaped hands toward her and traced the Diet Coke stain on her jacket with his index finger, all she could do was swallow. Hard and tight. Something in her trembled, but not in fear. In anticipation.

The horrid hormones actively pecked at her now, with sharp little beaks. *Go away!* she hissed. *Chick Filet. McDonald's . . .* but these were fierce, fightin' poultry. Pullets with an attitude.

Crash's index finger moved to her lips, and gently traced the shape of them. Oh, my . . .

And then he settled that finger in the middle of her bottom lip and slowly slid it inside about half an inch. She couldn't help but close her mouth over it and taste the flavor of it, of salt and man. She could feel the tiny ridges and whorls with her tongue, and had the insane impulse to take the whole finger into her mouth and suckle it.

But he withdrew it and placed his lips on hers instead.

Vanessa felt a shock flow through her, down to her toes.

Liquid heat followed the shock in ripples. She tilted her head and leaned into the kiss, exploring his lips with her own. She heard his quick intake of breath, felt his body close the gap between them and press hard against her.

Never had a kiss been this intense, not ever.

Crash explored her mouth with his tongue now, and she began to do the same, touching her own tongue to the edge of his teeth, then venturing beyond.

Heat continued to pulse through her, intensifying in embarrassing private places. She stiffened, and his response was to place his hands on either side of her jaw. He delicately stroked her skin and her ears with feather-light touches, ending his invasion of her mouth with a gentle nip at her lower lip that sent another flash of heat through her.

He dropped his hands, took a step backward, and stared at her, his breathing ragged.

She stared back warily. Dear God.

Outside the closed door, two T.A.s walked by, deep in conversation. She didn't hear their words, only the warning of their presence. It was a reminder that she and Crash were in her office, her professional workplace, behaving in an utterly unprofessional way.

Shame suffused her face as she recalled that she'd hauled him here to put him in his place, to ensure that he stop his silent harassment of her.

She'd meant to talk to him about his flirtation with her students, and here she was behaving worse than any of them. She was hot and bothered and damp and panting. She closed her eyes. She was teetering on the verge of shameless hussydom.

Had she smacked the man for sheer nerve? No. Had she told him to get the hell out of her office? No. Had she threatened to report him to the college? No. Instead, she'd encouraged him and kissed him back!

What in the blazes was wrong with her? When he'd touched her clothing, she should have socked him one in the jaw. When he'd popped that finger in her mouth, she should have bitten it off.

But no. She was obviously sex-starved enough to fall for his innuendos and the cheap thrill of his . . . okay, so it wasn't cheap. It was a thrill of the finest quality.

Her own behavior was cheap, however. Sleazy. It was just plain *sleazy* for her to be making out with a student in her office with the door closed. What did that make her? How could she have responded to him like that?

She was deeply ashamed. She'd been brought up to be a decent, honorable, upright person. Not the sort of woman who skulked around campus, preying on her students and climbing them like trees.

Her behavior had always been unimpeachable. She was stable and conscientious—not the type to be blinded by lust. Yet here she stood, with mussed hair, throbbing lips, and for heaven's sake, *fogged spectacles*.

"Vanessa," said Crash, quietly. "I shouldn't have done that. I'm sorry."

She couldn't look at him. "I think you should go."

"That's probably a good idea." He moved toward the door. "We'll just forget this ever happened, all right? And from now on, I'll . . . behave myself in class."

Chapter Eleven

CRASH SMACKED himself repeatedly in the forehead with the heel of his hand. Lip-locking with Miss Celery had not, not, *not* been a good idea.

Yes, he found himself inexplicably attracted to her. Yes, he'd been guilty of deliberately making her uncomfortable in the seminar. But it had backfired on him in a most unexpected way. He'd noticed that the more hot and bothered she became, the more aroused he got himself.

That wasn't supposed to happen. He was supposed to be firmly in control, not uncontrollably firm.

And why was he interested in kissing someone who was using and double-crossing his grandmother? That was the part he really didn't get. Because he just didn't buy her story about not being involved on the college's behalf.

Crash told himself to put her out of his mind. What he needed to focus on at the moment was his job, and his job today was to be a competent tandem-master to the overweight, green-faced kid who sat next to him.

Bart Olson, nineteen years old, was about to make his first jump ever, strapped securely to Crash's back.

He'd explained it to Bart: Once the plane got to a level of 12,500 feet, their pilot, Mike, would circle the drop zone and give the okay. They'd open the door and brace themselves for the onslaught of freezing air.

Then the group of five who were practicing the formation would jump, one at a time, in five-second intervals. After they'd gone, the individual parachuter would go.

Finally, Crash and Bart would make their leap. Tandem jumpers always went last.

Crash took a look at his student's face and shook his head, suppressing a smile. The poor kid's teeth were chattering in fear, and his hands were clenched into white-knuckled fists.

The group of formation jumpers grinned in sympathy. "Hey, kid," one of them shouted, "you'll be fine. You've got the best instructor I've ever met."

"Yeah?" warbled Bart. "Then how come his name's *Crash*?"

The others gave a whoop of appreciative laughter, and Crash was forced to explain how he'd come by his name. "Let's just say that I had a spectacular spill the first time I made an individual jump."

Bart's green face drained to white.

"But that was a long time ago. Ten years, okay?"

"So . . . did you break anything?"

"Just the tib and the fib on one leg, and my wrist."

Bart swallowed convulsively.

Crash shrugged. "Sorry—not trying to scare you, just being honest. Never have broken anything since. I was stupid. I flared too early, tried to run it out, and then tripped and fell. Tried to break my fall with my right wrist, snapped it, and then fell on my face."

The kid's eyes were now wild.

Crash clapped him on the shoulder, and told him, "You're not gonna do that. First of all, you're with me for the next ten jumps, and I'm not going to let that happen to either one of us—I'm a lot more skilled now. Second, I'm gonna train you better than I was trained. And third, you're a better listener than I was at your age. I was fearless, and that's just dumb."

The kid nodded.

"You, on the other hand," Crash continued, "I can smell your fear. And it's going to make you smart. You're going to remember what I tell you."

Bart's eyes remained wide, and his stomach quivered. Crash wondered if he was going to back out at the last minute. It had happened before—a full-grown man had screamed like a colicky baby and beat on his shoulders until he'd backed both of them away from the door. It was rare—most people who didn't have the guts wouldn't even get on the plane—but it did happen.

The other thing that happened occasionally was a nice case of the hurls. Crash really, really didn't want to get puked on today, but as he looked at the kid, with his green face and quivering stomach, he had to admit it was a possibility. Uggh.

The plane reached altitude, and they watched the others make their jumps without further conversation. When the last individual had gone, dropping down and away into the prop blast, it was their turn.

Crash gave Bart the signal, and they moved to the door, Crash gripping the bar immediately inside it. The kid didn't shriek or pound on him, so Crash released the bar and leaned out. As they dropped, he immediately turned toward the front of the plane, riding the prop blast. Then he turned them into position for a tandem fall: belly-to-earth.

God, he loved the adrenaline rush, the exhilaration of it, and he exulted in it for a brief couple of seconds, until he felt the kid's puke soaking into his turtleneck. Aw, *hell.*

Then they were enveloped by the familiar feeling of weightlessness. As Crash had tried to explain to Bart, you really didn't feel as if you were falling, you just . . . floated.

Though you were whizzing through the air at approximately 120 mph in a free fall, you had nothing to judge your speed by, so you couldn't tell.

After sixty seconds, Crash checked the altimeter on his wrist and signaled to the video guy with a wave-off that he was about to pull the cord for the pilot chute, the smaller chute that would stabilize them before he opened the main canopy. Done.

And now Big Bertha. Done.

For the next three minutes, courtesy of gravity, Crash and Bart floated down to earth. Crash steered them in expertly, pulling the brake toggles down toward his knees with perfect timing. They hit the ground, skipped a few steps in the grass, and felt the drag of the parachute landing behind them.

"That was soooo cooool!" Bart shouted in his ear. But after they'd unhooked from each other, he had a hard time looking Crash in the eyes. He was obviously remembering his stomach's midair rebellion.

Crash could smell it on himself now, but refused to let his face register any disgust. The poor kid didn't need to see it. He grinned at his student, instead. "So, you liked it, huh?"

Bart nodded, his face red but his eyes glowing. "Uh . . ." he began. "I'm really sorry—"

"Happens all the time, buddy. Don't give it another thought." He put an arm around the kid's shoulders and gave him a man-to-man slap on the back. "Let's get this chute packed."

Crash dragged his lawn chair into the seminar room and shrugged apologetically at Vanessa. "I'm sorry. I'm not doing this to be obnoxious. I can't sit in one of those medieval torture devices the college supplies as desks."

Vanessa looked at one of them, then back at him, and nodded. She made his mouth water today, dressed in a long royal blue skirt that hugged her slender curves. It had a slit in the back of it, so that her legs played peekaboo when she walked. Yum.

The snug silk sweater she'd paired it with was really very modest, but clung to her willowy torso in a most appealing way. He discerned the ridges of her bra under it . . . oh, damn! He was doing it again, giving her the one-eyed once-over, when he'd promised not to.

Her cinnamon eyes flashed at him behind the wire-framed glasses, and those perfectly formed pink lips compressed. Two spots of color accentuated the freckles high on her cheeks.

Okay. He'd sworn to behave himself, and behave he would. It was just that he could remember exactly how she'd tasted. Like sweet vanilla, with a touch of nutmeg. She'd been delicious, and hesitant, then passionate.

What bothered him was the shame he'd seen on her face afterward. Had he put it there, or was it something she carried around inside?

Was it due to professional or personal reasons? He wasn't sure. But he couldn't forget the taste of her, or the texture of the fine, delicate skin of her cheeks, or the tremor that had rippled through her when he stroked the shell of her ear with feather-light touches.

He forbade himself to look at her body any longer, and was soon distracted by more slides of his grandfather's work. Today, instead of lonely cityscapes, Vanessa was projecting a series of nudes with unbound hair. They assumed odd positions, not sexual, but private.

Naked, he thought, not nude. Natural, not idealized. They were pale and vulnerable against dark interiors, and always gazed, faces unseen, at an open window. The women had a peculiar dignity, in spite of their lack of clothing, but neither the rooms nor the suggested view outside their windows held any warmth or promise.

They were alienated figures, figures trapped in their circumstances, not resigned, but not desperate, either. They were lonely. Achingly lonely, and drawn against architecture and wide spaces that seemed far more important than they.

Vanessa put one nude in juxtaposition with a male figure.

The woman was inside, but leaned toward the wind billowing past her curtains. She crouched on an unmade bed as if she were slipping out of it, stirred by the forces of nature.

The man sat outside, on the stoop of a commercial building that was nameless, as if the business done inside didn't really matter. He was fully clothed, but had folded his arms across his body in a gesture of self-solace.

They both looked as if they wished to escape the mundane, the daily grind of their lives.

But whereas the woman looked toward nature, the man simply turned his back on commercial culture. He seemed hopeless; she seemed mesmerized.

When Vanessa turned the lights on, she suggested that all the students pull their desks into a circle. It was only then that Crash began to understand he was in trouble. Tanya, Jennifer, and Deirdre had all given him saucy greetings before class had started, but he'd been too busy looking at Vanessa to notice that he was under siege.

Pushing all thoughts of his grandparents out of his mind, he now recognized that he was in mortal danger.

Tanya wore no bra in the air-conditioning, and

had become adept at jiggling her luscious fruit whenever he looked her way. Good grief!

But shifting his gaze to Jennifer was no better: she'd applied some kind of shiny lip gloss that made her mouth appear wet with succulent juices. Her tongue was much in evidence, too. He averted his eyes.

Deirdre didn't seem the type to—Mother of God! He squeezed his eyes tightly shut until he was sure she'd crossed her legs again. Sharon Stone had nothing on Deirdre.

Where were their mothers? Their fathers? Their keepers?

Desperately, he looked elsewhere in the room, praying for innocence or chastity. What met his eyes was not reassuring.

A blonde in a squeaky-tight pink sweater took her time slowly peeling and eating a banana, while the girl next to her wore sprayed-on black leather pants and sat with her legs splayed open, stroking her own thighs.

Alarmed, Crash blinked hard and swiveled his head to find the wholesome, preppy girl who always wore her short bobbed hair in a plaid headband. Jayzus! His eyes scurried away from her, too, when he got a load of the tiniest tennis skirt ever manufactured. Her long, tanned legs looked ready to strike and wrap 'round their prey: *him*.

He felt like a helpless bunny surrounded by wolverines. These women wanted to hold him down and have their wicked way with him. His mind shied away from an image of himself, missing for days, found by the law, naked and bruised and handcuffed to a dorm-room radiator.

There had to be someone in this room who wasn't ready to take a bite out of him ... his eyes fell, with supreme relief, on the girl with the buzz cut and the nose ring. He'd never seen such a beautiful sight in all his life, even though she'd added a safety pin to her left eyebrow and was cleaning her black-painted nails with a Swiss army knife.

He shot her what he thought of as his most appealing grin.

Her eyes darkened with hostility, and she clamped the knife between her teeth to send him an international gesture. Then she went back to cleaning her nails.

Crash took a chance and slid his gaze to Vanessa, who kept her expression carefully deadpan and repeated her question about the differences and similarities of the two paintings she'd shown last.

When the room remained silent, she sighed. "Do I need to turn the lights off and show the two slides again?"

Crash shook his head vigorously. He was suddenly more afraid of the dark than he'd been at age four. There was danger in the dark—no telling what these teenage sexual predators would do.

"Crash? You have a comment? An insight?"

He thought fast. "Uh. Yes. Yes, I do . . ."

Vanessa waited patiently. "And that would be . . . ?"

"Uhhh—well, the architecture overwhelms the people in both paintings."

She nodded. "So what does that tell you?"

He stared at her, helplessly. He really hated this psychological art shit. But anything to keep the lights on, or he'd have to crawl into the guerrilla feminist's lap for protection from the other women.

"Are you seeing any close-ups of the people's faces?" Vanessa prodded.

He shook his head.

"Okay, so even though the woman on the left was naked, it's not an intimate portrait of her, right? You can't even see her face. And the guy on the right—do you see any real individualizing characteristics in *his* face?"

"Nope."

She waited for him to expand on that.

Silence.

She got up and walked ominously to the wall switch.

"No! Wait—he wasn't a social guy, my grandfather. All he wanted to do was paint. And you can see that in both of those slides. The people aren't as important as the whadyoucallit—the composition itself."

Vanessa's smile was brilliant, and he basked in the glow for a moment. She really reminded him of autumn, his favorite time of year. It was in her coloring: afternoon sunshine, red and golden leaves, the creamy skin under the sweet freckles like the promise of snow to come.

Autumn was in her whole demeanor, too—crisp and cool, with a cloudless cerulean intellect.

Crash blinked. He was an outdoors kind of guy, but this was a little ridiculous! He needed to get a grip on himself.

"The people weren't as important as the composition," Vanessa repeated. "Exactly. So why do you think they're there at all? If he didn't care about them, why put them in?"

Crash objected to this. "It wasn't that he didn't *care* about people. He did. He just couldn't escape his own alienation. I think he felt trapped, saw people all around him caught fast in the circumstances of their own lives, unable to change anything."

Vanessa was radiating some emotion—pride? And looking at him as if he were a toddler who had just formed his first complete sentence. Oh, for God's sake! What was *that* all about?

"So what you're saying," she murmured, "is that he cared very much for others. The alienation we're seeing in the paintings isn't out of disinterest, but comes from empathy."

This was getting a little too intense for Crash. "Uh, yeah. Whatever."

A frown crossed her face but then disappeared,

like a cloud chased by a stiff breeze. She seemed satisfied, for she nodded and moved on to discuss the formal composition of the two paintings and the significance of the window motifs in each.

Crash yawned, trying to hide it behind his hand, but his ennui evaporated as Vanessa turned off the lights once again. Uh-oh.

Tense, he sat bolt upright for a good ten minutes, and then told himself not to be stupid. Like any of these girls would really try to molest him in class—"*aahhhcckk!* What the hell?"

A hot, sweaty hand had gripped his upper thigh without warning. He knocked it off.

"Mr. Dunmoor, is there a problem?" Vanessa's voice inquired.

"No, no. No problem."

She continued to discuss the angles and planes of the new paintings.

A different hand gave a healthy squeeze to his right buttock. Crash leapt up, knocking over his lawn chair. "*Damn it!*"

"What is going on?" Vanessa snapped the question this time.

"Nothing," he muttered, shooting the woman next to him a glance full of suppressed violence.

She simply gave him a bland stare.

Crash righted his chair, moved it back about two feet, and sat again. Aw, hell. Where had his pen gone? Trying not to creak or cause any further disturbance, he leaned forward and felt along the industrial carpet for the runaway Bic.

He should have been ready for it, should have blocked it like a man, but the vixen got him. Out of the shadows came another set of fingers, and this one *flicked* his nipple.

"That's it!" Crash yelled. "Back off, you perverted private-school princesses!"

Vanessa flipped on the lights, and stood glaring at him, her hands on her hips. "If you don't stop interrupting my class—"

"I'm in danger of being gang-raped by this gaggle of nymphomaniacs!"

"Dunmoor, I realize you have an inflated ego, but that is ridiculous."

"Oh, yeah? One of these lovely young ladies just flicked my nipple in the dark. Another one grabbed my ass! How would you react? I find it humiliating, and I'm not putting up with any more of it." Crash slammed his notebook shut and stalked out of the room.

The rest of the class erupted into howls of laughter, while Vanessa stood stunned in the doorway. "I'm ashamed of every last one of you," he heard her say, in a shaking voice. "How could you?"

Chapter Twelve

"MISS EUGENIE, this simply isn't working out," said Vanessa. "We've got to find an alternative solution."

She sat in a folding metal chair next to the old lady's hospital bed.

"Why? Is my Christopher not behaving himself?"

Vanessa recalled the scene in her last seminar and struggled for words that would do it justice. "Noooooo," she said cautiously. "That's not exactly it." She picked at her cuticles, managing to create a nasty hangnail on her left thumb. "It has more to do with my other students' reaction to him."

Miss Eugenie grinned. "Crash *is* one hot hunk of burning love, isn't he?"

Vanessa choked.

The old lady reached out a bony index finger and poked her playfully in the ribs. "Aha!"

"There's no 'aha' about it."

"Ha! The 'aha' shows in your blush, girl, so don't try the 'huh-uh' business with *me*."

"Huh? I mean, what?"

"You find my Christopher very attractive, don't you?"

Vanessa opened and closed her mouth like a fish. "He's handsome, if that's what you're asking."

Miss Eugenie shook her head, as if clearing memories, and clucked her tongue. "Those quads," she said, dreamily. "His grandfather's were the same. Thick, and meaty and muscular. A man's stamina is all in the thighs and buttocks."

"I—uh—can I get you some water?" Vanessa asked, bolting into the old lady's private bathroom. She fanned flaming cheeks.

"Thomas was good for an hour, at least . . ."

Vanessa knocked both faucets on, trying to drown out Eugenie's mischievous voice, but it continued inexorably, at a higher volume. ". . . all the Dunmoor men are very well hung. I haven't seen Christopher nude since he was about seven, but judging proportionally . . ."

Vanessa splashed water onto her face and stuck her index fingers in her ears. Aghast, she looked into the mirror to find that her freckles had all run together, the dots connected by a blanket of scarlet.

Water dripped down her forearms, soaking into the sleeves of her sweater and pooling at the inside of her bent elbows.

"Are you all right in there, dear?"

"Yes," she croaked.

"I'm a dirty old woman, aren't I?"

"Um, no. Not at all."

"Liar," said Miss Eugenie cheerfully. "Come on out of there. I promise I'll stop."

Vanessa mopped at her face with a wad of paper towels, and tried to blot the worst of the water from her sweater sleeves. Then she emerged.

The old lady cackled. "I had no idea you were uptight about these things. It's usually old birds of *my* generation that I shock into pathos."

"I'm not uptight," said Vanessa.

"Yes, you are, dear. But that's all right. It's very sweet."

"I'm not sweet, either."

"Right. You're a regular old sourpuss, a nail-spitter. An absolute ghoul."

"That's me. Now, about this teaching situation." Vanessa cleared her throat. "It's not so much Cra—Christopher that's the problem. It's the young women."

"Flirting desperately with him, eh?"

That was one way of putting it. She nodded. Even

though the old lady probably wouldn't bat an eye, she didn't feel like telling her about the nipple-flicking incident. "Their attention certainly isn't on the subject matter I'd like to teach them."

"I'm a little surprised that the liberated women of Seymour College would pay much attention to my grandson, good-looking though he may be."

"Women today know what they want." Vanessa searched for a tactful way to put things. "And they're not . . . shy . . . about going after it anymore." *In other words, we've come a long way, baby. Maybe a little too far.*

Miss Eugenie lapsed into thought for a moment. "Fine. I'm sure that you'd like to have order back in your class, and I certainly understand that. So, there's nothing else for you to do but tutor Christopher privately." Her eyes gleamed.

Tutor Crash *one on one*? Vanessa's blood ran cold, then hot. Then it just ran, draining out of her face entirely. She could feel it. "That's really not a good idea," she managed.

"It's an excellent idea," maintained Miss Eugenie. "It solves your problem."

Yes, but it creates an entirely new one. Once again, Vanessa opened her mouth, then closed it. How could she tell the old lady that she and Crash had, uh, embraced in her office?

Shelly's voice suddenly mocked her. *Embraced? Nuh-uh. You did not embrace that man. You sucked face, you mashed with him, and you all but got down in a horizontal boogie.*

"I don't think he likes or trusts me, Miss Eugenie. I'm probably not the right teacher for him."

Hah, Shelly would say. *You're just afraid he'll make you bark like a dog.*

Vanessa's eyes popped, and she chased all thoughts of her friend out of her head. Dear God, it was true, though. Crash was the type of man who could elicit barnyard animal noises from a nun. And she was no nun. In fact, she seemed to be developing all the characteristics of her mother, the shameless hussy of yesteryear.

"Crash doesn't like or trust most people. So don't feel that he's discriminating against you, my dear Vanessa."

She was outrageous. "I'm afraid you don't understand. Crash thinks that I'm in league with the chair, and that I'm only using you in order to get my paws—or the college's paws—on your paintings. He's very protective of you."

Miss Eugenie broke into peals of laughter. "Poor boy. He's without a clue, isn't he? He has no idea that *I* was using *you*, both for Thomas's sake and for my own. You're not only a top scholar and evocative writer, but excellent company for a lonely old bird."

Vanessa shook her head at her, unable to suppress a smile.

"Now," added the old lady, "I should make it clear that the usage ended when I discovered how much I liked you."

"Thank you. The feeling is mutual. But I still don't think I'm the right teacher for Crash."

Miss Eugenie had looked fairly healthy and robust until this comment. Now she adopted a helpless expression, sinking lower into her bank of pillows. "Oh, but you promised, my dear. And," she paused, "then there's the tiny matter of that binding legal document. Not that I would be so crass as to throw that in your face."

She was something else. "Of course not."

"Regardless of how you may feel at the moment, you're *good* for Crash."

Vanessa blinked rapidly and said nothing. What *could* she say to this lovable, lipsticked locomotive?

"You're getting him to confront the past, battle his demons."

"Miss Eugenie, perhaps you could tell me more about these demons? It might help me get through to him. What happened with Crash and your husband?"

The old lady went completely still and closed her eyes.

Vanessa waited, assuming she was contemplating how to phrase things. But as the moments stretched on, it became clear to her that she wasn't going to phrase anything at all.

A tiny faux snore whistled past her thin magenta lips, and Vanessa grappled with the knowledge that once again, she'd been outmaneuvered. Drat Miss Eugenie!

Chapter Thirteen

CRASH FROWNED as he knocked on Vanessa's office door. He shouldn't have left the damned seminar earlier that week, but he'd been a little taken aback at having his nipple flicked and his butt grabbed.

It was one thing to know you were a healthy, virile male, and another to be treated like a piece of meat. Good God! Back when he was in college, they'd been known to grow a little weed in their closets. The women of Seymour College probably grew Grade A Jumbo cucumbers.

"Come in," Vanessa called.

He turned the knob and entered, closing the door behind him.

"Hi," she said.

"Hello. You wanted to see me?"

"Yes. I think we need to talk. Have a seat." She

crossed her slim legs, and he tried not to ogle them too obviously. "I spoke with your grandmother about the situation, without going into detail."

He sank into the other chair in the small room. "Oh, yeah?" *Which situation, the one with the girls, or the one with us?*

She nodded, and her cheeks pinkened. "I told her we really couldn't go on with those kinds of currents in the classroom."

Okay. So we're gonna ignore the other currents. "And what did she say? I know I'm not so lucky that she ditched the whole scheme."

"Ah, no. No, she didn't. She would like me to tutor you privately."

He was silent for a moment. This was complicated. "How do you feel about that?"

Vanessa stood up and paced to the other side of her office. She picked up and put down again various objects: a ceramic cat, some loose change, a letter opener. "As your grandmother pointed out, we have both signed a legally binding document. Under the circumstances, I'm not sure we have much of a choice." She raised her brows and flashed him a tight smile.

"She had the grace and charm to point that out, did she?" Crash laughed, without much mirth.

"Miss Eugenie is ... an unusual woman." Vanessa seemed to be riveted by his knees. No, his ... thighs?

Did he have a stain on his pants? Crash looked down to check, even though he knew he didn't.

Vanessa's hair glinted under the fluorescent lighting, and he thought again how much her coloring reminded him of autumn. His libido took the bit in its teeth and ran, and his next vision was of the good Dr. Tower buried naked in a pile of brilliant fall leaves, while he used his handy, uh, divining rod to locate her.

Crash blinked. What the hell was wrong with him? He'd had scantily clad nineteen-year-old tramps grabbing his body parts the other day, and they hadn't turned him on at all. They'd annoyed and embarrassed him. But here he was, sitting in a prim, bespectacled professor's office, wanting to rip open his shirt, beat on his chest, and grunt like an ape man.

None of it made any sense. It was any normal man's fantasy to be attacked by several nubile coeds at once. Most of the guys he knew would probably have shouted, "Take me now, you insatiable sluts!"

But no—he had to be attracted to a woman who wielded a pointer. A woman who had the power to test him, grade him, decide his future.

He reminded himself that he didn't give a rat's ass about that. He was only in this damned situation to humor his grandmother. For all he cared, Thomas Dunmoor's canvases could be plastered on the walls of the men's room at the local bus station.

"So," said Miz Tower.

"Yeah?"

"If we're going to work together one-on-one . . ."

One-on-one. Now that conjured a fresh batch of images for his libido to toy with. Red on top, Red on bottom. Mmm. Red's bottom. Squeezable, huggable, soft.

". . . I'd prefer to meet on the same day as the regular seminar, since I'll have the notes and slides prepared. Will that work for you?"

"Sure. What time?"

"Why don't we say four?"

"Fine." He nodded, still scanning her face. The woman had cheekbones like an empress, but the freckles softened their sophistication and gave her a kissable allure.

Kissable. Right. No, wrong! He had no business kissing her, or remembering how it felt to kiss her the last time he was in her office. But the memory manifested itself anyhow, stubbornly refusing to fade.

The kiss arced across the room, invisible, intangible, but somehow still apparent. It shimmered in the air between them.

Vanessa shifted in her seat and brushed a wisp of hair behind her ear.

He studied her, doing his best to fight this unwelcome attraction. The woman had been pumping information out of Miss Eugenie for months, purely for her own personal gain. She was an academic, writing a book, and she'd needed subject matter to analyze, dissect, and theorize about. She'd chosen his grandfather and preyed upon his lonely widow.

And in the end, the focus would not be upon Thomas Dunmoor, the American Scene, but Thomas Dunmoor, American Seen. Seen through the wire-framed glasses of the erudite Dr. Tower. Seen from the angles and perspectives *she* dictated.

It wasn't really out of academic curiosity that her book would be written. It wasn't out of appreciation for old Tom. The book was a measure of success for Vanessa. It was a landmark in her scholarly career, assuring that she'd advance to a certain level of professional status.

Crash eyed her pretty face again after deliberating this, and waited for his fascination to wane.

When it didn't he reminded himself that she was part of an unscrupulous plan to snare his grandfather's heritage for her college, so that she'd be rewarded with even more professional respect, and tenure, and who knew what else. Maybe they'd create a Thomas Dunmoor Chair of American Art, and seat her lily white rear in it.

Whatever. The woman was out to advance her career, and that was all there was to it. Seeing her in Eugenie's hospital room with that pompous ass of a chair had made it quite obvious.

So why, Crash asked himself, did he care? If he didn't want the cursed paintings, then why stand in the way of the college getting them?

It was just the underhandedness of it that pissed him off. And he'd always had a fierce competitive streak running through him. Why let them win? He decided just out of sheer orneriness that they weren't going to. He'd ace this course, collect the pile of "priceless" paintings, and torch them. Why the hell not? Old Tom deserved it.

"Crash," said the underhanded Miz Tower, "may I ask you something personal?"

"You can ask," he said, folding his arms. "But I reserve the right not to answer."

Her glasses had slid down her nose, and she pushed them up, eyeing him gravely. "What happened between you and your grandfather?"

"It really doesn't concern you." Damned if he was going to supply his family skeletons as fodder for her book.

"What you mean is that it's none of my business," she said. "Which, technically, it's not. But it does *concern* me, for professional reasons."

He curled his lip. "Well, I sure am glad your concern doesn't stem from just plain old vulgar curiosity."

She regarded him impassively, ignoring his sarcasm. "Would you like to know my reasons?"

He shrugged.

"This might be interesting to you personally, as well. Your grandfather spent a lifetime painting cityscapes, and landscapes, in which people were incidental, their faces often not seen. The viewer could feel the alienation of these people, but not their importance. So why, then, toward the end of his life, did he turn suddenly to painting portraits? Portraits as raw as any Thomas Eakins ever did?"

He got up and moved in the direction of the door. "I don't know."

"I think you have an idea," she said. "Why, Crash? What brought him at last to focus on people's faces, on their personal characteristics, on the hopes and dreams in their eyes? What closed the emotional distance between him and the subjects?"

"Maybe he lost something," he said cryptically, yanking open the door. "Maybe he lost something and wanted to bring it back."

There was blessed open space beyond that slab of wood on hinges. Clean air that he could escape into, air that didn't envelop Vanessa Tower or her magnetism or her damned questions. "Have a pleasant weekend, Miz Tower. I'll see you next Tuesday at four."

Chapter Fourteen

GIFF SMILEY wasn't smiling. He was analyzing the mysterious Shelly's reaction to his floral offering. Looking at it from a purely objective point of view, it said a lot about her.

This was a woman who, upon receiving a personal gift, dismantled it and put it to use for business, which indicated first of all that she was not a person given to romantic flights of fancy. She'd taken no time at all to enjoy the flowers, to exult in the surprise. She didn't allow herself the pleasure. Or she was too suspicious or defensive even to feel pleasure.

Second, the dismembering of the arrangement, the placing of the individual flowers on the tables of her café, had demonstrated a fierce practicality. Her business was more important to her than her personal life.

Giff thought about all that, and how to reach her. He didn't want her body without her heart. Well, maybe just a little.

And the way to Shelly's heart was going to be through her café. He knew it instinctively.

So, what did that mean? Instead of a dozen roses, should he send her a dozen . . . salt shakers? Pounds of sugar? Jars of cinnamon?

He had no idea. It looked as if a trip back to Ambrose was in order. Maybe it would help him figure out what she needed, both personally and on a business level.

Giff wasn't sure why he'd fixated on Shelly. After all, there were plenty of Sleazy Nasty Babes in the world, and probably thousands of come-hither belly rings. But there was something different about Shelly; something that caught his attention, twisted it into knots, and wouldn't untangle.

First of all, she wasn't truly sleazy or nasty, though she was definitely a Babe. A Babe to make this Beantown boy babble.

He'd grown up in a town full of baggy khaki pants and topsiders and Fair Isle sweaters. Duck boots and woolly caps and oversize turtlenecks. It was a uniform, among his crowd, for both male and female. Generally speaking, the sexiest it got around Boston's old money was maybe a sleeveless white cotton top and bare tanned legs—never, ever seen in a heel above an inch high. Maybe two inches for formal occasions.

Shelly's three-inch-high spike-heeled boots, faded snug denim, and tiny, skin-baring T-shirt screamed of L.A., or Miami, or New York. You certainly didn't see the likes of her in Beantown's top boardrooms.

Instead, you saw loosely tailored suits, a lot of chunky legs in sensible square-toed loafers, and chin-level blunt-cut hair. Oh, and pearls. How could he forget the ubiquitous pearls?

The women he worked with on a day-to-day basis wore barely any makeup, much less screaming red lipstick or three coats of mascara.

Shelly's skin was perfect, and the cosmetics really didn't look tawdry on her, but an unwritten code against her "look" existed in the circle of women he knew.

Therefore, it was all the more mesmerizing to him. She was exotic, forbidden, and oh-so-tempting.

While her eyes might be expertly shadowed and lined, they weren't empty. They hid secrets, and some sort of intangible grief, and a fierce determination to succeed.

Giff mulled it over. Shelly wasn't going to tell him her secrets, or share her closet grief with a stranger. But he had a feeling he could get somewhere with that drive to succeed.

It took him roughly an hour and a half on I-95 to get to Ambrose from his brownstone in Boston. It was a short hop from the exit to Main Street, and he maneuvered his classic old Mercedes-Benz roadster past the various shopfronts and side-walks filled with students.

Joe to Go looked warm and inviting on this cool autumn day. The picture window was framed in cherry red, and the walls inside were painted a fresh, vibrant yellow. Alternating black and white tiles gleamed spotlessly on the floor, and the legs of the wooden tables and chairs were painted the same cherry red as the window trim.

Giff drove past it, turned right into the adjoin-ing alley, and parked behind the shop. He got out of the car, locked it, and looked down at himself ruefully. He'd put on blue jeans, but his house-keeper Hannah had gotten hold of them, with the result that they were now starched and ironed. He could barely move in them.

She'd done the same thing to the three T-shirts he owned, stretching them across stiff pieces of cardboard and folding them with military preci-sion.

He looked ridiculous. He should have stopped in nearby Amherst and mugged a college student for his clothes. Since Seymour College was female-only, that wasn't really an option here.

He resigned himself to the comic crease marks and walked around the building and into Joe to Go.

Shelly wiped down the deli case and glanced at the suit with the hangdog eyes. Well, he wasn't wearing a suit today, but that was him. She was sure of it—that was the guy who had sent her the exotic flowers. He was tall, with dark eyes and a pricey haircut that fell casually in a lock over his forehead. She was also sure he didn't live around here. Nobody in Ambrose wore expensive suits, hundred-dollar ties, or starched-and-ironed jeans.

The jeans were really a laugh. He had crease marks down the center of each long thigh. Then the knees of the denim bubbled, since he'd stretched them out by sitting, and the creases resumed from shin to hem. Christ Almighty, she'd almost expected to find a *cuff* at the bottom of those poor tortured Levi's.

She bit back a smirk, since the guy did seem sweet, and he'd almost had an orgasm when he'd tasted her Wild Blueberry Danish. Shelly figured that was quite a compliment and almost made up for his pants.

She wiped the last smudge off the glass and rolled her shoulders to ease the strain of hours of work. She got to the coffee shop at five o'clock each morning in order to start the baking for the day. By 5:10, the radio was blaring classic rock n' roll, and she and Ursula, her assistant, were up to their elbows in butter, flour, fresh fruit, eggs . . . the list went on.

She didn't freeze anything and didn't touch any artificial ingredients. She used nothing substandard, and her baked goods were appreciated even three towns over. She had customers who placed special orders from Springfield.

Those special orders were flattering, but truth be told she didn't have time to fill them. She was exhausted, but she couldn't quite justify hiring another person, even part-time. And she owned a coffee shop, not a bakery.

Shelly started the batter for a batch of ham-and-cheese croissants, stealing another sidelong glance at Starchie. He was madly scribbling on her napkins with an expensive-looking pen. Whatever.

He seemed absorbed in his task, and curiously pleased with himself.

A lot of her customers stayed for an hour or so, reading a newspaper, doing crossword puzzles, or just yakking over their coffee with a companion. But she sensed that Starchie had an ulterior motive for being here, and since he'd sent her flowers last week, she suspected that it had to do with her.

Starchie needed to be discouraged and disabused of any romantic notions, pronto. If he was composing bad poetry on her expensive logo-printed napkins, she was going to be seriously pissed. She mentally calculated what she spent per napkin, and noticed that he'd used at least ten of them at this point.

If each of her approximately eighty customers a day regularly used ten napkins apiece, why, that would be eight hundred napkins! Didn't he understand that he only got *one*? It was all in her budget, down to the last penny.

Shelly washed her hands, found a dog-eared notepad, and walked over to his table with it. "Wouldn't it be simpler to use this?"

He looked up at her and smiled. His eyes crinkled at the corners when he did that, and made him very attractive. Starchie's eyes were hazel, and sparkled with intelligence—just not fashion sense. She reminded herself of that quickly.

"Thank you," he said.

His handwriting was generous and loopy. Thorough, too. He'd used ten napkins, but at least he hadn't wasted any space on them.

"What are you writing?" she asked.

His eyes crinkled even more. "A business plan."

"Oh." Thank God her guess of bad poetry was off the mark. He was just an average guy, spending his Saturday morning in her café. Relieved, she asked, "Would you like more coffee to go with the notepad?"

"I would." He got to his feet and retrieved his cup, following her back to the counter.

She poured.

"Thank you, Shelly."

She set the coffeepot down with a snap. She hadn't told the guy her name. A shiver went through her, and the hairs on the back of her neck rose. Oh, no. It couldn't happen again. The past was the past and wouldn't repeat itself. Or would it?

"Look, asshole. You tell me right now how you know my name."

Shock registered in his eyes. "I, uh—"

"How do you know my name?"

He put out his hands, palms forward, as if to show he was unarmed. "Calm down. I sent you flowers last week, okay? The florist across the street told me your first name. That's all. I don't know anything else about you."

Shelly swallowed and nodded. "Why did you send me flowers?"

"Believe me, I didn't mean to upset you. I . . . I think you're beautiful. I wanted to put a smile on your face."

She took a deep breath. "Thank you," she said, with an effort. "But don't, okay? Don't send me any more flowers. You come here for coffee and a Danish, okay? Nothing else in Joe to Go is for sale."

"I never meant to imply that it was." His eyes searched her face, reflecting concern, not anger or hurt as she'd expected. His face was kind, not creepy. No menace there. "I'm not going to bother you like that," he said. "You take care of yourself, all right? Good-bye."

Starchie turned, scooped up his plethora of napkins from the table, and walked calmly out of her shop.

Chapter Fifteen

MAYBE HE lost something. Maybe he lost something and wanted to bring it back.

Vanessa puzzled over the words, and even more over the muffled pain in Crash Dunmoor's oh-so-matter-of-fact tone. What was this mystery all about? Miss Eugenie pretended to fall asleep when she asked about it, and Crash either refused to answer or talked in riddles.

She remembered his words on the roof of the cabin, the first day she'd cast eyes on him. The first day this horrid lust had carpet-bombed all her defenses.

Her blood was still thrumming as hard as her curiosity five minutes after he'd left her office. There was something very wrong with her, so wrong that she almost understood how one of the girls in her seminar had flicked his nipple. Crash

Dunmoor was just one of those men that you wanted to take a bite out of. He was a human Cadbury bar, with nuts in all the right places.

And now Miss Eugenie had her inspecting his quads. *A man's stamina is all in the thighs and buttocks . . . all the Dunmoor men are very well hung.*

Thanks a lot, Miss Eugenie. Vanessa jumped up and paced the length of her office. Her body was in league with her mind to conspire against her. Her breasts felt full and heavy, the tips sensitive against the confines of her bra.

Her skin was on fire, and she'd developed a hot pulse in an unspeakable place. Steam was probably curling up from the hem of her tweed skirt.

It was all *hideous*. She'd never felt like this before, not when she'd dated Harry from the bank, or Wayne from the English Department, or what was his name who worked in one of the research labs. Fred.

Fred had been nice, she thought desperately. He had a pleasant mouth that curved up in a Cupid's bow. Slightly chapped lips. Dry.

Not mocking and rapacious, hiding white teeth that could rip through cotton panties with a single growl . . . oh God help her! Where had *that* come from?

Her hair was escaping its knot, just as her libido was. She pulled it down and twisted it back up so ferociously that tears sprang to her eyes. Then she clipped it into place with a vengeance, as the voices of her aunts on that long-ago Christmas Eve came to mind.

Shameless hussy! Devious slut . . .

She was proving to be no better. To distract herself, she sat down in front of her computer and clicked her mouse on the AOL icon. The machine hummed and warbled, finally flashing the familiar rectangular screen in front of her. "You've got *male!*" she read.

"No, no I *don't*," she said aloud, through gritted teeth. "Nor do I want one." She clicked on the mailbox symbol, but not before reading one of the featured topics for the day: Are you emotionally honest?

Vanessa said a bad word, one she didn't normally use. She quickly scanned through her messages, responded to a couple, then closed out.

Crash's parting words echoed in her mind again. *Maybe he lost something . . .*

She had to get to the bottom of this family mystery. Not only for personal reasons, but professional ones. She could hardly complete a treatise on the work of Thomas Dunmoor without knowing why he'd shifted his focus so dramatically at the end of his life. And if nobody was going to tell her, she'd have to do a little detective work on her own.

She gathered her things, locked her door, and headed for the main library on campus. It was time to resort to old newspapers. The walk along the college's pretty paths allowed her to stretch her legs and breathe in lungfuls of crisp, early-October air. She sorted through known facts in her mind.

Thomas and Eugenie had raised only one son, Robert Dunmoor. Robert had been married in his thirties to a woman named Ester, who'd shared his interest in and devotion to humanitarian concerns. They'd both died while working with the Peace Corps in Africa.

Crash had not been with them. He'd stayed behind, presumably with his grandparents.

Something was bothering Vanessa, though. The day she'd met him at his cabin, Crash had started to say a name. "Ste—" Steven, she'd thought, wondering if he was an uncle or a brother. If he was an uncle, he would have had to have been on his mother's side, since Robert was the only son of Eugenie and Thomas. And that didn't make sense, in the context of the conversation she'd been having with Crash about his Nordic Dunmoor ancestors.

Vanessa stopped in the middle of the path, watching a squirrel retrieve an acorn and scamper off with it.

A snippet of conversation with Miss Eugenie came back to her, something about taking care of "the boys" in Robert and Ester's absence. Not boy, but boys. Had Crash had a brother? A brother named Steven?

Since her human resources weren't telling her, she'd resort to microfiche. Vanessa reached the heavy ornate wooden doors of the Seymour College library, and hauled on one of them with all her body weight. She was going to figure out the Dunmoor mystery even if she had to stay in the library for the next ten days straight.

Mountains of microfiche later, Vanessa had found what she was looking for: the birth announcement of Steven Thomas Dunmoor, 8 lbs, 4 oz., 21 in. to Mr. and Mrs. Robert Dunmoor of Newton, Massachusetts. He was eighteen months older than Crash. Vanessa picked at her cuticles, bit off a hangnail, and stared at the tiny baby. He was adorable, gazing at the camera with an utterly confused expression on his face.

This was Crash's older brother? She tried to imagine Crash himself ever being that small, that helpless, that innocent. Nope. No way. The louse had sprung, fully grown, out of a pod from Mars.

Shaking the thought out of her mind, she continued to research for hours, looking for any other clues about the family.

It was after nine o'clock at night before she found it: an obituary notice for Steven Thomas Dunmoor. He'd been killed in a recreational diving accident off the coast of Thailand at age twenty-four. He was survived by a brother, Christopher Alan Dunmoor, and his grandparents, Thomas and Eugenie Dunmoor.

"A graduate of Groton and Yale," the obituary read, "Mr. Dunmoor was a semester away from receiving his MFA at Columbia. Following in his renowned grandfather's footsteps, he had built a reputation for himself as a young artist to be reckoned with."

Vanessa dug for change in her tan nylon bag, finally locating a couple of quarters. She narrowed her eyes at the microfiche machine and carefully read the instructions on how to copy something from it.

She framed the article as best she could, dropped her change into the appropriate slot, and pressed the button. It seemed to work, and she gave a sigh of relief, until she grabbed the piece of paper and saw that it had cut off two inches of print on the left side. Aaarrgghhh.

She adjusted the supposed picture frame, and dropped her other quarter into the machine. This time it cut off two inches on the right side. Of course.

Vanessa glared at the stupid, rotten *beastly* machine. She was out of quarters, so she'd just have to Scotch tape the two pages together in the middle.

Her neck and shoulders ached with tension, and her bottom had gone to sleep after hours in the hard wooden chair. She shoved the two copies into her bag, stood up, and made her way out of the library, past the scores of Seymour students still studying.

The night breeze was cool and refreshing after the stale recycled air of the building, and she unknotted her hair to let her scalp relax. She ran her fingers through the strands and then rubbed at her temples, ditching her glasses for a moment. Then she allowed herself to think some more about Thomas Dunmoor and the family members to whom he'd said good-bye.

Maybe he lost something, Crash had said. *Maybe he lost something and wanted to bring it back.* Of course. He'd lost first his son, and then his other grandson, the one who had also been a painter. But he'd somehow lost Crash at the same time. They had obviously fought, and the clash was so fierce they had cut off the relationship for good.

The old man must have been bitter and lonely, except for Eugenie. And he'd ached enough inside that he'd begun a series of portraits, both of himself and of others. At the end of his life, perhaps when it was too late, he'd tackled the issue of his alienation from others.

Vanessa had often wondered about the portraits and knew she hadn't seen all of them. She'd focused on other aspects of Thomas Dunmoor's work, the earlier paintings for which he'd become known.

Now she was burning with curiosity on every level, personal and professional. Miss Eugenie had kept an entire portfolio from her when they'd gone through the studio. She'd tucked it under her arm, saying that it didn't amount to much, and brought it back up to the house, where she'd slid it into a closet.

If Vanessa hoped to write the definitive book on the old man's work, she couldn't leave out the last period of his life. The artistic and emotional shift was too significant to be ignored.

She needed to get her hands on that portfolio. She had a hunch it was the key to understanding not only Thomas, but Crash.

Chapter Sixteen

CREIGHTON CONCH slicked back an errant strand of his thin, graying hair and stood frowning at his reflection in the men's room mirror. His pate gleamed under the industrial lighting, and he surreptitiously whisked a ladies' compact out of his trouser pocket. Glancing around quickly to make sure he was alone, Conch flipped it open and ran the powder puff over his balding dome.

He turned to the side, and used the smaller mirror to check that he'd taken care of all relevant glints. Then he pursed his lips and let out a sigh. Gianni, his hairdresser, had taken his sideburns up half a centimeter too high, curse him. The results completely changed the shape of his face and made him look far less distinguished than he really was.

His eyebrow pencil was at home, so he wouldn't

have time to fill in the whiskers properly before his presentation. Damn.

Conch retracted his lips to better display his teeth in the mirror, pleased with the results of the bleaching process he'd undergone. His pearlies sparkled as white as the industrial porcelain sink under the mirror, and he looked at least ten years younger. Nodding in approval, he sprayed some breath freshener between each set of molars and smacked his lips closed.

The mint would mix nastily with the champagne they'd all be drinking tonight at the reception, but it couldn't be helped.

Conch shimmied his knees, attempting to shake loose the crawl of his silk boxers, but it did little good. With a frown, he unbuckled his dress belt, unfastened the tab of his pants, and reached a well-manicured hand around his love handles to make the adjustment.

When the door of the men's room swung open, revealing the president of Seymour College, he was sorry he hadn't stepped into a stall. Conch flashed his new-and-improved teeth and removed his hand from his pants.

The president nodded at him, one eyebrow lifted, and went to stand in front of a urinal.

Conch found himself in a dilemma. He didn't get a lot of face time with the president, and this was a godsent opportunity, it really was. So even though he didn't have to pee, he sauntered to the adjoining urinal and stood shoulder to shoulder with the man.

He was only able to squeeze out a few measly dribbles, but it gave him the opportunity for conversation. "Lovely evening, eh?"

The president made a noncommittal noise.

"I am so looking forward to this little soirée, and to presenting Mrs. Hewitt with her certificate of appreciation from the music department. The antique sheet music she donated is worth probably eight thousand dollars, at a conservative estimate."

The president continued to pee.

"That's a drop in the bucket, however, compared to the deal I'm working on at the moment."

"It's always inspiring to hear how you exert yourself on the college's behalf, Conch."

"Yes, well. It's a labor of love, you know." The dean cast his gaze modestly downward, only to get an eyeful of his superior's package.

A muscle jumped in the man's jaw, and he stowed and zipped with perhaps more force than necessary.

Conch scrambled to make up for his faux pas. "A drop in the bucket, as I was saying. I'm about to finalize a deal worth 2.6 *million*."

"Impressive," said President Reeves, looking down his nose at him. Why did the blasted man have to be so tall?

"Thank you. Yes, I quite look forward to making the official announcement." He scanned Reeves's face, looking for some sign of approval, and discerned none. That would soon change. "The donation involves a body of work by the late Thomas Dunmoor."

"Well, keep me posted."

"I most certainly will." He extended his arm for a handshake, in a gesture of courtesy and male bonding. "So nice to see you this evening."

"Wash your hands, Conch," said the president, making his own move toward the sinks.

Vanessa stopped on the path and checked her watch. Oh, no! Involved in her research, she'd completely forgotten to attend an event in the music building tonight, a reception that Creepy Creighton expected all the fine arts faculty to go to. The old windbag was making some sort of presentation and knew none of the students would actually show, so he'd recruited the unlucky staff on this Monday night.

Well, it was too late now. She'd just have to hope that he hadn't noticed her absence.

Vanessa looked at her watch again and realized that it had been several hours since she'd eaten. She was getting shaky and knew she had to do something about food immediately. A dinner of cold cereal or tuna fish, alone in her house, didn't sound at all appealing.

One of Shelly's ham-and-cheese croissants and

a cup of hot herbal tea sounded better, and she could use some of her friend's bracing company.

She cut around the student union and headed down Main Street to Joe to Go. Shelly only stayed open until nine, but she was there until ten, closing out the register and cleaning up.

The lights were still blazing, and her friend was wiping down tables, scrubbing them as if they were infected with the plague. The expression on her face was a little manic. Vanessa knocked on the door, and Shelly jumped fourteen inches into the air, coming down hard and twisting an ankle. Not hard to do in those boots.

Her friend glared at her and shot her the finger, but her face broke into a grin as she hobbled to the door and unlocked it. "What brings you out tonight, Professor Primrose?"

"Starvation," said Nessa. "Got any of those ham-and-cheese croissants left? My only other menu options involve Top Ramen or something green and fuzzy at the back of my refrigerator."

"Yeah?" asked Shelly, locking the door behind her. "Has it turned into a form of modern art yet?"

"Close. I'm going to give it a few more days, then try to sell it at auction."

"Let me see what's left in the back. We may not have any ham and cheese, but I think we've got some plain croissants stuffed with chicken salad."

"Mmmm, even better." She watched her friend still hobbling. "Is your ankle okay?"

Shelly waved off her concern. "Fine." She grabbed her roll of paper towels and spray cleaner off a café table, flipped off the front lights, and gestured for Vanessa to follow her.

"So how're your classes? How's the jerk? Is he giving you any trouble?"

With a wry twist of her mouth, Nessa filled Shelly in, and she shouted with laughter. "Professor, you sure have gotten yourself in a jam. Next thing you know *you'll* be flicking his nipples. Or letting him flick yours."

"Shelly! That's not an option. He's a *student*. Do you know how much trouble I could get into? It doesn't even bear thinking about."

"Oh, you're thinking about it, all right."

She could feel the heat moving into her face. "No, I'm not. Okay, I am. But it can't happen. I'm just having a random attack of the hornies."

Shelly laughed. "Thank God for vibrators, right?"

Vanessa had never actually seen one. "Um, yeah."

"Jayzus, you've gotta be kidding me. You don't have one, do you?"

She opened her mouth and closed it again, shaking her head. If she tried to lie, Shelly would probably ask her the make, model, and speed.

"Well, we can fix that."

"No, no, that won't be necessary."

"Then you're going to jump him?"

"Absolutely not!"

"Then it's necessary."

"How do you even know where to get one? Who introduced you to the things, anyway?"

"God, you've led a sheltered life, haven't you." Shelly pulled an open bottle of chardonnay out of her walk-in fridge, along with a plate of the stuffed croissants. She poured two glasses of wine, and slid a couple of sandwiches out from under the plastic wrap, plunking them onto plates.

They sat down at a little table in the back for their meal, and Shelly unzipped and ditched her boots, rubbing at her ankle. Then she tucked her feet up under her.

"See, the thing about you, Nessa, is that you look so upright and proper that nobody would even say the *word* 'dildo' around you. Nobody but me, anyway." She grinned. "Me, on the other hand—people have never been careful around me." She dug a forkful of chicken salad out of her croissant, popped it into her mouth, and chewed.

Vanessa inhaled a mouthful of wine. Professor Primrose. Yick. But she supposed the nickname suited her.

Shelly swallowed her food and continued. "Let's see, I first learned about vibrators on the job. I was fifteen, and bussing tables for a greasy barbecue joint in Worcester. The owner, Big Betsy, was one scary woman. Mean, too, except twice a day after she took her breaks. Eleven and four, on the dot."

Nessa screwed up her face, not sure she wanted to hear this. She took another gulp of wine.

"Big Betsy had a walk-in fridge, just like that one, and at eleven and four she'd go in there, sleeveless, and close the door. She wouldn't come out for a good ten, fifteen minutes, and nobody would bother her. You learned that if you needed dairy, you just got it way before she went in.

"Anyway, Betsy would disappear into that walk-in, and when she came out, there wasn't a goose bump on her. She was usually sweaty, in fact, and she had this kind of glow about her. She'd go back out and start taking orders again, and work into her regular mean self."

Shelly began to laugh. "One day, she had a big falling-out with the cook. They had a screaming match in the kitchen, and then she stormed out front again to take care of the lunch rush."

"Ethan, the cook, marched over to the walk-in and started throwing stuff out of it, on the floor. Lettuce, butter, sour cream—you name it. He was hitting every shelf, looking for something. Finally he found it: the biggest, nastiest-looking vibrating dildo you've ever seen. Ethan took that thing out into the main restaurant, waving it around and shouting at her while entire families fled the place . . ."

Vanessa was horrified, yet she couldn't help laughing.

Shelly sobered. "I didn't like Big Betsy much, but I did feel kind of sorry for her. That was the end of her restaurant." She sipped at her wine. "Anyway, that was the first time I saw a vibrator."

"Uh-huh. Well, thanks for sharing, but I don't want one."

Shelly eyed her, chewing another mouthful of chicken salad. "They're much better than men. They don't burp, fart, or leave dirty socks on the floor."

"I'll still pass."

"They don't tune you out for sports or leave beard bristles in your sink."

"Okay, okay," Vanessa said. "I know where you stand on the subject of vibrators." She picked up her chicken salad croissant. "So, heard anything more from the exotic flower guy?"

Shelly went completely still. "Yeah," she said finally, "he was in here on Friday. I kind of snapped his head off."

"What? Why?"

"He knew my name. It gave me the creeps."

"The whole town knows your name, Shel. You run a popular coffee shop. People come in and greet you."

"He's not from here, and he was very . . . intense, and he hung around for a couple of hours, reading a newspaper and making notes all over my napkins."

"It does seem pretty dastardly for him to read a newspaper while drinking his coffee. Did you call the police?"

"Nessa, it's not funny. There are things about me you don't know." Shelly drained the rest of her wine and went to get the bottle for refills. She was edgy again, and her eyes looked strained.

"Hey," said Vanessa. "I'm sorry. I was only teasing."

"Yeah, I know."

She laid a hand on Shelly's arm. "What? What's wrong?"

Her friend took a deep swallow of chardonnay, plucked her clear plastic plate from the table, and tossed it, Frisbee-style, into the trash. Most of her food was still on it. "You done?"

Nessa nodded.

She did the same with her plate, though it sported nothing left but half a fluorescent green pickle. "A few years ago, before I moved here from Boston, I had . . . trouble . . . with a stalker." Her face had gone carefully blank. "He knew my name, my address, my license plate number. He knew where I worked. He knew where I bought groceries, Chinese takeout, even underwear." She swallowed. "He'd been following me for months, and I'd never noticed. I was so, so, *stupid*. How could I have been so stupid?" she asked.

All Nessa could do was murmur sympathetically, afraid to hear what came next.

"He got into my apartment. I let him in, actually. *I let him in.* He said he'd just moved into the complex and wondered if I had that day's *Globe*—the movie listings."

Shelly lifted her wineglass once again to her lips. Her hand shook. "I won't talk about what happened. Let's just say we had a 'date' on his terms."

Nessa got out of her chair and put her arms around Shelly, who didn't—couldn't—respond. Her thin shoulders shook, and she seemed to soak up the embrace as best she could.

"I'd remembered hearing that you should . . . work . . . with a person like that, try to play into his fantasy world. That you could be safer that way. So I pretended to like him." She took a deep shuddering breath. "I said I'd see him again. Then I talked him into going to get Chinese food. Just going to the ladies' room, I said, when we got to the place. Be right back!"

Vanessa began to cry as she held Shelly.

"There was a pay phone back there. I called 911, and a black-and-white picked him up with a bag of moo shu pork in his hand. He couldn't believe I'd called the cops."

Shelly finished a third glass of the wine, leaving the bottle empty. Vanessa still wouldn't let go of her. She gave a small hiccup. "So, Professor, I don't trust men a whole lot. I know they're not all like that, but . . ." She gulped.

"I'll probably end up like Big Betsy, in twenty years. I'll keep a turbo-charged v-v-vibrator next to the cream in my walk-in." She began to laugh hysterically, and Nessa rocked her, just rubbing her back and making soothing noises.

"Psycho Shelly, here. The flower guy comes in, wearing s-starched jeans. And then he knows my name. And I flip—all I could think about was how weird must a guy be, to starch his jeans? And I was afraid it was starting all over again, that I have some radar that attracts violent wackos, even though I moved on purpose to a tiny college town populated mostly by women."

Vanessa rocked her some more, and finally Shelly pulled away and stood up.

"Thanks." She unrolled a paper towel and blew her nose on it. "Anyway, that's why I don't think getting flowers from some unknown guy is romantic. And I called poor Starchie an asshole."

Vanessa choked. "Starchie?"

"Flower man. Like I said, he wore starched Levi's. Very weird. But what was even weirder was that he wasn't mad at me for calling him an asshole. He just looked at me like he was concerned, or sad, or something. Like he understood, even though I know he didn't."

"Hmmm," said Vanessa.

"Then he said he wouldn't bother me that way."

"Good."

"But now I'm wondering if I wish he would." She stopped, seeming surprised by what she'd just said.

"Come on," Vanessa told her. "Let's lock this place up. Then maybe you can stay at my house tonight. You don't want to be alone, do you?"

"No," said Shelly. "Thanks. I don't."

Chapter Seventeen

THREE FIFTY-SIX, Vanessa's clock read. Four minutes until she would have to contend with Crash and his long, lean dangerous body. Those high-voltage shoulders, the dynamite buns, and that explosive sexual current he emanated.

A sudden sharp pain in her knuckles made her aware that she was gnawing on them like a beast. Vanessa jerked her hand out of her mouth and inspected the resulting tooth marks. They were a testament to her spiraling insanity.

What kind of woman chewed on her own hands while waiting for a student in her office? Granted, she was hungry, having eaten nothing since the chicken salad croissant the night before. Today had been too busy.

Poor Shelly. She'd taken her home, given her a

chocolate chip cookie and a tall glass of milk, and tucked her into the guest bed under a bright quilt that Aunt Tabitha and Aunt Gertie had made together.

Shel had protested that she didn't need to treat her like a baby . . . but she did. Nessa wanted to draw innocence around Shelly again like a fleece blanket and feed her all the childhood comfort food she could swallow. Gummi bears—she'd get her some gummi bears today. She remembered an age, long ago, when a sticky clan of gummis inside a small cellophane bag could change the world. Red bears spread love, green ones made things grow, yellow ones radiated sunshine . . . but she was stuck on orange. What had orange gummi bears done for the world in her six-year-old mind? She couldn't remember.

"A penny for your thoughts, Professor." Crash's voice startled her out of candyland.

He stood in the doorway, looking good enough to lick.

"Oh, they're not worth that much," she assured him.

"*Your* thoughts? I'm sure each one is valued at a thousand pennies, at least. After all, they're highly trained and intellectually acrobatic. You do have a Ph.D. after your name."

Yes, and when you're around, those three little letters stand for either Physical Desire or Phantasm of Debauchery. Aloud, she said, "Trust me. Today my mind is completely unworthy of the degree." She pulled her lips into a professional smile.

He tilted his big, dirty blond head and slanted her a gaze that said he knew what she meant.

She hoped not, and screwed her smile on tight. "I've reserved a viewing room in the slide library for the next two hours, since I don't have any wall space in here." Vanessa gathered her things: a flimsy waxed paper cup of iced tea, her bag, her lecture notes, and the pointer she kept with two umbrellas in a tall, narrow container.

She gripped the smooth wood of the pointer like a weapon of self-defense and took a long draught of the cold tea to try to drown her leaping pulse.

She was calm, cool, and controlled. She was not a bit ruffled at the idea of spending two hours in a dark, private, soundproof room with Crash Dunmoor. Why should she be?

They had gotten that one useless, shameless kiss out of the way already. He'd probably just been trying to shock her, pull off some bizarre chauvinistic power play. He would have been delighted if she'd shrieked and complained to the chair, and thus made herself into a prize idiot.

But she could be proud: She hadn't done that. She'd handled the situation on her own.

Vanessa locked her office door and marched down the mint green tiles of the hallway, ignoring the suspicion that Dunmoor was staring at her ass.

She told herself again that she had nothing to fear. It didn't matter that her buns were growing warm and tingly under his impudent gaze, or that her breasts seemed to have just gained two pounds apiece. If he kissed her today, they were in danger of exploding through her bra and wrapping themselves around his neck.

What was she thinking? If he got within a foot of her today, she'd knock his leonine head right off. He wasn't going to kiss her.

She shuddered. Was shameless lust something you could genetically inherit? *No, Vanessa Lynn. You are not like her. You will not be tempted by your body into degenerate behavior.*

Nothing would happen between her and Crash Dunmoor except an exchange of knowledge. She'd planned ahead, by wearing not only tight granny panties, but Super-Spandex, Thigh-Thinning, Tummy-Terrorizing panty hose under her skirt. And a pair of Lycra bike shorts, to boot. If Crash so much as laid a finger on her, it would bounce right back and poke him in the eye.

Granted, between the panties, the hose, the bike shorts, and the elastic waistband of her skirt, she was about to pass out thanks to low blood circulation. But that was her cross to bear. The bullet-proof sensation was worth the shortness of breath.

"Have you been working out?" Crash asked, from behind her.

She gritted her teeth. "No. Why?"

"You just look very . . . trim." He sounded thoughtful.

He would never know her secret. "Thank you. By the way, I appreciate the mark of respect, but you're welcome to walk next to me, rather than twenty paces behind."

He chuckled. "You're most magnanimous, Miz Tower."

"I do try."

They reached the doors to the slide library, where tens of thousands of slides were stored in narrow drawers, similar to a card catalog system. Vanessa strode to the front desk and requested her carousels from the librarian. She signed them out, and they walked to the viewing room she'd reserved.

Boxlike, the room was white-walled, sterile, and airless. Furnishings consisted of a six-seater birch-veneered table and black molded-plastic chairs. Two projectors squared off with each other at the end of the table.

The moment Crash entered the room, it shrank by several feet until it felt about the size of a shower stall. Vanessa couldn't seem to get her breath, even though the walk from her office wasn't more than a hundred feet. The cursed spandex was crushing all her internal organs, and was exacerbating a stomachache brought on by sheer hunger. How on earth had women ever worn corsets?

She slid her things onto the table, then set the carousels in place on the projectors. She turned them on to make sure they were adjusted correctly and focused. Then she switched them off again.

Crash, meanwhile, had sprawled into one of the black chairs. He leaned back with his head pillowed in his hands behind his head, his elbows extending like angel wings. Huh—some angel.

The angels she'd read about didn't have wicked green eyes, or dirty blond manes, or sculpted quads. They fluttered around in filmy white robes, not Levi's that fit like a second skin, down to the very last bulge. Ahem.

That started her down another imaginative path. Did manufacturers of men's trousers take measurements to ensure that a customer's joystick was well accommodated? For example, what did the Levi's 550 label say about a man, as compared to a 501?

She glanced at Crash, but whatever label he wore on his jeans was pressed flat against the plastic chair back. *All the Dunmoor men are very well hung . . .* Vanessa blinked. *Go away, Miss Eugenie, you've caused enough trouble already!*

She opened her mouth to try to suck some air into her lungs. Her pulse throbbed madly, and the damned man was doing nothing but *looking* at her.

What if he were to touch her face again, the way he'd caressed it during the kiss they'd shared?

What if he grazed his sandpapery jaw along her lips, then dipped his head to put his own lips at the hollow of her throat? What if his lips trailed downwards from there until they nuzzled the slopes of her breasts . . . Oh, God, she had to get more air than this, but the layers of spandex and elastic wouldn't allow it.

Crash's green eyes narrowed and moved over her like laser beams.

Could he see that her nipples had hardened? That they were going to start spinning and drill their way out of her clothing to meet his mouth? Oh, this was too embarrassing.

She gasped for breath again and felt perspiration gather on her brow. Her stomach ached fiercely now. She really should have eaten something.

"Vanessa, are you all right?"

"What? Oh, yes, I'm fine." She pulled her lecture notes out of her bag and tried to focus on the typed words, tried to think of concepts such as "artist" and "grandfather" and "Cape Cod" and "ruthlessly driven personality." She tried to remember what a Thomas Dunmoor painting looked like, but all she could focus on was his grandson. His presence pulsed through every fiber of her being. She was wrapped in a sexual awareness so intense that it was hypnotic. And he hadn't touched her. Oh, how she ached for him to do so . . .

"Vanessa?" He'd gotten out of his chair and come to stand behind her. He touched her arm, and her skin burned under his fingers.

She turned to face him, and fell headlong into the green of his eyes, drowning helplessly.

He cupped her chin in those strong, warm hands, and she felt a tingle spread over her face and neck until it reached even the tips of her ears.

Breathe! You've got to get some air into your imbecilic lungs, Vanessa. But then his thumbs were at the corners of her mouth, and he covered her lips with his. He was searching, wondering, trying as hard as she was to figure out what this thing was between them, she thought.

And then she ceased to think. Their tongues tangled, teeth nipped, skin brushed skin. Desire became the ringmaster, and nothing else mattered.

His neck supported her arms, his hard chest supported the heavy, aching softness of her breasts, his mouth drove against hers. She was dizzy with want and need, too dizzy to care that she was shameless . . . that her stomach was in torture . . . that she really couldn't breathe . . . she felt Crash's hands move down her back to cup her bottom, which should have felt good, but instead she felt nothing. She was falling . . . and everything faded to black.

Crash knew the difference between passion and deadweight. One moment he'd been kissing a definitely responsive hot armload of woman, and in the next she passed out on him. Christ, was she okay?

He laid her gently on the table and felt for her pulse. Thank God it was there, slow and steady. What had he done to her? What kind of monster was he?

His mind raced. He should loosen her clothing, and put something cold on her forehead, and then he should get help fast. No! If he disturbed her clothing, somebody might get the wrong idea and call the police.

Crash raced out of the viewing room and shouted for the librarian to come in, fast. The woman ran.

"She fainted or something. I need you to stay here while I loosen her clothes, okay?"

"Ohmygod, ohmygod, ohmygod," she said. Her name tag told him she was Jan Bowers.

"Everything will be fine, Jan," he told her. Then he tugged at Vanessa's blouse, but it was as if the damned thing was cemented inside her skirt. What the hell? He tugged again, and saw layers under the waistband of her skirt. A black layer, a flesh-colored layer, and then a white layer.

"I'm not trying to be a perv here, okay Jan? We need to get this stuff off her."

Jan nodded, her eyes wide.

Crash slid up the light wool skirt and raised his

brows. He took one look at what Vanessa was wearing, and dug for his Swiss army knife.

What in the name of God was the woman trying to do to herself? He tugged the elastic out a couple of inches from her waist, and sliced off the weird black pants. Then came the most industrial panty hose he'd ever seen. Crash made quick work of those. Last was a pair of white granny undies that were so thick and ugly they defied description. To spare Vanessa's modesty, he only made a slit on either side of the waistband, and left them on.

Then he and Jan carefully pulled down her skirt, which he made sure was unbuttoned and unzipped at the waist.

Next he lifted her slightly with one arm, and reached around with the other to deftly unhook her bra under the blouse.

"Stay with her," he said to Jan. Then he grabbed her paper iced-tea cup and ran for the water fountain he'd seen earlier.

He filled it, commandeered some paper towels, and brought them back to the room, where Vanessa's eyelids now fluttered open. He dipped one of the paper towels into the cold water and laid it across her pale forehead.

"Should we call 911?" Jan asked.

"Let's see how she feels. Vanessa, sweetheart? What's wrong? Does anything hurt?"

She turned her face toward him. "I . . . couldn't

breathe. Must have fainted." A light flush spread across her freckled cheeks. "No, nothing hurts, except my stomach. But it's better." She placed her hand there, and then noticed her clothing was in disarray. Her eyes widened, and she raised her head to look down at herself. The black stretch shorts and her panty hose lay on the table next to her, where he'd tossed them.

"What have you eaten today?" Crash demanded.

The flush flamed into a mortified crimson and she squeezed her eyes shut. "How did my . . . my underwear g-get off me?"

"What have you eaten today?" he repeated.

"Nothing. About my underwear—"

"I sliced it off you. You needed air. Do you mean to tell me you haven't had *anything* to eat all day? It's almost four-thirty!"

"You cut my underwear off with a knife?"

"To hell with your underwear, woman! Why aren't you taking care of yourself properly?"

Jan took the cup of water from him, and held it to Vanessa's lips. "Drink," she said gently. "Can you hold the cup?"

Vanessa nodded, and struggled to sit.

"I've got some saltines in my office, dear. I'm going to get them."

"Thank you, Jan." Her face was so red it was almost violet.

He would have laughed under any other circumstances, but he couldn't just now. He'd been too worried.

Though when he eyed those scary industrial panty hose and the black nylon thingies, he guessed he could understand her blushing. They truly did take the prize for ugly. Even more hideous, though, were the panties she still had on.

Crash shook his head. If they ever figured out what was going on between them, maybe he could give her a little aid in the lingerie department. However, to judge from the appalled expression on Vanessa's face, he shouldn't bring up the subject just now.

The only kind thing to do was to distract her. So he cleared his throat and announced thoughtfully, "I've had women moan before, when I've kissed them. I've even had an overenthusiastic woman chomp on my tongue. But never, ever, have I had a woman pass out on me just because I kissed her. Damn, I'm good."

"Crash Dunmoor, you are the most insufferably arrogant *louse*—"

"You have to admit, it's an extreme reaction."

"—I have ever met in my unfortunate life!"

"Louse?" he repeated. "But those are tiny little suckers. I'm pretty large, and I much prefer a woman's breasts to her scalp . . ."

"Don't flatter yourself. I passed out from lack of food and lack of oxygen, not, I repeat NOT, because of you, Dunmoor!" Her voice shook.

"Aw, come on," he mourned. "I don't get *any* of the credit?"

"No! And I can't believe you pulled my skirt up when I was out cold and *cut* . . ." Words failed her.

"Jan was here the entire time," he said, sobering. "Just ask her. Why do you wear all that stuff, anyway?"

"That is none of your business!"

He couldn't argue with that.

Vanessa set the cup of water down and slid off the table.

"Careful," he said. He took a step toward her, and reached for her arm.

She evaded him, leaned on the birch veneer instead, and managed to give a good imitation of stalking to where the offending undergarments lay. She whisked them up and stuffed them deep into her nylon shoulder satchel. Then she turned her back on him for a moment, in order to compose herself, he guessed.

"I suppose I should say thank you," she finally managed. "For . . . for . . . uh, reviving me."

"You're welcome," Crash said.

"Where are my boots?" She looked incredibly sexy, all rumpled and barefoot and gruff with embarrassment.

"Over here." He bent down and handed them to her.

Jan appeared with her box of saltines. "I called my doctor, Vanessa, and he advised that you should go in for some blood tests, just to make sure everything's okay."

He watched the good professor's face as she obviously debated whether or not to say something. After a few moments, she folded her arms across her body, and blurted, "I am *not* pregnant."

Jan blinked. "Of course not, dear." She carefully avoided looking at Crash. "Now, just have two or three of these." She passed over the crackers.

"Thank you." Vanessa took two out of the box and crunched on them. "It would have to be an immaculate conception, you understand," she said around the food.

Jan's eyebrows rose.

"Because," Vanessa swallowed, "I'm not even dating anyone at the moment."

Shut up, he thought, *you're making it worse.*

"Certainly not *him*," she continued, gesturing at Crash with her thumb. "He's a student. Special dispensation, you know . . ."

Jan smiled and nodded.

"Dr. Tower," he interrupted, "why don't I drive you home so that you can rest." He turned to Jan. "Thank you for your help. I'll make sure she gets back safely."

"All right. Take care of her now." The woman patted Vanessa on the shoulder, then turned and left the viewing room. "Don't worry about the slide carousels," she called. "I'll get them."

Vanessa stuffed her bare feet into her boots and

said nothing further. He gathered her bag, her pointer, and the cup, and they walked from the building.

"Where's your car?" he asked. "I'm on my bike today."

"You don't need to drive me home."

"Yes, I do. You just passed out. Have some sense and give me your keys."

"They're in the zipper pocket. The car's on the opposite side of the building, not far."

The Cruiser suited her, he thought again, as they reached it and he unlocked the passenger door. She got in gracefully and he handed her the bag, slipping the pointer into the backseat.

Such an old-fashioned instrument. These days, only an art history professor would use one, to indicate areas of a projected slide. But it made him think of her in a pioneer schoolhouse, rapping errant students' knuckles with the thing.

He opened the driver's side door and slid in, and soon they were purring down Main Street in the Cruiser. It handled smoother than he'd thought it would, and he decided he liked it.

Other than giving him directions, Vanessa stared straight ahead and said nothing. He hummed and wondered how long it took a woman to get over the public exhibition of her most gruesome drawers.

Five minutes later he pulled into her driveway. She lived in a small, white Cape Cod with black shutters and a cherry red rocking chair on the porch. The mailbox to the left of the door was also painted cherry red.

Several full paper lawn-and-leaf bags stood in a neat row at the curb, like senior citizens waiting placidly for a bus.

Crash imagined Professor Vanessa in a big plaid flannel shirt, the sleeves rolled to her elbows and the top three buttons undone. Long legs clad in faded denim, she'd lean over to reach with the rake, spilling her coppery hair over her shoulders in the sunlight.

He imagined sliding the jeans down her smooth white thighs, and discovering a sapphire blue thong instead of those, those . . . testaments to moldy virtue she had on at the moment.

"Keys?" said Vanessa's voice, probably not for the first time.

"Keys. Right." He transferred them from his palm to hers, and she slid a large brass one into the lock on the front door.

Lucky key, he thought. The lock squeaked as she turned it, so he figured it was having a nice time, too. Aw, Jayzus! He could practically hear old Sigmund Freud howling with laughter from the heavens. *Bite me, Siggie.*

She opened the cherry red door and stepped inside. He saw cool blue walls, white trim, and braided rugs scattered on hardwood floors.

"When would you like to reschedule?" he asked her.

"Reschedule? Oh, the tutoring session." Her brow furrowed. "Let me check my day-runner."

He handed her the tan nylon bag he still held, and she dug into it, retrieving a compact little zippered book. She flipped through the pages, chewing on her lip.

"Damn. Maybe Friday—no, that's no good. Monday—no. Tuesday. But we'd have to do an extended four-hour class in order to get the material for both weeks in, which gets really long and tedious . . ." She thought for a moment, then turned and stared into the dining room.

"Look. Why don't we do this: If I remove a couple of pictures, I have a big blank wall in there. If you'll go get the carousels from Jan, we could do the class here, in about half an hour."

He frowned. "You sure you're up to it?"

"I'll be fine—I'll heat some soup while you're gone."

"You just happen to have two slide projectors in your house?"

She stared at him. "Well, of course I do. I teach art history, for heaven's sake."

True. He inspected her from head to toe, trying to gauge for himself if she could physically manage this. She'd just passed out, and now she wanted to teach?

"We'll do it on one condition," he said.

She raised her brows.

"Any talking you do will be from a comfortable chair. You will not get out of it. You will not strain yourself in any way, shape, or form. Agreed?"

She sighed. "Okay."

"There's actually another condition."

"What?"

"I will bring you some real food on the way back, and you will eat it, not a can of soup that's had all the vitamins boiled and packaged out of it."

She folded her arms. "Awfully dictatorial, aren't you, Crash?"

"You bet. Is it a deal or not?"

"Deal."

Chapter Eighteen

SHE CLOSED the door behind him and leaned on it weakly for a moment. Then she went to the window and watched Dunmoor get into her car and back out of the narrow driveway.

Crash looked incongruous on quiet, quaint little Maple Street, with its neat, square lawns and perfectly aligned mailboxes. He looked like the kind of guy who lived on a boat—wild and free. He seemed undomesticated, defiant of regular haircuts, regular paychecks, regular anything.

An untamed, testosterone-driven legend, she thought again. That was Crash Dunmoor. And he had cut her underwear off with a knife.

Just thinking about it made her cringe. Except then a flash of heat shot through her. The concept of Crash and the knife was so deliciously barbaric, so savagely sexual, so darkly forbidden.

If only she'd been wearing a leopard-print thong and had had herself waxed into oblivion. But no, she was Vanessa Lynn Tower, and therefore she'd been wearing granny panties, support hose, and the modern equivalent of a girdle.

And to think she'd been wearing all of that in self-defense, so that she couldn't possibly have any sort of sexual sensation around Crash Dunmoor. Irony had galloped up while she wasn't looking and bitten her in the butt.

She wiggled her bare toes inside the boots. Yuck. Her feet were sticking to the leather lining. Well, at least that was one thing she could fix, even if she couldn't change Crash's perception of her as a prize idiot.

She sat down on the stairs and unzipped, then removed the boots. Oh, hell. Now that she wasn't worried about her dignity anymore, she might as well put on her big yellow chicken-foot slippers. No way a man could come on to her in those things.

That way she and Crash could actually focus on the subject matter he needed to learn and not this bizarre, completely unsuitable, unasked-for and unwanted, *disastrous* attraction. It was ludicrous, moronic, and senseless. She would dismiss it immediately.

Vanessa sat down in one of the armchairs in front of her fireplace and stuck her feet—in their big yellow fuzzy slippers—on the ottoman in front of her.

God, but he was hot.

Half an hour later, when a knock sounded at her door, she hadn't had a single other coherent thought.

She shuffled to the door, muttering invective to herself, and opened it to find a large paper sack filled with the heaven-sent scents of the best food on earth: Italian. Takeout from the Hot Tomato, to be precise.

Crash bumped her passenger-side door closed with a cock of one hip, and followed with the slide carousels.

If Jan had had any doubts before that they were sleeping together, they'd now been laid to rest. The woman would be checking her for bow-leggedness when she returned the slides.

"Nice shoes," said Crash, when she held open the door.

"Thank you," she said, pouncing on the sack of Italian food. "They're the most elegant items in my closet. Eat your heart out, Manolo Blahnik."

"Shoe designer?" he guessed.

She supposed he could be forgiven for not reading *Vogue*. She nodded. "The Hot Tomato's my favorite. What's in the sack?"

"Frutta di mare over linguini, cannelloni Florentine, antipasto, and hot buttered bread."

"You get a gold star on your homework today." Her stomach growled audibly.

"I'll take that as a thank-you," he said, and poked her tummy with his free index finger.

The familiarity of it took her breath away, but then she gave a mental shrug. The man had been under her skirt this afternoon. She guessed a poke in the belly wasn't a stretch after that.

She waved him into the kitchen, where he stood looking around at the pristine space.

"You don't cook much, do you?"

She thought of the frozen dinners in her freezer, the scores of cans in her cupboards. The ongoing battle she had with a recipe for one of Aunt Tabitha's cakes. "No, not really. I never learned." But she was literate, damn it, and she'd done everything the recipe had instructed. Four times, now.

Once she'd burned the cake. Then she'd under-baked it. The third time, ecstatic that it came out looking normal, she'd still crumbled it while trying to roll the filling inside. She'd forgotten you had to use a pastry cloth.

In a rage, she'd made it a fourth time, only to roll it too tightly and have all of the filling squirt out of it. Her hands covered in jam, whipped cream, and melted chocolate, she'd finally decided that her father could have a store-bought birthday cake. Julia Child she was not.

She got two plates out of a cabinet while Crash

pulled the food out of the bag, along with a bottle of chianti.

She eyed it suspiciously. Was he trying to get her drunk and take advantage of her? *Oh, relax, Vanessa! He couldn't possibly want to seduce Big Bird in granny panties.*

Without comment, she dug out a corkscrew and two stemmed glasses, and set them on the counter.

"Silverware?" he suggested, pulling the lids off the cartons. He looked good enough to eat himself, standing there broad-shouldered and long-legged in her kitchen.

Duh. They weren't going to eat linguine and cannelloni with their hands, now were they? She pulled out forks and knives, just as her stomach—or was it her libido?—growled again. Roared, actually. Then licked its chops.

She swiped a piece of butter-soaked bread and jammed it between her teeth, so she wouldn't be tempted to take a bite out of his thigh.

"I do love a woman with a healthy appetite," Crash murmured, flashing white teeth at her.

She ignored him and led the way into the dining room, where she set the plates and silver on the table. Then she went to forage for napkins. When she returned, she found that he'd put a portion of each entrée on her plate, along with some salad. A full glass of wine glowed, ruby red, beside her food.

"I figured we'd share," he said, after swallowing some of his own wine.

"Yes, but I can't possibly eat that much!"

"Try," he ordered. "No more fainting. Like I said, it was flattering, but also worrying."

"Can we drop that particular subject?" She reached for her wine and took a large sip. It tingled in her mouth and sent a shiver of sensation down her spine. "I must say, I don't usually drink before I teach."

He shrugged. "I don't normally quaff wine before studying, either. I don't normally study, period. But Grandma Eugenie blackmailed me into this, so here I am."

"Here we are." She raised her glass, and they toasted wryly to circumstances.

The wine burned a pleasant warm trail to her stomach, and the food was superb. She'd always loved seafood, and the calamari, scallops, shrimp, and mussels were fresh, the garlic and spices drawing out their natural delicate flavors.

The cheese inside the cannelloni had been whipped to smooth, delicate perfection, and its accompanying tomato–meat sauce trumpeted the talent of the Hot Tomato's chef. Vanessa sighed with pleasure before she remembered that she should probably make conversation, instead of just inhaling her food.

"So, Crash, why sky-diving? How did you get into it?"

He shrugged. "I suppose it was the one dangerous sport I had yet to conquer. I've done them all, you know: from white-water rafting to sailboat racing to scuba diving. From race cars to downhill skiing to getting my pilot's license and flying professionally for a while. Six years ago, I got the itch to jump out of a plane. And now here I am, teaching other people how to do it."

"I'm not asking this question to be rude," she said, "but all these sports require ... money. If you left home twelve years ago, then how ... ?"

"Stud service," said Crash without a blink. "I pleasured bored married women."

When her eyes widened and her face registered disgust, he laughed. "Just kidding. Gotcha, didn't I? No, Vanessa, I had no money. But I did have skills, and I did have basic business sense. I founded my first outdoor adventure company at age twenty-four, a year after leaving. Sold it three years later at a big profit. Founded another one. Sold it, too. I move on once they're turning a healthy profit."

"I see. And how long will you be in Massachusetts?"

"The sky-diving season around here is really over by the end of October. Everybody will pack up and move down to Florida."

"Including you?"

"I'll hang around here, finish the class, and do some maintenance and marketing work to prepare for spring. I've got other instructors now who can take care of the existing business."

Interesting man, Crash Dunmoor. She took another bite of cannelloni and watched him enjoy his own food. "The liability must be scary."

He nodded. "Oh, the insurance is high. No doubt about it. But we're extremely careful, and we train people until they can practically go through the steps in their sleep."

"Aren't you ever afraid?"

He hesitated. "Afraid's not the right word. You always get a rush of adrenaline, no matter how many times you've made jumps." He drank some more wine. "Accidents do happen, but they're usually the result of human error. And we do our best to avoid that."

She shuddered. "I could never jump out of a plane."

"Sure you could. I'll take you sometime, if you'd like."

"I don't think so."

Vanessa took another sip of wine. As it slid down her throat, a hundred other questions about Crash flew to mind. Personal questions. Where, exactly, had he spent the last twelve years? If he'd gone from rafting to skiing to sailing to flying . . . "You've moved around a lot, haven't you?"

"Oh, yeah. When I first left"—a shadow crossed his face— "I headed for the opposite coast. Spent a couple of years in San Diego."

"The sailing?" she suggested.

He nodded, then grinned. "And the beach babes."

"California girls." She kept her voice light, though for some reason her stomach knotted.

"Mmmm." It was his turn to sip his wine. "Next was Tahoe—the skiing."

"Don't forget the snow bunnies."

His eyes crinkled at the corners. "Maybe a couple."

This time, her stomach gave a bona fide lurch.

"And after that, I headed to Colorado for some white-water rafting. Oh, I should mention a brief stint on a west Texas ranch, where I got my face kicked in by a horse. That helped me decide I wasn't much for animal husbandry."

Or husbandry in general, she thought. He hadn't mentioned any ranchers' daughters, but of course he must have sampled a few of the famed Texas women.

"So you've never been married." She didn't need to phrase it as a question.

He laughed outright. "Who, me? No. I don't think I'm the type. How about you?"

She shook her head.

"That surprises me."

"Why?"

"Because you're so . . . stable."

Boring?

"Let me guess," Crash mused. "Your parents

are still married after thirty years. Your mother stayed at home with you. You're the oldest of three."

"I hate to burst your bubble, but you couldn't be more wrong." Vanessa sighed. "I'm an only child, and my hippie mother ran off with a Brazilian guy when I was two. I haven't seen her since."

Crash stared at her. "I'm sorry."

She shrugged. "It's the way it is." She wasn't about to explain to him that when she got married, she'd be damned sure it was for keeps. There would be no abandoned children in her future, no lost half-pint souls.

"So it was just you and your father?"

"And his two sisters. They moved close by to help take care of me. One's widowed, the other divorced, and they still live in Natick, where I grew up." Vanessa smiled. "They still fuss and carp and try to outbake each other, and they take turns behind the wheel on outings because both of them love to backseat drive."

Crash laughed. "And your father? What does he do? Did he ever remarry?"

"He teaches architecture at B.U. And no, he didn't remarry. Though he's started seeing someone now." She paused and fortified herself with another sip of wine. "My turn, now. Tell me about *your* family."

His face went blank, and he fidgeted with his wineglass, rolling the stem between his long, brown fingers. "I grew up mostly with my grand-parents," he said carefully, neutrally. "Lost my parents at an early age. They had an opportunity to go to Mali with the Peace Corps. It was only supposed to be for a few months, but they were killed there."

Vanessa waited, but he said nothing else. She took a deep breath. "What about your brother?"

His hands tightened on the glass. "How do you know about my brother?"

She blinked rapidly. "Uh ... Miss Eugenie mentioned him," she lied.

"Did she." Crash set his glass down. "Yes, I had a brother named Steven. He was an artist, like Tom. He died in an accident a few years back."

"I'm sorry ..."

"Yeah. Me too." He obviously didn't want to talk about it, and she hated to press him.

Silence fell between them, and she stood up to take their now-empty plates to the kitchen. "We should get started, before it gets too late."

Darkness had fallen, and she turned on a few lamps to ward it off.

Crash carried an armchair from the living room into the dining room, while she readied the slide projectors and drew the blinds. The wine buzzed pleasantly through her system, and she felt the urge to have just one more glass.

As if he'd read her mind, Crash handed her a refill just as she'd finished setting the slide carousels in place. Then, with a mocking flourish, he handed her the pointer. "You seem to enjoy using this."

She flushed. "It's a useful tool."

"Mmmmm." He sipped his wine, his free hand tucked loosely into his pocket.

She turned on the projectors and flipped off the lights. His dark shadow moved to stand beside her armchair.

"You can sit, if you'd like. Bring the other comfortable chair in."

"No, I'm fine. I'll stand for a while."

"All right. Today—tonight—we're going to look at the work of some of your grandfather's teachers, to examine their influence on his painting. Specifically, we'll look at Robert Henri, whom he most respected. And then we'll move on to compare Dunmoor's work to that of his contemporaries, noting his specific choices and his inclination to create an art that was peculiarly American, and not European-influenced . . . it was a matter of pride for him."

She flashed the first two slides onto the wall, and launched into her lecture. A sidelong glance at Crash revealed an inscrutable expression. Was he bored? No—too alert for boredom. Resentful? Edgy?

Vanessa focused again on the images in front of them, and kept on talking.

She finished with a comparison of two more nudes, one by Thomas Dunmoor, and the other by a European contemporary of his. "As you can see, your grandfather paints his figure with a not-unaffectionate sense of realism, showing her flaws, but not magnifying them as she stands in the sunlight. The French artist has elongated and idealized his model, artfully draping her hips . . ."

Crash cleared his throat and stood up, having spent the last forty-five minutes in a chair. "Vanessa, I'm sorry, but I can't look at these nudes any longer. The one on the left is my grandmother, as you must know. I just don't want to look at Grandma Eugenie naked, okay? Even if she is forty years younger in the painting."

Vanessa bit her lip to stem a renegade gurgle of laughter and switched to the next sequence of slides. "Okay. But how do you know that's your grandmother?"

"Are you kidding? She would never have let any other woman model nude for him. She'd seen too many examples of torrid studio affairs. Miss Eugenie's mama didn't raise no fool."

This time she laughed outright. "Okay. Last two slides: one is the Woolworth Building, which your grandfather saw every day from the window of his studio. The other is a view of Notre Dame, which the other artist saw every day from *his* workspace. Perhaps these different settings say a lot about the individual visions of each artist: the pragmatic vs. the polished; one groundbreaking and one steeped in tradition."

She put down her notes and settled back into the chair with her wine, which she hadn't touched while teaching.

"You love what you do, don't you?" Crash said quietly.

"Yes. So many people dismiss art history as a debutante's major, useless and easy. It's nothing of the sort. It's a discipline that combines art, philosophy, history, and psychology. And it's an international discipline, one that absolutely requires a knowledge of other languages like German, Italian, French, and Spanish."

He moved to her chair in the darkness and retrieved the pointer from its position in the corner. She hadn't used it at all this evening.

"Professor Vanessa," he murmured. His voice was almost tender.

Her toes curled inside the chicken slippers, and that was *before* he leaned over and touched his lips to hers.

Chapter Nineteen

HER HORMONES went wild, clucking and squawking and running into one another at full speed. All too appropriate for a woman wearing chicken slippers. Crash Dunmoor was nuts, but then so was she, because she was kissing him back, and with great enthusiasm.

His hands cupped her face again, and her heart squeezed. They were so powerful and so gentle at the same time. They were adventurer's hands, hands that had been everywhere and done everything—including, she suspected, a lot of women.

She lived her life through books. Except for a couple of short trips to Europe, she was an armchair traveler, a dreamer. She sank willfully into other people's creations and lives, analyzing and enjoying them, but never participating.

What could a doer and a dreamer possibly have in common? Yearning, she supposed, as she gave herself up to his mouth and tangled her tongue with his own. He had little stability; she had too much.

Her brain stopped processing thought as their mouths melded, and she only knew sensation. His strong jaw angled over hers, and his lips sought and gave pleasure in a dance of exploration. His teeth nipped lightly at her lower lip, and razor stubble burned her cheek as he moved to the sensitive areas of her ears and throat.

Shivers coursed through her, and every nerve in her body came alive, many congregating in the tips of her breasts and between her thighs.

Crash had gone down on his knees in front of the chair. He moved his hands now from her face and neck to her shoulders, and then down to her breasts. He cupped them in his fingers, using his thumbs to slowly pleasure her nipples through the fabric of her blouse and bra.

Her breath caught, and her head fell back. He pursued her with his kiss, and she found herself wishing fiercely that no fabric separated their bodies.

As if she'd spoken aloud, Crash tugged her blouse from the waistband of her skirt and slid his hands up to her breasts. His fingers crept under her bra, and she keened with pleasure as he found her nipples and rubbed them erotically. He unhooked the bra easily and went back to his ministrations.

Heat flashed through her and pooled in waves at her center. Just as she almost gave in to it, Aunt Gertie's voice snapped, "Shameless hussy!" and Aunt Tabitha echoed her with, "Devious slut!"

Vanessa braced her hands against Crash's chest and pushed him away. "Oh my God," she said. "I can't do this!"

He sat back on his heels, took one of her hands in his, and asked the most simple of questions. "Why not?"

"Because . . . because you're a student! This could mean my job, could destroy my reputation. And I don't know you all that well, and you're related to Miss Eugenie, and . . ." She looked at him desperately.

He stood up, brushed off his knees, and looked down at her. "I scare you."

"Yes, you do."

"You want to keep me at a distance."

"Yes, I do."

"You still want me, but you don't want to take the risk."

"Yes, I—no, I don't. This is not a good idea."

"Oh, I think it's the best idea to come around in a long time. But you want distance." He rubbed a hand over his jaw, and suddenly his eyes lit upon the pointer, on the floor by her chair. The green of his pupils gleamed wickedly in the dim light. "Okay, we'll do it your way."

Crash picked up the pointer and backed up a couple of steps. He loomed large over her, legs spread and desire in plain evidence against his left thigh. Another flash of heat went through her at the sight. Oh, dear. She really was shameless. And what was he doing with her pointer?

She gasped as the tip of it circled her right nipple, and sensation surged there.

His lips curved, and his eyes gleamed again. A wild, testosterone-driven legend. The legend of her fall . . .

Vanessa sucked in another breath as he moved the pointer to her left nipple, tracing it slowly. She leaned her head back again and closed her eyes. Perhaps it was time to lose the chicken slippers. She kicked them off.

Crash transferred the pointer to the hollow between her breasts, jerked down, and she felt the top button of her shirt pop. Her eyes flew open.

His breath was audible, and he held her eyes prisoner as he gently rubbed her skin with the wood, and then deliberately popped another button.

You want distance, he'd said. *Okay, we'll do it your way.*

She felt helpless in front of him, mesmerized, though she knew instinctively that he would stop if she asked him to do so.

She didn't.

He popped the third button, and then the fourth.

Her breathing was rough and shallow now, as she waited to see what he would do next.

Instead of popping the fifth, he trailed the pointer up again, between her breasts, and onward to the collar of the blouse. He pushed it off one shoulder, then the other.

Scarcely believing she was doing it, Vanessa shrugged her arms out of the sleeves and faced him in her unhooked, loosely draped bra.

He took care of that next, edging the straps down her arms until it fell to her lap and she was bare to his gaze.

"You're breathtaking," he said. "Perfect, absolutely perfect. Beautiful."

She could do nothing but stare at him, wide-eyed.

"Stand up, Professor," he said softly.

And she did.

"Now, I want you to reach under your skirt and slip that god-awful underwear down your legs so I don't have to see it again."

Vanessa swallowed and gave a weak laugh. She hesitated.

He touched her breasts with the pointer again, rubbing her sensually, lifting first one, then the other with the tip.

"Ditch it, sweetheart, or I'll have to rap your knuckles," he teased.

Vanessa took a deep breath and slid her fingers under her skirt. She found the waistband of the panties, and pushed downward. Her own skin felt hot to the touch.

Next she reached behind her, under the back vent of the garment, hiked it up a foot, and pulled the panties down until they fell to her ankles. She stepped out of them and kicked them aside.

Crash nodded in approval and slid the pointer up her calf, caressing the skin. Then he went higher, teasing her knees, and lower to her other calf.

She didn't know if it was the wine or the tension or his hot gaze on her; perhaps it was his simple pleasure in gazing at her body, but she felt as if she were going to explode.

Crash raised the pointer between her legs, lifting both front and back of the skirt, until he reached the bare, pulsing center of her.

She cried out at the contact, at the strange wonder of it. The wood was cool, smooth, and slippery.

His breathing ragged, he moved the polished wood back and forth against her. She arched her back helplessly, feeling it slide between her thighs and buttocks and glide sensually for what seemed miles along her most sensitive spot. The sensation was too much, and she shattered then and there, standing in front of him.

Then she clapped a hand over her mouth, appalled.

"Hey, hey, hey," said Crash, soothingly. "What's that all about? There's no reason for shame. Come here." He tossed the pointer aside and took her in his arms, closing the distance between them as easily as that.

"Oh my God," she whispered.

Then he kissed her, his hands roaming hungrily over her body, unfastening the waistband of her skirt and pushing it off so it puddled around her feet.

He pulled his shirt over his head and dropped his jeans to the floor, after removing a foil packet from the pocket. He kicked off his shoes.

She stared at his naked body in wonder. She'd never seen anything as gorgeous before, unless she thought of the monumental nudes on the ceiling of the Sistine Chapel.

She had to touch, had to explore all that coppery magnificence, the hot pulsing muscle, and the beauty of his most private areas.

With lips, tongue, and teeth, he pleasured her breasts until she thought she would come again, all the while rolling on the condom he'd fished out of his jeans. Then he lifted her bodily.

To hell with shame. She wrapped her legs around his waist and sank onto him, gasping at the sensation of it.

Crash groaned, and pulled her bottom toward him until he was sheathed one hundred percent. He filled her with hot slickness, withdrew, and plunged into her again, igniting the core of her into molten lava.

She clung to his shoulders, rocking with him, drinking in the sight of all that hard muscle holding her so easily. That in itself was a powerful aphrodisiac.

The undersides of her arms slid against his biceps, his triceps, while his strong forearms held her thighs, spread her for him. The lava churned within her as she rode him, building to an unbearable heat.

Hot, wet, and helplessly desiring release, she ground wantonly against him, feeling her inner thighs tremble. He slowed their rhythm, sliding almost all the way out of her, and then penetrating deeply, tenderly, completely.

Vanessa whimpered, bit her lip to try and stop the sound, and then keened as orgasm gripped her, shook her, destroyed any semblance of control.

Waves of pleasure still tossed her as Crash stiffened and drove home in his own release. He held her against him as they both quivered with aftershocks.

* * *

The return to consciousness was slow and unwelcome. She focused on the blue-painted walls, first, then the white trim of the chair rail, and finally the slide projectors, which were still on.

Woolworth's stood on the left, Notre Dame on the right, and both buildings swarmed with people. Because of the slides, Vanessa had the uncomfortable sensation that they were in public.

She had a naked man between her legs, and she was stuck to him like some kind of sexual burr. How had this happened?

She opened her mouth to demand that he put her down, but Crash impeded her speech by kissing her thoroughly. And it would be, well, *rude* not to respond. So she did, telling herself that it was purely in the name of good manners.

Her insides felt like half-melted butter, all soft and gooey and spent. Crash lifted her off him and set her down, where it took her a moment to find her balance. He wrapped his arms around her while she did so, buried his face in her hair, and let out a long, satisfied sigh.

"I should turn off the slide projectors," she said.

"Why? You don't like making love in front of Woolworth's?"

"Well," she confessed, "I think I'm also afraid that God is looking through the rose window of Notre Dame, and getting quite an eyeful."

He laughed and released her. "You crazy woman."

Yes. She was definitely crazy. And she needed to go find her sanity, put it on a leash, and drag it home.

Chapter Twenty

SLUT! HUSSY! Jezebel! Fallen woman! Aunt Tabitha and Aunt Gertie weren't holding anything back, and Vanessa cringed. She was down on her knees next to the bathtub, where she was scrubbing the pointer with steel wool and Lysol.

She didn't think she'd ever be able to use the damned thing again—it would always remind her of her fall from professionalism, her metamorphosis into some kind of sexual witch riding a broomstick of lust.

How could she have allowed last night to happen? Dear God, sleeping with a student.

She had allowed herself to be seduced by her own pointer. And it was all Crash Dunmoor's fault.

No it wasn't.

She was just as much to blame for what had

happened between them. She could have ordered
him out of her house. But had she done that? No.
She'd taken off her panties for the damned man.

*Oh, God. I am a slut. I ditched my panties and
humped a pointer, and my self-respect has fallen and I
can't get it up. I mean, it can't get up. I mean—oh, shit.
Who knows what I mean?*

She jerked the pointer out of the bathtub and
tried to snap it across her knee. No such luck.
Aaarrrggghhh! She stomped with it out of the
bathroom, down the hall, through the living
room, and out the front door. She marched it all
the way into her garage, where she took a hand-
saw to it and sliced it into three pieces. Then, puffing, she threw it into the trash and slammed the
lid on it.

Now she felt stupid, but better.

She trudged back into the house, got a cup of
coffee, and went to her computer to check e-mail.
The machine warbled and honked while making
the Internet connection.

She sipped her coffee, feeling soothed by the familiar hot beverage.

"Welcome," said her computer. "You got
nailed!"

Vanessa spit her coffee onto the screen and
cursed. Then she sprinted for a paper towel. Her
imagination was running away with her.

Her only consolation was that she wouldn't
have to see Crash Dunmoor for a week, and when

she did, he would be taking the first exam of the semester, so she wouldn't actually have to *speak* to him. Not much, anyway.

She'd have to look at him, though. And she'd remember what happened between them, and how beautiful his naked body was, and how affectionate and tender he'd been. She'd remember that he'd brought her dinner. And that he'd still wanted her, even after seeing not only her granny panties but her chicken slippers.

Huh. That just proved what an indiscriminate horn-dog he was. Not content with going after anything in a skirt, he went after anything in chicken slippers, too. The man had probably been with thousands of women, of every size, shape, and color.

So she'd better not think she was special. She'd just been an irresistible challenge for him, one that he'd surmounted. She winced at her unfortunate wording, since it reminded her that *she'd* mounted *him*, technically speaking.

Crash had kissed her good-bye, his lips lingering on hers, and she'd wished fleetingly that he would spend the night. But he'd left, mentioning that he had to be at the drop zone by six the next morning.

Don't be silly, Vanessa. Men with names like "Crash" don't stay overnight in little Cape Cods on Maple Street. The Crashes of the world were more likely to be found bedded down in sleeping bags in the wilderness. Or snoozing temporarily in some runway model's glass-and-chrome condo. Or maybe catching z's in an airline seat on a red-eye back from some exotic island.

She went upstairs with her coffee and made her bed, straightening the lemon yellow flannel sheets under her blue-flowered comforter. She propped the pillows and shams against the white ironwork of her headboard and sternly banished the image of Crash handcuffed naked to it.

She sighed and started the shower. She had an exam to prepare, student papers to grade, and her book was crying out to be finished. She needed to put Crash out of her mind and figure out how to get her hands on that portfolio of Miss Eugenie's. It was imperative that she see those portraits.

"What portraits?" asked Miss Eugenie, the picture of blue-haired innocence.

Vanessa sighed. She couldn't let her get away with her tricks this time. "Miss Eugenie, you know very well what I'm talking about. I saw two of them years ago when they went up for auction, but they were so atypical that I didn't give them much thought."

The old lady made a face at her, but said nothing.

"You've given me the task—or the opportunity— to write a definitive book on your late husband and his painting. Yet you're keeping secrets from me, holding things back. I know you kept an entire portfolio from me. How can I ignore, or gloss over, a major tragedy in Thomas's life, one I believe caused a fundamental shift in his work?"

Miss Eugenie plucked at the white knit blanket covering her legs. She was silent for a long moment. Then she admitted, "You're right. It's not fair for you not to know about the past. And as Christopher's instructor, you should know more about what you're up against."

Vanessa waited for her to gather her thoughts. When that seemed to be taking a while, she prompted her. "Crash had a brother, didn't he?"

The old lady nodded. "Yes. Steven. He was a year and a half older than Christopher. A very different personality."

"And he . . . died."

"Yes." Miss Eugenie's mouth worked, and a tear rolled down her wrinkled cheek.

Vanessa couldn't help feeling like the worst kind of jerk for making her talk about something that was so obviously painful.

"Steven and Tom were very close. Steven loved to draw as a child, loved anything colorful. He was bookish, a dreamer. He played the piano. Tommy would take him down to the studio, and the two of them would look at pictures for hours. Tommy taught him gesture drawing, contour drawing, shading . . ."

"And Crash?"

"Oh, Christopher." The old lady's smile was full of sadness. "He had ants in his pants. Couldn't sit still long enough to draw. He took apart radios and clocks. He rambled through the woods and sloshed through creek beds. He brought home animals, built forts. The poor child felt left out of the bond, the partnership really—that Tom and Steven had. He resented it and often tried to disrupt their activities.

"I remember one afternoon in particular, when Steven had spread out a huge piece of paper on the floor and was painting a still life that Tom had set up for him.

"It was very close to Halloween, and I'd made Christopher a Superman cape. He was tremendously excited. Down the stairs he came, swooping and shrieking in that cape, right into the living room where Steven was painting.

"Tom and Steven were dismissive, barely looked up. Christopher was hurt, and he wanted attention from them. He ran straight at the painting and jumped into the middle of it. He even scuffed his feet around."

Miss Eugenie rubbed at her arms. "A very ugly scene ensued. Tom yelled that he was wild and destructive. That he was incorrigible. And any number of other things . . ." She closed her eyes.

"Christopher ran out of the house and didn't return for hours. I was worried sick about him. He came back, but that day marked a turning point.

He no longer tried to be included in their relationship. He did his own thing. He played every sport available. He hiked, swam, boated, skied. Always outside, that boy. I think he would have slept outside if we'd allowed him.

"Tom didn't mean to be cruel or to exclude him. He simply had no patience, and nothing in common with him. I think the only thing they did together was chop wood for the winter . . . I spent as much time with Christopher as I could. But he had little interest in baking or keeping a house clean. We swam together, occasionally skied together. My old bones wouldn't take much of that, though." She lapsed into silence.

Vanessa's heart ached for the young Crash, the boy who'd lost his parents and then been shut out by his brother and grandfather.

"So Crash did his own thing." She wanted to keep Miss Eugenie talking.

"Yes. He made some friends at school. Boisterous and sports-minded, all of them. They tended to get into some trouble—not malicious trouble, but pranks and experimentation with alcohol. Thomas had no patience for that, either." She took a deep breath.

"Steven and Christopher went off to separate colleges. Steven studied art, and Christopher majored in business administration. They'd come home for the holidays and try to get along, but they lived in separate worlds. One year—I think

Steven had just started graduate school, and Christopher was . . . yes, a junior. Anyhow, one year the boys decided to start taking one trip a year together. A sort of male-bonding trip, in order to spend time with each other.

"The first year, they went skiing for a week and really enjoyed themselves. Tom and I thought it was a good thing. The following year, it was mountain climbing, and we worried a little more, afraid one of them would get hurt. Christopher had so much more experience in these outdoor endeavors, and because of his personality, he had a tendency to push the envelope.

"That time, Steven did indeed return with a broken arm. Luckily it was his left one, so it didn't keep him from school."

Miss Eugenie rubbed at her eyes with her gnarled knuckles, and Vanessa noticed how exhausted she looked today. There were no new cartoons, no big band tunes, and definitely no disguised felines in her bed.

"For the third outing, they chose a diving trip. Christopher had his open water certification and a couple of other more advanced ones. Steven had barely been trained in the basics. Tom and I were not happy, especially when they told us the expedition would take place in Thailand." She sighed, and Vanessa found that her own hands had curled into fists, her nails digging into her palms.

"They'd saved the money for it, however, and

we didn't refuse permission for them to go. Not that we really could have, since they were both over the age of eighteen."

The old lady stopped again, then seemed to gather enough steam to finish her story. "The first two days of the outing went fine. The boys and their equipment had gotten there safely, and they'd rented oxygen tanks and met up with the rest of the group.

"On the third day, though, there was an accident. Christopher and Steven were diving partners, and they were exploring the submerged wreckage of a ship. Christopher was trying to get a photograph. He'd told Steven not to go inside the wreck. But while Christopher was focusing, Steven went in anyway, and slipped into one of the old cabins. He was excited, and must have kicked out without looking, collapsing a heavy rusted iron staircase. It blocked the exit of the cabin he'd swum into."

Miss Eugenie began to cry in earnest, heaving dry sobs that sounded like rattling coughs.

Vanessa took her hands and tried to warm them.

"Steven was trapped, and though Christopher tried, he couldn't get him free. Desperate, he swam to the surface and recruited others to help. But by the time they removed the debris, Steven was dead. There wasn't anything they could do to save him.

"Christopher brought the body home. Thomas couldn't even look at him, much less speak to him that day. It was awful: the silence, the avoidance of eye contact. The boy went out hiking, and didn't return until after dark.

"Thomas sat in his wing chair and stared out the window at nothing for all those hours."

Miss Eugenie pulled her hands out of Vanessa's and clamped them under her arms, so they were hidden by the flannel of her nightgown.

"My heart was breaking," she said. "I made them sit down at the dinner table together, and Christopher tried to explain, tried to apologize. Tried for any sign of understanding or forgiveness from his grandfather. He even told him—" Her voice broke. "He even told Tom he wished it had been him, trapped in the wreck."

Vanessa felt tears traveling down her own cheeks.

"Tom just stared straight ahead. 'Why did you let him?' he asked. 'Why did you allow him out of your sight? What were you doing fooling around with a camera when he was that inexperienced a diver?'

"Christopher's face turned ashen. I can still remember it to this day. And then Thomas said worse. 'You've always been reckless, boy. Do you see now that recklessness has consequences?'

"I was so horrified that I couldn't say anything myself. Not then. When Christopher had packed and was walking out the door, it was too late. I told him Tom was just in shock, that he hadn't meant it, that even now he was regretting what he'd said.

"But Tom was in the studio, alone, painting with the door locked.

"Crash kissed my forehead. 'I've got to go, Grandma,' he told me. 'I can't stay here. I can't look at him.' "

Eugenie Dunmoor leaned back against her pillows, honestly weak this time. Her face creased in lines of distress, and her fragile shoulders shook with emotion.

" 'Grandma,' " he whispered, " 'I wasn't reckless. I didn't gamble with my brother's life. You *know* that. Why didn't you stick up for me?' "

The old lady said nothing more after that, but the walls of the hospital room echoed softly with her sobs.

Chapter Twenty-one

LATE-OCTOBER sunshine streamed through the windows of Joe to Go, and Shelly took a moment to savor it. She'd finished the morning's baking and turned her attention to decorating the place for Halloween.

She'd already armed herself with purple garland studded by fuzzy faux tarantulas, and orange garland with tiny white ghosties attached. She had plans to carve a few pumpkins into happy ghouls and serve a special dark-roasted coffee that she would feature as "Witches' Brew."

Shelly herself always painted her face green and wore a black, pointed hat on October 31. It had become a tradition that her customers expected. She also gave out an award for best customer costume.

She draped the colorful garland around the windows and the bakery case, then amused herself by hanging some gruesome rubber masks on the walls.

Finally, she donned a white apron and went into the back to sculpt her grinning pumpkin heads. Ursula was doing fine taking care of the customers.

Shelly hefted the first pumpkin onto her cutting board. She cut a circle six inches in diameter around the stem of the big veggie and scooped out the seeds and pulp. He was a tall, narrow fellow, so she'd focus on the eyes.

Carefully, she inserted her knife and cut out first one eye, then the other, poking out the two shapes with her fingers. It was only when she began to cut the triangular nose that she noticed what she'd done inadvertently.

The pumpkin had hangdog eyes.

Shelly looked at her knife and wondered if it was possessed.

She carved the mouth next, and wasn't terribly surprised when it came out looking like Exotic Flower Man's.

She put her hands on her hips and stared at the pumpkin. Then she repaired its cranium and thanked God that it didn't have dark, wavy hair that fell in a long forelock over one eye.

Nor did it have generous lips that didn't possess even a hint of a coercive nature.

Nor, Shelly reminded herself severely, did it have long, black, silky eyelashes.

She told herself to get a grip and moved on to the second pumpkin, which was reassuringly short and squat. She'd finished carving round eyes and a definitely feminine mouth on it when Ursula called to her.

"Shelly, can you come to the front? Someone's here to see you."

"Sure." Sighing, she untied her apron, slipped it over her head, and hung it on a hook. Then she washed her hands and strode up to the counter.

Starchie stood there in a navy suit of impeccable quality, wearing what was probably a 150-dollar tie today. Under his arm he carried a leather portfolio.

What the hell? Had she conjured the man?

"Hello, Shelly." Starchie extended a hand.

"Um, hi." She wiped her wet hands on the seat of her jeans, and extended one in return. "I'm afraid I don't know your name."

"It's Giff."

Giff? As in, rhymes with Biff?

"Giff Smiley."

Worse and worse. Smiley? Get real. Nobody had a name as dopey as that. "Nice to meet you. Sorry if I was a little abrupt the other day."

"It's quite all right. I didn't mean to unsettle you. Shelly, I'm here today on a matter of business. I wondered if I might take a few minutes of your time."

She narrowed her eyes at him. "What's this about?"

"Is there somewhere we can talk in private?"

She thought of the walk-in refrigerator and swallowed a laugh. "Um, not really. I mean, you can come into the back, into the kitchen, if you'd like. That's about as private as it gets around here." *And I'm not going anywhere with you alone.*

"All right." Giff Smiley nudged a hip against the little swinging door near the register and came behind the counter, where he looked utterly ridiculous against the backdrop of canisters, bakery tissue, and take-out boxes. He squeezed past Ursula's generous form, smearing powdered sugar onto the pocket of his suit.

Shelly shook her head as he bent forward to inspect her espresso machine and managed to drag his pricey tie through a puddle of milk foam. The man needed to take up bow ties. He didn't seem to do well with the regular ones. Then again, they were probably dry-cleaned and pressed every time he wore one.

She handed him a paper towel and gestured him all the way to the back, where he took in the numerous racks of baking equipment and materials.

"Wow," said Smiley, smiling. "I've never seen such a big container of chocolate chips."

"Want some?" she offered. In spite of his protestations, she twisted the lid off the industrial-sized plastic jar and filled a Dixie cup with chocolate morsels. She set it on the butcher block and rounded up a couple of mismatched chairs, sliding them across the bare concrete floor.

He waited until she was seated before sitting down himself, and she allowed herself some amusement at that. Her butcher block wasn't a formal dining table, for God's sake. Shelly popped a couple of chocolate chips into her mouth and stole a look at his socks, to see if they were starched and pressed. She wondered if the man ironed his newspaper in the mornings.

Giff placed his leather portfolio on the scarred surface of the wood and rested his arms on it. "I came back in today with a business proposal involving your café . . ."

Vanessa stopped by Joe to Go for an invigorating dose of Shelly's company. But her friend's personality was taking a coffee break, leaving her body staring vacuously into space.

Shelly leaned on her cash register, her chin propped dreamily in one hand. She didn't even blink as Vanessa walked in the door.

"Hel—*lo!* Service with a smile, anyone?" Vanessa snapped her fingers in front of Shelly's face.

"Hey, Professor. I'm a little loopy right now."

She glanced around to see if anyone was listening. "I just received a, um, proposal."

"Ooh," said Vanessa. "I do hope it was an indecent one."

"No, no—I get those all the time. What a bore. This one was unusual because it was *decent*. Business-oriented. That's what has me stumped. And you'll never guess who it was from: Flower Man."

"Flower Man? You mean Starchie?"

"Yeah. That attorney of Mrs. Dunmoor's. His name is"—she choked on a giggle—"Giff Smiley."

Vanessa recalled the young lawyer with the coffee-drenched tie. "I remember him. Oh, Shel—he's good-looking!"

Shelly wrinkled her nose. "Yeah, maybe in a Brooks Brothers sort of way."

"Oh, give him a break. A guy like that would look ridiculous in black leather."

Shelly pursed her lips. "You're probably right."

"So what kind of business proposal did he bring you?"

"Come into the back. Hey, Ursula?" Shelly called to her assistant. "Do you mind covering the front for a few? Thanks."

Vanessa followed her friend into the cramped kitchen quarters of the café, making a beeline for the Dixie cup of chocolate chips she spied on the butcher block. She turned away from the shelves full of other temptations: industrial-sized bags of

Reese's Pieces, M&M's, and baked almonds. "God, how do you stay so thin? I'm going to have to break down and hate you one of these days."

Shelly waved this away. "Nah. You're too fair-minded. And I only stay thin because I'm always on my feet. Anyway"—she stole a few chocolate chips herself—"this Giff character says he wants to help me expand Joe to Go into other locations in the Boston area. What do you think about that?"

"Shelly, that's wonderful!"

"Hmmmph. Is it wonderful, or is it too good to be true? I mean, what if he's some con artist?"

"Eugenie Dunmoor's too sharp to hire a con artist, and he's the third generation with a family-run firm. But if you're worried, check him out. Get references."

"He's going to send me some, along with other paperwork. I said I'd think about it."

"What else is bothering you, Shel?"

Shelly fidgeted and reached for more chocolate chips. "Don't you think it's weird that he started off by sending me flowers? I mean, there's more to this than just business. He has a personal interest in me. I can feel it."

Vanessa rattled the remaining chips in the Dixie cup, and thought for a moment. "Maybe so, but I doubt he'd be talking about this kind of money just because he has a crush on you. He must think it's a worthwhile investment."

"I guess so. Don't get me wrong: I don't want to

lose the opportunity, but the situation makes me uncomfortable."

"Are you attracted to him?" Vanessa asked the question point-blank.

"I—I've never in my life gone for his type."

"You're not answering the question. Are you attracted to him?"

Shelly squirmed again. "I don't know. Maybe. But you remember the old adage about mixing business with pleasure."

"He's a lawyer," Vanessa pointed out. "He's already got a full-time job. It's not like he'd be under your feet every minute of the day."

Shelly shrugged.

"And if you get another attorney to look over things, make sure you're legally protected, then your butt will be covered." She cleared her throat. "After that, it'll be your choice whether or not you decide to, um, *un*cover it on a personal level." She grinned.

"Nessa!"

"What? You asked for my opinion. I gave it to you. I think you need to start dating again. It's time."

Shelly eyed her. "You're different these days. I can't put my finger on it . . ." She snapped her fingers. "I've got it. You boinked Crash Dunmoor, didn't you?"

"I don't know what you're talking about."

"Ha! You go, girl! Professor Primrose is getting pollinated."

"I have to go," said Vanessa. She wasn't ready to talk about Crash, or how he made her feel.

"Admit it!"

"Bye, Shel. Do yourself a favor and give Giff a chance."

Chapter Twenty-two

CRASH INHALED the cool scents of loam and wet leaves and the blue atmosphere. He stood on the edge of his mountain, ready to do a base jump. And for the first time in the history of his sky-diving career, he wondered why.

Why did he like to fly through the air? Why did he enjoy testing life to its limits? Why was he incapable of feeling fear?

His answers to these questions came easily, as he perched at the edge, prepared to duel gravity.

He chose air over water. It might not support him, might not buoy him, but neither could it trap him and drown him deviously. If he came face-to-face with death through the air, at least it would be honest, quick, and over.

He tested life to its limits because it had tested

him to his. He'd lost both parents, his brother, and his relationship with his grandparents. What else could life destroy? He wouldn't give it the bloody satisfaction.

And as for fear . . . he actually laughed aloud at the thought. To feel fear, you had to care. You had to have something at stake: love, or happiness, or at the very least obligation.

He had nothing at stake. As Crash pulled his goggles down, and prepared to make the jump, though, he realized that he still couldn't answer the overall question. Why?

What was the damned purpose of jumping off this particular mountain, on this particular day, at this particular time?

Vanessa.

Oh, don't be ridiculous.

Vanessa, his mind repeated.

What, I'm jumping so the wind will chase her image away? Yeah, right.

Something like that.

I don't believe this. I wasn't even thinking about her.

Exactly. Deliberately. You're planning on blocking her out with a lot of adrenaline and blue sky. It's been your way for years.

Bullshit.

It was then that Crash jumped—clean, swift, and sure. And he reveled in the weightlessness, the sensation of leaving his body behind. He was free, he was all spirit and pleasure and adrenaline. The only other time he'd felt like this was—

Oh, hell. Hell and damnation.

The only other time he'd felt like this was in Vanessa's arms, having left his body behind in his release.

Crash barely remembered to pull his chute, and he had a piss poor landing. Rough. Stiff. Wholly unsatisfying.

Vanessa.

He thought of her as he packed his chute and loaded it once again into the container. He'd definitely had his share of women. He couldn't help what he looked like, or that women seemed to have some irrepressible desire to tame him. He'd been chased with everything from homemade cookies to tears to threats—and he'd shrugged them all off.

What he couldn't seem to shrug off was the image of Vanessa, naked to the waist and coming sexually undone without his laying a finger on her.

He hardened just thinking about it. Then he remembered what it had felt like to bury himself to the hilt in her, have her warm, creamy thighs enveloping him. He'd sunk his hands into the flesh of her bottom and thrust beyond the brink of sanity.

Her perfect pink mouth had been open in wonder and passion, her gorgeous coppery hair falling about her shoulders, and her lovely breasts bare to his gaze.

What turned him on the most, though, was that he somehow knew she'd never been like this with any other man. Prim Miz Tower had come unraveled for him, and him alone.

He wondered what she was doing at this moment, while he packed a chute with a hard-on in the middle of a deserted clearing.

He didn't need this weird attraction to a professor who wore bulletproof underwear and chicken slippers. He really didn't.

And yet he was salivating over when he could make love to her again. He'd like to take her upstairs in that little Cape Cod on Maple Street and see what her bedroom looked like. He wondered what she wore to sleep at night. Was it a high-necked flannel nightgown? With ruffles at the wrists?

Or a black silk number that plunged dangerously in both back and front?

His renegade imagination finally settled on creamy satin pajamas with a spaghetti-strapped camisole top. Her hair was unbound, and her glasses nowhere in sight.

But before he could focus on lasciviously getting her *out* of those satin p.j.s, or all the delightful, wicked things he could do to her while she was only *half* out of them, concern intruded.

It forced him to wonder if she'd gotten enough

protein today and whether at any point she'd felt an attack of hypoglycemic weakness.

Concern also gave him the perfect excuse to call her without seeming . . . too attached. Unmanly.

Oh, yes. This was excellent.

Vanessa jumped as the phone rang and eyed it as if it had horns and a tail. Telemarketer, she told herself. Not Crash. Why would Crash call? To say thanks?

By all rights, she should call *him* to say thank you. *What a delightful evening,* she'd say. *Dinner was delicious, and the two earthshaking orgasms were quite a special touch. Do stop by more often, won't you?*

The telephone rang again, insistently.

Actually, she needed to tell him *not* to stop by, not ever again. She felt sleazy about the whole encounter. Had it been the best sex of her life? Absolutely. But it had happened with a student, and that was shameful.

It didn't matter that he wasn't a normal, everyday student. What mattered was that her integrity was on the line, her objectivity as a teacher and as a party to this bizarre scheme Miss Eugenie had bound them to.

Right after she got rid of this telemarketer, she needed to call Crash and set things straight.

She grabbed it on the fourth ring. With a sigh, she picked up the receiver and held it to her ear. "Hello?"

"Vanessa." Crash's voice purred through the receiver, pure jungle cat. Pure sex.

"Hello, Crash." She forced her voice to stay cool and calm. *What can I do for you? Rip off my clothes and run at you with some hot baby oil?*

"Hi. I was calling—"

"We can't see each other, Crash. Not outside the next few tutoring sessions, which will remain firmly focused on your grandfather's work."

"Er—"

"Our . . . encounter . . . was an aberration. A mistake. A complete betrayal of the teacher-student relationship."

"Actually—"

"And don't think," she continued, taking a deep, bracing breath, "that I'm hung up on you now or anything silly like that. I'm an adult, not a schoolgirl."

"Vanessa, I was actually calling to see how you were feeling physically."

A long, pregnant silence ensued.

"You know, internally."

Vanessa cringed.

"Oh, hell. I mean, *health-wise.*"

She cringed some more. "You were calling to see if I was okay?" And she'd treated him like a scab and a sex hound.

"Yep."

"Oh."

"So, are you?"

"Yes, I'm fine." She cleared her throat. "Thank you for asking."

"You haven't had any more fainting spells?"

"No, no. That's really only happened to me three or four times in my life. I'm usually careful to keep crackers and cheese or a yogurt with me." *And I don't normally wear the modern equivalent of a corset or kiss explosively hot men like you.*

"I have a book on hypoglycemia, which I'd be happy to drop by your house."

"That's very nice of you, but—"

"Are you home for the evening?"

"Um . . ."

"Does that mean yes or no?"

"This is really not a good idea, Crash."

"I'll take that as a yes." And he hung up.

She sat looking blankly at the receiver and tried to muster some outrage to blanket the quickening of her pulse. She failed miserably.

When she heard the roar of his Harley outside, and his steps on her front porch, she went to the door and opened it.

He gave her a wicked, unshaven grin along with the copy of *Hypoglycemia and You*, a book she already had. When he kissed her, she felt drugged and unable to resist.

And when he took her by the hand and asked where her bedroom was, she showed him.

* * *

Vanessa sat in her office, chewing on a pencil and grading seminar exams. Her door was open, and she heard Creepy Creighton's labored breathing before he even said a word. Just hoofing it down the mint green hallway was enough to get him puffing.

She schooled her face into a polite expression and disciplined her lip not to develop a curl. "Good afternoon, Dr. Conch. What can I do for you?"

"Vanessa, my dear. Glad I caught you." Conch stepped into her office and closed the door.

Uh-oh.

Then he made himself comfortable in her visitor's chair, crossing one stubby, chubby thigh over the other and shooting his cuffs.

She repressed a smile at the fact that his belabored breathing inflated his pocket hankie like a spinnaker sail.

"I just thought," he puffed, "that I'd check on the progress of young Dunmoor in your seminar."

I'm so glad you didn't ask about the prowess of young Dunmoor in my bedroom. She looked away, praying that her forehead hadn't sprouted a scarlet "S" of pimples, right in the center where she deserved it. "S" for "slut." "S" for "shameless." "S" for "stupid."

She folded her hands on top of her desk. "Crash Dunmoor? Oh, he's doing fine."

His Creepiness frowned. "What exactly do you mean by fine?"

Vanessa stared at him. "I mean that in terms of class participation he's got around a B, and—"

Conch beamed. "Excellent."

"—in terms of identification quizzes he's got an A—"

The chair pursed his lips.

"—and I'm in the middle of grading the midterm exams, so I'm not finished with the essay parts, but it looks like he'll be somewhere between a B and an A."

Her unwelcome visitor cleared his throat. Then he steepled his fingers together and began to twiddle his thumbs. She'd never actually seen a person do this before, but her boss had it down pat.

"My dear Vanessa . . ."

I am not your dear, Conch. Call me that again and you may end up dearly *departed.*

". . . I'm sure I don't need to stress to you how important, how beneficial, the Thomas Dunmoor collection would be to Seymour College." He gazed at her with a look of great significance.

What an absolute schmuck he was. She decided not to make this easy on him. She'd play dumb.

She blinked rapidly three or four times. "Yes?"

"We need this collection in order to be able to compete with the college art collections at Williams, Amherst, and so on."

You mean you need this collection to garner your next promotion and pay raise.

"We need it because we have a gap in the particular area of American art that Dunmoor addressed in his work."

Vanessa nodded and smiled, blinking again to look dim.

"And this makes you terribly significant, Vanessa."

"Me?"

"Yes. For you, essentially, hold the fate of Seymour's Fine Arts Department in your hands."

That's right, establish a need, then flatter me, then steamroll me with pressure. You've got your Machiavellian tactics down pat, don't you, Creepo? "Oh my goodness, I never thought of it that way." She blinked again.

Conch sat back in his chair and uncrossed his fat little knees. He laid his pudgy hands across his paunch. "I know I can count on you, my dear, to ensure that young Dunmoor gets nothing higher than a B+."

Fury boiled over in her veins. *You slimy son of a bitch!* Aloud, she said sweetly, "Oh, Dr. Conch, surely that depends upon Christopher Dunmoor himself and his performance?" She rose from her chair, forcing him to do the same if he were to keep up his pretense of being a gentleman.

"I know that a man of character and principle like yourself," she continued, "would never wish the college's objectivity or morals to be questioned."

"Of course not," he said.

"I keep very careful notes and records of my grading, you know, just in case anything is ever called into question." If he didn't take that as a warning, he was more of a fool than she thought.

"Excellent, excellent. I'm so glad." He smiled, but with eyes full of daggers.

She looked at her watch, blatantly. "Goodness, the time! I've overstayed my office hours and must run to an appointment. Have a nice evening, Dr. Conch." She had to get him out of her office before she leapt on him and pummeled his face.

She brushed past him and opened the door, leaving him no choice but to go through it.

His shoulders stiff with displeasure, he did so, giving her a glance of perplexed reassessment.

And then he and his plump little buns, in their too-snug pants, receded down the mint green hallway.

Chapter Twenty-three

EUGENIE DUNMOOR wished she had the strength to drop to the white linoleum and give God twenty push-ups. Sadly, that was out of the question. But she needed some reassurance that blood still flowed through her veins, and not just the nasty beige fluid dripping through the IV stuck in her arm.

She was bloody tired of daytime television, and if she listened to any more CNN, she'd get so depressed that she'd throw herself into one of the hospital flower beds to be eaten alive by garden slugs.

A stack of the latest romances and mysteries winked at her from the bedside table, but she'd devoured every single one of them and even reread some particularly enjoyable scenes.

"Thomas, Thomas," she whispered. "I'm bored

out of my wicked mind." She gazed down at her wedding ring, a simple platinum band ornamented with a half-carat diamond. It seemed almost hidden by the wrinkled skin of her hands.

"When was it, Thomas, that my hands began to look like the useless teats of an old cow? Red, wrinkled, rough—and worse—dangling idly, of no use to anyone."

Her hands had once been lovely and strong, the skin soft and dewy, her nails polished. She'd had come-hither hands, seductive hands. She'd snapped her fingers, and the men had come running. Well, all except for Thomas. Since he was shy, he'd required a bit of subtle chasing.

She'd managed to position herself next to him at a dance just as the band struck up a delicious tango. Then with a sequence of steps and smiles, she'd enslaved the poor man. She'd caught him like a fly in the bottle of her life.

Eugenie grinned at what Tom would say to that. Okay, so maybe she'd been a fly in his bottle, too. They'd been such lucky, happy flies, though—and flies with great views. Most of the time. Every couple, every family, had their great tragedies. Losing their son had been . . . unspeakable. Losing their grandsons even harder.

But she wasn't going to dwell upon that. She had Christopher back now, and it was so much more pleasant to remember falling in love with her big, handsome Thomas.

Eugenie gingerly moved her legs to the side of the hospital bed and slipped them over the edge. When she felt the floor under her feet, she nudged her blue velour slippers into reach and wiggled into them.

Since she was hooked to the bag of yucky fluid anyway, she took advantage of the support the IV stand could give her, and clung to it while she rolled it over to her portable sound system.

She pawed nearsightedly through the bunch of compact discs next to it, and brightened when she came to the one featuring tangos and salsas. She put it on, carefully turning the volume to low.

"Why, yes," Eugenie said aloud. "You may have this dance."

When the first chords struck, she was ready: poised dramatically with her dance partner, the debonair and charming IV stand. Perhaps its evening clothes left something to be desired, but she decided not to be choosy.

Closing her eyes, she transformed her own homely cotton hospital nightie into a devastating turquoise silk flapper dress. She added a matching band around her forehead, which sported a delectably drooping peacock feather.

Her blue velour slippers morphed into strappy evening sandals of shocking height, and she could feel garters against her thighs, holding her seamed stockings in place.

The final touches were a long perfect strand of

creamy pearls and lipstick so lusciously crimson it would put a stoplight to shame.

Bah rup dup dah, bah rup dup dah, hummed Miss Eugenie, *Bah rup dup dup dup dah dah dah.* "Why thank you, sir. You're a wonderful dancer yourself. Yes, I'd love a martini afterward . . ."

While Thomas had never felt like a cold steel pole, nor had he ever had wheels, she could see his rare smile. She basked in it, letting the music intensify her memories and play the riffs of emotion on that long-ago evening.

There'd been notes of discovery, danger, fascination. The treble of attraction and the bass of uncertainty.

Eugenie extended an ankle in its seductive high heel, meaning to give Thomas a slightly naughty view of tempting thigh. Unfortunately, reality intruded upon fantasy. Fifty-odd years and several illnesses separated her young legs from her old, and she slid awkwardly on the IV cord, losing her balance.

She clung to the rolling stand, which toppled backward with her. She'd break a few bones for sure—

"*Grandma!*" exploded Christopher's voice behind her. And she was blessedly caught by her grandson's strong arms.

"What in the blazes are you doing?" Crash demanded, placing his grandmother gently into her bed and righting the IV stand. She weighed about as much as a feather pillow. He shook his head in concern as he tucked her under the white blankets and felt her forehead, which was warm.

"The tango," she said, chin quivering, but still jutted out at a rebellious angle.

"The *tango*? Grandma, you're not even allowed to walk around the garden!"

"*Allowed*? At my age, nobody tells me what to do."

"Your doctor certainly can."

"Bah." And Grandma Eugenie proceeded to give him her pithy opinion of doctors, whom she declared had not progressed much beyond nineteenth-century leeching.

"That's not true," said Crash, "and you know it."

His grandmother crossed her arms over her bony chest and glared at him. She was probably just embarrassed at being caught, and on the brink of injuring herself. The mortification made her gruff and argumentative.

He tried to imagine what it was like to be suddenly under orders, after five or six decades of active adulthood. He imagined his healthy, strong body degenerating and letting him down when he wanted desperately to do something physical.

What if some M.D. he'd never met told him he could no longer skydive, or hang glide, due to calcium deficiency in his old bones? Hell, he'd probably ignore orders and do what he pleased. Just like Eugenie.

He looked at her with sympathy.

"Horrible to get old," said his grandmother. "I don't *feel* old, in my mind. And sometimes it's so surprising to look down at this decrepit old body and realize that it belongs to me."

Crash made soothing noises.

"No, you don't understand. I used to be quite sexy. I had *marvelous* breasts!"

Horrified, he felt his face turn deep red. He truly didn't want to think about his grand-mother's breasts. Not that old Tom hadn't immor-talized them on canvas for every Dick and Harry to ogle.

"I had full, kissable lips," Eugenie continued, without mercy.

He squinted in revulsion.

"And the best ass on the Cape, in the summer-time!"

Oh, Lord, this was too much. Must he think about Grandma shaking her booty on the beach, too?

"So if I choose to forget about this old wineskin that houses me now, and tango back to my twen-ties, then who are you to deny me?"

"Hey! I didn't deny you. I caught you before you bashed your head on the metal bed frame, okay?"

She had the grace to look away, but still clung to a pout.

He supposed he couldn't blame her. Being caught dancing with an IV stand in your eighties was probably just as horrendous as being caught in your underwear, making muscles at the mirror when you were twelve. He recalled sulking for a good few hours after that, especially when she'd laughed at him.

"Thank you," she said finally.

"You're welcome. You scared the crap out of me, though, Grandma."

"I doubt it. You've always been full of that, Christopher." The pout had vanished, and she was grinning now, clearly glad for the chance to give him a hard time.

"Thank you. I believe I come by it genetically."

She snorted. "So how are you liking your class?"

"Oh, it's just wondrous and amazing."

"I'll ignore the sarcasm dripping from that statement. How do you like your instructor?" Her eyes brightened with speculation.

"Why? How would you like me to like my instructor?"

"Don't beat about the bush."

"Don't plant the bush in the first place."

Miss Eugenie threw up her hands. "I asked you a simple question."

"Miz Tower is very nice."

"I want you to know that she's never tried to manipulate me, or use either our professional or personal relationship to suggest I leave the paintings to her college."

Crash nodded. "I'd come to that conclusion on my own."

"Vanessa is an admirable young woman."

Indeed she is. I admire her naked even more than I do clothed.

"Pretty, too, don't you think?"

"Yes, in a scholarly way." He kept a poker face. The last thing he wanted was to discuss Miz Tower's physical attributes with Eugenie. He felt oddly protective of their relationship—or whatever it was. What did you call a situation in which you'd slept with your instructor twice and wanted to do so again very badly?

He couldn't call her his girlfriend—that was too official, not to mention presumptuous. But he couldn't refer to her as his boink buddy, either—that was too casual and disrespectful. The term "lover" seemed overdramatic.

But was it? If he and Vanessa hadn't shared passion, then he didn't know the meaning of the word.

Miss Eugenie was scanning his face like a laser, and looked as if she were going to launch more questions, so he preempted her.

"How's Lancelot?"

"Poor thing. He's very lonely, even though my neighbor feeds him and checks on him every day. He needs a new home."

Uh-oh.

"Mildred can't take him because she already has three cats of her own, and her husband Roy has threatened to leave if she brings home another one."

Why, oh why, had he asked about Lancelot? "That's too bad," said Crash.

"He's house-trained," she confided. "If he has one of those kitty doors, he goes right outside to do his business, so there's no messy box to take care of."

"Isn't that special."

"He's a very nice cat. He'd keep your feet warm at night."

And if you order now, we'll throw in a free set of Ginsu knives! Plus a faux-wood block that adds a touch of class to any kitchen. "I'm sure he would, Grandma, if he ever got the chance."

To his surprise, Eugenie said nothing more, and because of this he began to think of himself as a heel. What kind of grandson wouldn't take in his ailing grandmother's pet while she was in the hospital?

It wasn't that he had anything in particular against cats, but he didn't want anything dependent around that tied him down. He liked his freedom.

Crash stood up and kissed Eugenie on the cheek. "I've got to get back to do a tandem jump with a kid. I'll come again tomorrow. In the meantime, no more tango for you! Promise?"

She sniffed. "Fine."

"I'm serious. God only knows what would have happened to you if I hadn't been here to catch you."

"This from a boy who jumps out of planes for a living. Go on with you!"

"Good-bye, Grandma." Crash waved at her, and made plans to measure for a cat door.

Chapter Twenty-four

CRASH PULLED into the driveway of the little Cape Cod on Maple Street to find his sexy professor committing an act of violence.

He unstrapped the leather chin piece of his helmet and squinted at her. She wielded a rubber mallet in her right hand, and an unfortunate Mr. Pumpkin Head in her left. *Thwack!*

Take that, Mr. Pumpkin Head. He was a brightly painted wooden silhouette attached to a stake, but Vanessa was driving him into the ground near her porch as if he were her worst enemy.

Thwack! Thwack! Thwack! At the rate she was going, Mr. Pumpkin Head stood in danger of being buried to the neck.

"Vanessa?"

She whirled, mallet at the ready. Though she'd

clamped her gorgeous hair to the top of her head, the ends stuck out in fiery feathers that quivered with rage. She wore a pair of ancient gray sweatpants hiked to the knee and a Seymour College T-shirt with a hole in the side.

"Hello, Crash." She pushed her glasses back up her nose and struck Mr. Pumpkin Head again. He insisted on grinning in spite of this ill treatment: The guy was a professional. He had a good attitude, even under duress.

"What's wrong?"

"Wrong?" *Thwack.* "Why would you think something's wrong?" *Thwack, thwack.*

"Just instinct, I guess. That, and the fact that you've now buried Mr. Pumpkin Head's shoes entirely."

"Huh?" She looked down. "Oh."

"Are you always this violent when you decorate for a holiday?"

"No," she said, tossing the mallet on the porch. She put her hands on her hips. "Just when slime oozes under my office door and materializes into a hobgoblin."

"Why don't you invite me in for coffee and a quickie, and tell me the whole story?"

"Coffee only," she said. "No quickie. We've got to talk about that."

"How about coffee and a long hot shower?"

"No!"

"Okay. I'll settle for a soft drink and copping a cheap feel."

She narrowed her eyes at him and gestured toward the front door.

He opened it and went through, breathing in the homey scents of furniture polish and freshly laundered kitchen towels. Vanessa's kitchen was still blue, white, and immaculate. No food smells emanated from the oven or a Crock-Pot. Hmmmm. Maybe he should have picked up some more takeout, Thai this time. Then again, he probably shouldn't be trying to seduce an angry woman armed with a mallet.

"So what's this about slime oozing under your office door? I realize that Halloween's coming up, but that didn't make much sense to me."

"Yes, well, you're not haunted by Creepy Creighton Conch."

Crash thought for a moment. "The chair?"

Vanessa nodded shortly. "Himself."

"I take it you don't like the guy."

She snorted. "Look up the word 'asshole' in the dictionary, and you'll find his photo next to it."

Whew. Proper Vanessa was pissed, all right. He'd never heard her use this kind of language.

Even more curious, he asked, "So what did he do?"

Vanessa's face reflected a brief struggle with discretion, but anger overrode it.

"He had the nerve to tell me that the future of the Fine Arts Department rested with me, and said he knew he could *count on me* not to give you anything higher than a B+."

"Oh, he did, did he?"

"Yes! It was all I could do not to spit in his face. Oh, if I'd only had a tape recorder. I'd have killed for a tape recorder."

Her face was flushed in the fading afternoon light, outrage written clearly across the freckles. The last of Crash's doubts faded away in that moment, and her fairness warmed him.

Though she would benefit from the college's acquisition of his grandfather's paintings, she wouldn't play dirty to get them.

She crossed the kitchen to the freezer and yanked out a bag of ground coffee beans. Then she stomped to a cabinet over the coffeemaker to retrieve a filter, which she stuck in the top of the machine.

Crash fixated on her trim ankles and the expanse of creamy skin he could see between her battered old gym shoes and the elastic of her sweats. Sexy, supple calves. He imagined them rubbing against his back.

She spooned coffee into the filter with short, staccato movements, sloshed water into the coffeemaker from the glass pot, and punched the ON button.

"Conch," she ground out. "The *chair*. He's in a

position of honor and leadership. He's supposed to be a champion of *education*. He should value the beauty of knowledge and its capacity to transform the human spirit, but no! He's as twisted and hollow as his namesake. He's an empty shell of a man." She pounded her fist on the counter, knocking the coffee bag into the sink.

He moved across the room and put his arms around her, hugging her from behind as he took the bag, rolled it up, and pressed down the wire tabs so it would remain sealed. He put it back on the counter and kissed her head, inhaling the citrus scent of her hair. The angry rooster tails that sprouted out of her barrette tickled his ear and cheek.

"So how did you handle him?" Crash asked, enjoying handling her. He didn't understand why he was horny, not angry himself.

"I tried to play dumb, but ended by telling him that I knew he would never want the college's morals or integrity questioned—ha!—and that your grade depended entirely on your performance."

"Mmmmm," he said, unable to resist fondling her bottom through the sweatpants. God, she felt right in his arms. And she was so much fun to tease. "Well, if it's my *performance* we're talking about, especially around midnight, then I'm bound to get an A."

She stiffened and shoved an elbow into his gut.

She turned with a dangerous glint in her eye. "*What* did you say?"

Oh, shit. He should have known better than to make light of this subject. "Kidding," he backtracked. "Just kidding."

"That's not funny." Her breasts heaved up and down under the T-shirt, and her face had drained of all color.

"Vanessa—"

"That's not funny at all. How *dare* you imply that I'd exchange a good grade for sex?"

"I didn't mean it—"

"My job is everything to me. I don't teach for the money, Crash, or for prestige. I'd be stupid if I did. I teach because I believe I can make a difference and impact students' lives. I teach to share the beauty of my field—art is something that's largely ignored by this century in favor of technology." She stopped to take a breath.

"I've spent my life wading through books and paintings. Who would I be, if not a teacher? Why would I ever degrade or jeopardize my position for some—some low-down sexual exchange with a student?"

It was then that he got angry. "Is that what you think we have? A low-down sexual exchange?"

"No! Be clear on this, Crash Dunmoor: *There's no exchange about it.*" She stood white and trembling against her kitchen cabinets, the only color in her face two high spots of crimson. Temper snapped in those cinnamon eyes, but something else chased it. Something he couldn't put his finger on.

But at the moment, he didn't care too much about defining that nameless emotion, because he felt hot and nauseous, and then oddly, coldly furious. "Okay," he said, still fixing her with a hard stare. "That leaves us with low-down and sexual."

She crossed her arms over her chest and said nothing.

"Why are those two linked, Vanessa? Why is 'sexual' necessarily 'low-down'? We're two consenting adults, and it's not the Dark Ages. A woman's worth more than her chastity in the twenty-first century."

"That may be so, Crash, but I'm not worth more than my integrity. And I won't have it said that I graded a student with anything other than objectivity."

He laughed. "People say whatever they like. Gossip doesn't take orders."

"No one has any reason to suspect that our relationship is anything but teacher-student-based, and I intend for it to remain that way. Anything physical is over between us, as of now."

"Don't I have any say in this at all?"

"No, you don't."

Crash folded his arms and glowered at her.

She glowered right back.

"I never figured you for a coward," he said.

"A *coward*?"

"You heard me. You're hiding behind your precious integrity, hiding behind the possibility that people might gossip. What I'm not sure of is *what* you're hiding. All I know is that you're afraid. You don't want to come out from behind your books and paintings about the world and actually *live life*, instead of analyzing other people's interpretations of it."

"There's more to living life than having a sexual fling with a student!"

"How do you know it's just a fling?" Crash bellowed, surprising himself. "In order to know if it's just a fling, you have to goddamn well *have* it!"

He wasn't staying around for coffee, that was for sure. He stomped out of her kitchen and down the serene blue-painted hallway, across the oval braided rug in the foyer, and out the door, which he slammed behind him. Why had he even stopped by? He couldn't remember.

Chapter Twenty-five

THE COFFEE was as black as her mood and as hot as her temper. Damn Crash Dunmoor and all pestilent men. Damn the chair. And damn the stack of exams she had to finish grading, Crash's among them.

Vanessa found the biggest mug she owned and filled it with coffee. How fitting that it was Shelly's Halloween blend, the one she labeled "Witches' Brew." She felt like a witch, looked like a witch, and had just acted like a witch to Crash. But his teasing comment had pierced the heart of her conflicted emotions.

What had possessed her to sleep with him? To jeopardize her entire value system and life for a roll in the hay with the likes of Crash Dunmoor? And what did he mean, she was afraid? She wasn't afraid, she was simply establishing boundaries, keeping control of the situation.

She'd always been a good girl, and she'd grown into a stable woman. She didn't give in to irrational impulses. Her whole life had been a demonstration that she was *not like her mother*—wasn't some irresponsible hippie who destroyed lives while indulging selfish whims.

Selfish whims like lust.

The four-letter word echoed in her mind, rolling in filthy primordial ooze and shame. Llllu-uuuusssssssstttttt. Like the black tongue of a snake, it flicked in and out of her consciousness, lying in wait behind razor-sharp teeth.

She didn't know how she'd turned into such a dumb little bunny, but lust had struck, paralyzed her, and swallowed her whole. Now it was in the process of digesting her.

Vanessa pushed the unpleasant thought away, only to have it replaced immediately with Crash's parting shot this afternoon. *How do you know it's just a fling?*

Well, that was an easy one: It was just a fling because Crash wasn't the kind of guy anybody married. Crash was built for speed, not comfort. Crash was a high-performance vehicle, and once his laps around a woman's track were done, he got an oil change and went to compete somewhere else. He'd as good as told her that himself.

In order to know if it's just a fling, you have to goddamn well have *it!*

That was just pique talking. The big lummox was annoyed that she hadn't allowed him to complete his laps; that she'd cut him off at two instead of letting him get up to speed before he raced away.

She gulped down some more Witches' Brew and stared at her tan nylon bag, pregnant with the litter of exams she had to finish grading. With a sigh, she pulled them out and curled up with them on her sofa.

She graded three decent essays, one mediocre one and two that were just plain wretched before coming to the blue book marked "C. Dunmoor." She put down her pen and picked nervously at her cuticles.

Vanessa prayed for objectivity and fairness to enter her mind. On the one hand, furious at the chair, she might be tempted to grade Crash more leniently. On the other hand, furious at Crash, she might be tempted to grade him harshly.

Perhaps she could give it to another professor in the department and ask for his or her opinion. But that might require an awkward explanation, and it seemed the coward's way out.

Crash had already called her a coward, for not living life. She was damned if he could call her a coward for not fulfilling her professional obligations.

She would read the essay.

Vanessa flipped open the blue book. He'd gotten every single identification and date correct, so he was well on his way to a decent grade. He had studied, and that vaguely surprised her. It indicated that perhaps he wasn't quite as indifferent as he'd like her to think.

The question she'd posed to the class for the essay involved two parts: First, she'd asked the students to describe what it was that made a Thomas Dunmoor painting American, and second, they were to choose a specific work they felt had great significance in his life and address why.

Crash adequately explained his grandfather's peculiarly American characteristics, as if he'd repeated them by rote. But for the second part of the question, he'd simply chosen a painting that had done well commercially.

Vanessa finished reading his essay with disappointment. Crash was taking in the facts, the dates, the mechanicals of the elder Dunmoor's work. But he wasn't grappling at all with the heart of the man. He held himself aloof from any contact with Thomas's spirit. While this was understandable, given the family tragedy, it wasn't what she'd hoped for as a teacher.

She didn't think it was what Miss Eugenie wanted, either. Thinking of the old lady reminded Vanessa that she needed to pressure her about the portraits. It was time she came clean with those.

For the moment, though, Vanessa had a job to do. And no matter how much the chair had upset her, no matter how much Crash himself unsettled her, she had to be fair.

She pulled the cap off of her pen, consulted her point sheet, and read the essay again. No two ways about it: Crash had written a good exam. But it was not a stellar one, and she couldn't give him an A.

She thought of the smug jubilation she'd see on Creepy Creighton's face, and itched to give Crash just three extra points, points that would tip him into the A minus range.

But revenge wasn't worth her integrity, and she didn't exchange A's for big O's; 87, she scrawled firmly at the top of the blue book.

She waited for her fairness to bring her some sense of relief, but fifteen minutes later she was staring aimlessly out her living room window, still feeling like a witch.

Evidently Crash thought she was a witch, too. "Eighty-seven? That's a B."

He was large, malcontent, and had invaded her office once again. He bristled with testosterone and sheer magnetism, and . . . and he wore far too many clothes. *Stop it, Nessa! Mind over matter.*

"Yes, that's a B." This wasn't the first time a student had disagreed with her over a grade, and she knew it wouldn't be the last.

Their eyes met, his challenging and hers calm, she hoped.

"I studied for that exam. I knew the material. I wrote the best essay I could. Are there spelling problems, Dr. Tower? Grammatical errors?"

He wore a rugby shirt today, open at the collar. A strong, angry pulse beat at the side of his bronzed, powerful neck. He seemed overly annoyed for a man who didn't care about this class and didn't care about the legal outcome of the grade.

"No. Your writing is technically flawless. And I can tell that you've studied—which frankly surprises me, given your outlook about this whole situation."

"My outlook?"

"Your unwillingness to be saddled with your grandfather's legacy."

"Ah." Crash folded his arms, and she had to look away from the muscular, golden flesh. Had to forget how it felt when he held her, or braced himself over her with those arms in bed. Why, oh why had she slept with him?

"So you're surprised that I studied, and there's no problem with my writing. I answered the questions. Why the B?"

Vanessa pressed her feet flat on the floor behind her desk and clasped her hands. "I gave you an 87, Crash, which is a high B. And I considered it carefully. Yes, you've studied. Yes, you know the material. But you're still skirting around the main issues, avoiding any mention of emotional or psychological content in the paintings."

The distance in his eyes spoke for itself. "I don't understand what place either emotion or psychology has on an exam. Tests are about cold, hard facts. The work itself consists of lines, shapes, and smudges on top of gesso on top of canvas or wood."

She shook her head. "You're taking a mechanical, almost mathematical approach to this course, and it won't work. Art is like literature in a sense: It requires interpretation and analysis that's not scientific. You're attempting to leave all the emotional content out of the paintings."

Crash shook his head impatiently. "Emotional content, Vanessa, is based on assumption. And assumption has no place on an exam."

"Assumption plays a role in every aspect of our lives, Crash! And we make those assumptions based on deductions. There—does that make you happier? Should I use a more scientific, linear word?" She pushed her glasses up her nose and thought for a moment. How could she get this into man-speak?

"Okay, Crash, it's like this: You study the facts, first, as you've done. That's the first step. Then you make deductions from those facts—the second step. Third, you assume something larger based on the deduction." She glanced at his stubborn, virile face.

He nodded, slowly.

"See, it's a three-step process, and you have to take all three steps."

"Okay, then show me how you apply this scientific formula to art history—or emotion, for that matter."

Excitement buzzed through her: She was making progress with him. "Fine. I can do that. *Fact:* Your grandfather lived through the Depression, when materials were hard to come by. *Fact:* During this time he produced mostly charcoal and pencil sketches. *Fact:* It wasn't until years after the Depression had lifted that he began using oil paints with any regularity. *Deduction:* He didn't have much money during those early years. *Assumption:* This early deprivation colored his later work."

She came around the desk, gesturing. "Then, if you were writing an essay on this topic, you'd support your assumption with several arguments, such as the fact that Dunmoor was always sparing with materials, never wasting any, never getting expressionist with globs and layers of paint. Do you see what I mean?"

Crash nodded again, and the anger and frustration drained from his face.

"Then you might go on to note how this shaped his character in other ways. Maybe he didn't waste *anything*, even words or emotion. In the essay you wrote for this exam, you presented facts only. You skipped the other two parts of the process, and that's why I had to take off points. But Crash, as I said, it's a high B, and you still have the final paper to prove yourself."

His gaze almost sizzled on her skin, and he stood so close that she noted gold flecks in the green of his irises. "You're a good teacher, Vanessa. I'll give you that."

A zing of pure pleasure arced through her at the compliment. His next words froze it solid.

"I was afraid you'd decided it was in your best interests to knuckle under to your boss."

Chapter Twenty-six

APPARENTLY CRASH DUNMOOR wasn't the only person who suspected Vanessa had the integrity of a cockroach. Jan Bower looked at her sideways when she went into the slide library.

"Hi, Jan," Nessa said pleasantly.

"Good morning, dear." The slide librarian's pale blue eyes radiated sincerity and concern.

It was not just Vanessa's imagination: Jan was inspecting her belly, no doubt checking for signs of roundness. It was her own fault, for declaring out of the blue that she wasn't pregnant.

Somehow it made things worse that Jan was a kind, decent human being and didn't have a catty bone in her body. "How are you feeling these days?" she asked.

"I'm fine, just fine. Thanks for asking." Vanessa signed out her slide carousels. "Uh, Jan, I proba-

bly should mention that I'm mildly hypoglycemic, and I was silly enough not to eat the day
that I passed out. So there's no cause for you to
worry—"

"Now, I'm not one to pry, dear. Nor one to gossip, so don't you worry about a thing." She patted
Nessa's arm. "But just so you know, there's always a box of saltines in my office, since I like
them with my soup on a cold day."

"Uh, thank you."

"And there's a new neonatal vitamin out. I
wish I could remember the name. My daughter
was just on it a few months ago . . ."

"Jan, really. There's no need. I'm not preg—"

They were interrupted by the telephone. "All
right, dear, I'll mind my own business now. You
run along."

And before Vanessa could say another word,
she'd picked up the receiver. "Slide library, Jan
speaking. How may I help you?"

Nessa entered her classroom loaded down with
materials, as usual. Her satchel slung over her
shoulder, she balanced a tower of books, the
guidelines for the final paper, and her carousels
for the day. She'd wrestled it all to the head of the
table and thankfully set it down, when she noticed something was off.

Normally, she walked into class amidst the

hum of conversations and laughter, which didn't subside until she raised her voice and began to call roll.

Today was different, and it took her a moment to put her finger on the reason. She'd heard whispers, giggles, and hooting right before she'd gotten to the doorway, and then once she stepped inside the whole room had fallen silent.

No doubt about it: Her sixteen female students had been discussing her.

"Good afternoon," Vanessa said, in as strong a voice as she could muster.

No one said a word, and sixteen pairs of eyes slid away from hers, to look at the floor, the ceiling, or out the window.

"I hope you're all well, and that you enjoyed the reading for today's class."

A collective rustle ensued, as students reached for their books and notepads. Still no conversation. Vanessa began to feel antsy and flushed. She really didn't enjoy being the focus of thirty-two eyes on a *good* day, and it was only her love of the subject matter that enabled her to handle public speaking.

She forced herself to go through the motions, calling roll and beginning the discussion. But dread leaked through her veins and pooled in her stomach. Her students were gossiping about her.

She led a very average, unexciting life. Nothing

about her was worthy of gossip, with one major exception. That exception was six-foot-four and blond, with green eyes.

If she was the topic of insidious whispers and the butt of tasteless jokes, it could only mean that the cat was out of the bag—and streaking through campus.

Evidently, the cat had *shredded* the bag. Vanessa arrived at her office door only to find Creepy Creighton there, tapping a highly polished tasseled loafer on the mint green tiles.

"Dr. Conch," she said, a chill traveling down her spine.

"Dr. Tower," he said. His gray eyes gleamed, predatory behind the navy blue glasses.

"To what do I owe this honor?" She unlocked her door, knowing the answer already. She could feel it in her gut.

He licked his already spit-shiny bottom lip. "We need to have a little chat."

"Do we?" Vanessa closed her eyes. He was going to fire her on the spot. Her career was over, her reputation in tatters, her precious integrity thrown to the four winds.

But what evidence did he have? This wasn't an Agatha Christie tale. No smoking gun—er, condom—lay in plain view for Hercule Poirot to find. Not that Conch was any Poirot.

Could she deny that she'd had an affair with Crash? Bluff her way through this? Put it down to vicious rumor? Of course she could. But that would be a lie.

A lie on top of a lay.

Brain, she said to her brain, *cut it out. This is serious, and no time to be irreverent. The little putz is going to can you.*

The little putz preceded her into her office and stood with his arms folded as she disposed of her things and took a seat behind her desk.

"Would you like to sit down?" She gestured to the visitor's chair.

"No, I believe I'll stand."

Yes, so you can look down upon me and feel superior. Well, let's get it over with. She waited.

"It has come to my attention that your relationship with Christopher Dunmoor is not purely professional." A satisfied smirk wiggled its way across his pudgy lips.

"And how has this come to your attention?"

"How doesn't matter, my dear Vanessa."

"It matters to me."

"So you aren't denying that you have a relationship with Dunmoor outside your tutoring sessions."

"I have a friendship with him, yes."

Creepy Creighton allowed triumph to dawn across his face. "Why don't you admit that it's more than a friendship? Let's be frank: He's been seen entering your home and not leaving again until the next morning."

And your flying monkeys told you this? "He's been seen by whom?"

"My source is confidential."

"Dr. Conch, if you're going to barge into my office with these accusations, the least you can do is tell me where they come from! This is ridiculous."

"Oh, no, Vanessa. It's not ridiculous at all. You're in hot water up to your pretty little neck." The chair's voice was menacing now. "And if you don't wish it to rise over your head and boil you like a lobster, you'll listen closely to what I have to say."

Emotions warred within her: anger, shock, disgust. "Are you threatening me?"

"Vanessa, your little grading games are threatening the future of our Fine Arts Department. So unless you'd like your little affair to be exposed to the president, the board, and the entire college, you'll give your lover the 'B' that will guarantee Seymour's inheritance of the paintings."

She'd always done the right thing. She'd always kept her mouth shut. She'd never been one to rock the boat. But a furious anger consumed her now. This particular boat—and its captain— needed to meet an iceberg.

"You are scum," she said distinctly to Conch.

"Perhaps you don't admire my tactics, Vanessa.

But at least I do my job, and not"—he chuckled nastily—"my students."

She bolted out of her chair. "Your job," she shouted, "is to champion education, not to betray it! Your job has nothing to do with swindling old ladies and their grandchildren out of their worldly goods. You're a vile, despicable, *odious* little man. *Get out of my office!*"

"And you're a stupid woman, one who's committing professional suicide. Think about this carefully before you act."

"Get out," repeated Vanessa. She rounded her desk and advanced on him.

He backed up as fast as his stubby legs allowed. "You can still do the right thing for the college. I'm willing to forget this conversation ever took place."

She wanted so badly to remove her shoe and bash its high heel through his revolting skull. "Well, I'm not. The right thing? You sicken me."

"You'll be publicly branded a whore. Is that what you want?"

She lunged at him, and he squeaked, hurtling backward and hitting his head on her closed door. Wildly, he fumbled for the knob to freedom, as she gazed at him through slitted eyes. "You can go to hell, Conch."

He got the door open at last and was soon on his way.

Vanessa turned, shaking with anger, and

walked back to her desk, where she slumped. Then she irrationally began to laugh. The expression on the little pip-squeak's face as he'd bonked his head on her door—absolutely priceless.

She stopped laughing just short of hysteria and got mad all over again that the unethical putz thought she'd still bow down to his blackmail.

Then she got even madder as she thought about Crash's last comment to her. *I thought maybe you'd decided it was in your best interests to knuckle under to your boss.* She wondered what he'd say if he knew that she'd knuckled *up* to him, and not under.

Vanessa reached for the bottled water she always kept on a corner of her desk, unscrewed the cap, and glugged some down. Why did she have to go and have principles? Boy, did they ever get in the way.

Her principles, just like her vocabulary, seemed old-fashioned in today's world, where everyone seemed to ignore them. People like Creepy Creighton lied, cheated, and stole all before breakfast, and toasted themselves with a self-congratulatory drink at lunch. They were everywhere, popping up like bad mushrooms.

She was obviously an alien, complete with domed head, oversize eyes, and principles.

She'd be much happier without the darned things. She could use Miss Eugenie to write her book, without being entangled in a friendship. She could have a wild sexual fling with Crash, give him a B, and not worry about his actually learning anything or making peace with his grandfather and the past.

Without principles, she could easily find a way to take credit for the college's acquisition of the Thomas Dunmoor collection. Then she'd have leverage to wangle a promotion and tenure and probably a few appointments to high-profile committees, where she could network for grant money and paid sabbaticals.

It was very clear: Her principles had to go. *So giddy-up*, she told them. *Vaya* con Diablo, *dammit. I want an easier life.*

Funny thing about principles. They were mulish. They were like her freckles, which refused to fade, tan, or be scraped off with a carrot peeler. She knew that because she'd tried it on her nose when she was seven.

Vanessa took another swig of water. No matter how she wished them away, she was stuck with her principles.

And that meant, when she did her job as a teacher and coached Crash to an A, she was going to be unemployed and the object of a scandal—one that would make her unwelcome at any other college.

Chapter Twenty-seven

SHELLY SAT at the butcher block in Joe to Go's kitchen, peering at the immaculately typed business plan Giff had given her. She'd read through it for the eighth time and couldn't find anything scary or objectionable in it, except for the whole concept of selling an interest in her business to someone she didn't know.

That in itself was scary and raised objections. But it might also be worth it. She decided she would have a lawyer of her own look over the papers, just to make sure she wasn't missing anything. But in the meantime, she'd check Gifford Smiley's references.

He'd listed six in all: three business and three personal. She drummed her fingers on the butcher block. She'd call the personal ones, and let her lawyer call the business ones.

The first reference, a Mrs. Lionel Kent, answered after three rings.

"Hello, Mrs. Kent? My name is Shelly Zimmer, and I'm calling to check references on a Mr. Gifford Smiley."

Silence. Then a gurgle of laughter. "Who did you say this is?"

"Shelly Zimmer."

"Zimmer. I see. And you're calling to check references on a member of the Smiley family? You're joking."

"No, I'm not." Shelly frowned.

"The Gifford Smileys of Boston?" There was another trill of merriment. "Oh, this is the most entertainment I've had all week."

"Why?"

"Listen, dear. You don't need to check references on the Smileys. They came over on the *Mayflower*, and they own half of Boston. Pillars of the community, all of them, with not a whiff of scandal to the name, more's the pity. Every single one of them even has a work ethic. It's sad, really. *Nothing* interesting to talk about." The woman paused. "Who exactly did you say you were, dear?"

"I'm—nobody," said Shelly. "I own a coffee shop."

"How delightful. Well, I must run now. Late for an appointment . . ."

"Okay. Thank you."

Shelly pressed the OFF button on her flour-smudged cordless phone and stared at it. She should have known. But half of Boston? The *Mayflower*? No wonder Giff's jeans were starched.

She eyed the next two references and wondered if she should bother calling them. If Giff and his family owned half of Boston, then why would he bother with her two-bit coffee shop? It didn't add up. She thought about the flowers again, and it really didn't add up. What was going on?

Just to be on the safe side, she called Mr. Andrew Helton next, and finally, Ms. Antonia Chatsworth. Both of these individuals had a similar reaction to Mrs. Kent's. Andrew Helton laughed, and Antonia Chatsworth went so far as to insinuate that Gifford Smiley was probably still a virgin. "He's that nice a guy. Can you imagine?"

No, Shelly couldn't. Her cynical side told her that of course people didn't list references they thought would say bad things about them. But there'd been genuine puzzlement in these people's voices, a sort of bafflement that anybody would look at Giff Smiley with suspicion.

She wiped the flour and a few streaks of chocolate off her phone and placed it back in the cradle. She supposed, that if the papers passed muster, she would give this thing a try.

Imagine Joe to Go in multiple locations and maybe eventually competing with Starbucks. Imagine being able to pay off her little two-bedroom house and maybe get a car that was less than ten years old. Imagine the sense of accomplishment she'd have. She, Shelly Zimmer, who'd considered it a big step when she stopped living in the huge, baggy sweatshirts that had disguised her shape for three years, and grown out the hair she'd cut off, and finally put on mascara again.

The belly ring had been her final hurrah toward reclaiming her life from fear and a sense of victimization. She fingered it now, recalling Giff Smiley's obvious fascination with it the first day he'd come into her shop.

Again, she felt that something about all this didn't add up. But who was she to look a gift horse in the mouth? Especially when she thought with increasing frequency about what it would feel like to kiss the damned animal.

Crash couldn't get the image out of his head. He lay on his back in the cabin's single bed, cursing dawn after a sleepless night. Vanessa's face, her expression frozen and hurt, kept appearing to haunt him.

I was beginning to think you'd decided it was in your best interests to knuckle under to your boss.

He shouldn't have doubted her in the first place, and he definitely shouldn't have verbalized it. But once the words were out, he couldn't retract them.

And if he were to be honest, he was still annoyed and hurt himself at her dismissal of their . . . fling. Damn it all, "fling" wasn't the right word. But what was?

They weren't living in a tepid little fairy tale, cardboard characters who decided, upon one kiss, to live happily ever after.

Happily ever after implied marriage, anyway, and he wasn't the type to marry. He especially wasn't the type to marry a professor who was bound to a tiny little college town.

The idea was laughable: he, Crash Dunmoor, driving a Volvo wagon and living in a Cape Cod on Maple Street. It was inconceivable. But even more unlikely was the idea that Vanessa could become a drifter, an adventurer, like him.

Crash rolled over moodily to escape a shaft of sunlight that was intent on torturing his eyes. What the hell was he thinking, anyway? You didn't decide to spend a lifetime with somebody after sleeping with her twice.

Ridiculous.

But the image of her hurt face popped into his mind again, and he decided that he had to at least apologize to her. He had been unfair.

And maybe, when he went to set things straight, her auburn hair would be loose about her shoulders, the blunt ends skimming the tops of her breasts. Maybe she'd turn sideways in a button-down shirt, and he'd catch tantalizing glimpses of silky white skin in the gaps between those buttons. Perhaps even a flash of lacy bra.

Maybe his tongue would unravel to the floor, and he could lick her legs accidentally while rolling it back up.

Jayzus, Crash, you are one pathetic sex-starved man. Get a grip.

A part of him jutted out obnoxiously, all too eager for him to do so.

Crash cursed and got up, shivering in the cold, damp air of the cabin, which was insulated as well as a sieve. Frigid morning air whistled through various cracks in the walls, and a draft as strong as a prop blast blew, uninhibited, under the door.

Crash thought with something akin to longing of Vanessa's tidy, well-built little home, with its braided rugs and ample cushions and throws.

Then he shoved the images away and pulled a sweatshirt over his head. He *liked* roughing it. He was a real man, not some corn-fed executive with a soft belly and soft hands.

Crash started his morning pot of coffee and wished fiercely that his erection would go away. After all, even real men had to pee.

Vanessa answered the door in her chicken slippers and her favorite beat-up plaid flannel pajamas. She almost shut it again when she saw Crash on the other side, especially since she'd been having recurring dreams of sky-diving naked with him. The only thing that stopped her from slamming the door was a flash of white in a window of the house across the street.

"Hello," said Crash.

"You," said Vanessa, peering beyond his shoulder. Yes, there was definitely movement in the window, and that sure looked like a nose beyond the curtain. She was a bright woman, and even before coffee she could deduce that where there was a nose, there were neighboring eyes.

"Er, yes. It's me."

Someone across the street was spying on her. Spying, and probably reporting to Creepy Creighton.

"Perhaps you've never heard of a modern technological device called the telephone," she said to Crash.

"Well, I thought that if I called first, you'd refuse to see me outside of class."

"What makes you think I'm not refusing to see you now?"

"Technically speaking, it's too late. You've already seen me. So can I come in?"

Vanessa's disgust at the surveillance peaked, and she decided that if someone were going to spy on her, she might as well make it worth his or her while. She'd always been a good girl, always done the right thing, but what had it gotten her? A boring life punctuated occasionally by bad sex.

If it was inevitable that she be publicly branded

a whore, she might as well play the part, even if she'd already put a stop to getting banged for the buck.

Without warning, she launched herself at Crash. She attached her lips to his. She wrapped her arms around his neck, her legs around his waist, and squeezed his buns with her chicken slippers.

"What the—hmmmmm," said Crash, slipping his tongue into her mouth. He grabbed large handfuls of her and squeezed back. *"Mmmmmm-mmm.* I guess I should show up unannounced more often."

"Shut up," she told him. "Now keep kissing me, and carry me into the house. Look as if you want to ravage me, and shut the door with your foot."

"Am I being graded on this?" he asked.

"Don't go there."

He did as she asked, melting all her internal organs with a look from those green eyes that said clearly, in any and all languages, "I want to take you hard against a wall."

Oh, my. Who needed coffee after a scorching look like that? *Zing bada boom.*

"Now," said Crash, "would you like to tell me what this is all about?"

"Not particularly. You can put me down now." She got the second sentence out with a lot of effort. It felt incredibly good to be held in his arms. And look at that! There was a wall right there.

"You're not playing fair." His voice rumbled

against her breasts, which caused her nipples to pebble.

The wall was a scant three feet away. All he had to do was take two measly steps toward it and then figure out how to get her pajama bottoms off while holding her vertical with her legs around his waist. Surely a man as experienced as Crash Dunmoor could accomplish that with panache, and before her pesky principles ruined everything.

Maybe, just maybe he had a Swiss army knife in his pocket, and he could cut her pajama bottoms right off!

Vanessa recalled with a frown that she had ended the sexual part of their relationship just a couple of days ago. And why was that? Oh, yes. The damn principles she'd felt so strongly about before Crash had kissed her again.

She could feel his avid interest bulging against her, uh, love button. And he smelled of mountain air and pine and hot male. She knew a quite undignified urge to lick his chest, and her mind grew foggy.

What the hell is a principle? And how do you spell that?

Crash's chest, that same one she wanted to lick, began to rumble again. This time he said, "You have no right to be so beautiful. You're gorgeous, even with sheet marks on your face and sleep in your eyes."

She knew somebody had to be paying him to

say these things, but they warmed her inside. And that avid interest of his was warming her outside. It was all too much.

"Wall," she gasped. "Take me."

"Excuse me?"

She wiggled against him, desperately.

"I thought you wanted me to put you down."

She shook her head and put her mouth on his.

"The wall, huh?" he said, breaking free. "I don't know. Those pajama bottoms of yours pose a logistical problem." He bit lightly at a nipple through her flannel top.

Oh, God. "S-solve it."

He laughed. Then he eased her down the length of him and set her on the floor. In one gesture, he slid the flannel pants down her legs until they pooled at her ankles, leaving her bare to the cool air and his hot, seeking fingers.

"How 'bout the stairs, instead of the wall?" Without waiting for the answer, he picked her up and set her on the landing, her bottom bare to the cold, polished hardwood. Then he stripped off her pajama bottoms completely, taking the slippers with them. He spread her knees.

The next impossibly delicious sensation she felt was the bristle of his cheeks scraping her inner thighs, which began to tremble. She waited breathlessly.

His tongue sought her out, a generous wet warmth that made her cry out involuntarily. His mouth closed over her and his hands cupped her bottom, and she fell headlong into a vortex of bliss. Shameless, wild, slutty bliss that she wanted never to end.

She returned to consciousness to find him grinning at her from between her knees. He looked quite at home there, unshaven, with his disheveled hair and devastating eyes.

She traced his prominent cheekbones with her index fingers and pushed some strands of hair out of his face. How did he do this to her? How did he make her forget who she was and what her life was about, and reduce her to nothing but longing?

Crash sat up and pulled off his sweatshirt, exposing all that bronzed, beautiful muscle sprinkled with golden hair. At the sight, all her jumbled questions receded, and she gave in to that naughty urge to lick his chest, starting with his small, taut nipples.

He groaned and stroked her hair, while she moved her hands from the smooth skin of his shoulders down his torso to his flat, muscular belly. She followed her hands with her mouth, flicking her tongue in and out of his navel. He watched her through slitted eyes, his breathing labored.

She nibbled at the waistband of his jeans, teasing him as she'd never teased anyone before. Finally, she took the tab of his fly between her teeth and tugged until the metal button was free.

He closed his eyes.

She tugged down the zipper, found what she

sought, and released him from the confines of the denim. Crash's breath caught audibly as she took him into her mouth.

Giving him pleasure brought her pleasure. She experimented with what gave him the most, using lips and tongue and fingers, until with a growl he flipped her back under him on the stairs and shimmied out of his pants.

"Did I not do that right?" she asked.

He stroked her cheek. "You did everything right, honey." He teased between her legs with the tip of himself. "I just want to be inside you." He unbuttoned her pajama top and took one of her breasts in his mouth, cupping the other almost fiercely in his palm.

"Look into my eyes, sweetheart," he said, and drove into her with one powerful thrust.

It was his eyes that paralyzed her, though her body rocked with his and responded helplessly, primally, to the chemistry between them.

She fell into the deep sea green of them, flailing and unable to tread water. She sank like a stone through their depths, finally coming to rest on the sandy floor of realization.

The reason her principles faded to nothing around Crash Dunmoor was quite simple. She still fought it, still denied it, even as her body crested involuntarily into orgasm: She was in love with the man. With a cry that was half ecstasy, half anguish, she collapsed onto his chest.

Chapter Twenty-eight

"I CAME OVER HERE to apologize," said Crash, looking a little cross-eyed. "I guess God really does reward humility."

Vanessa couldn't help laughing, even though she'd just realized she was the stupidest woman alive. What kind of cretin would fall in love with a man like Crash Dunmoor?

They'd finally made it from the stairs into her bedroom, where they now sprawled, drinking coffee.

"Apologize for what?" she asked. Oh, yes . . . she had been angry with him. She'd almost closed the door in his face.

"For thinking you might have gone along with the chair and his plans."

Creepy Creighton seemed very far away, very unimportant compared to the discovery she'd just made. How could she have allowed herself to fall in love with a student? Especially Crash?

Aloud she said, "I'd hoped you knew me better than that."

"I saw the hurt in your eyes as soon as I said the words. I'm sorry. It's just hard for me to trust people sometimes . . ." His voice trailed off, and his lips flattened.

I know. For the last twelve years, you've felt betrayed by the people whom you loved most in the world.

She wanted to say it aloud, wanted him to talk about it. She knew how damaging unsaid words and unshared feelings could be. After all, she'd witnessed the emotional paralysis of her own father for years.

What if he'd talked about how her mother's departure had made him feel? What if he'd gotten counseling? Perhaps he would have come out from the library and met someone before twenty-seven years had gone by. *Twenty-seven years.*

Her father, however, was a different type of man. He'd holed up, licked his wounds, then lost himself in scholarship.

Crash was the type to take refuge in action, to wander to the four corners of the world until new sights and smells and experiences chased the old ones away.

Unfortunately, immersion in the present never entirely annihilated the past. But she wasn't sure if Crash had figured that out yet, and he'd keep wandering until he did. Which meant it was doubly stupid for her to fall in love with him.

Then there was this sexual problem she had with him: She couldn't seem to stick with the word "no." She was not normally a wishy-washy person, nor was she undisciplined. But when Crash came around, she dissolved into pure animal instinct.

Every time she made love with him, she became more vulnerable, and also more . . . *wanton*. She knew it was an old-fashioned word, and probably an old-fashioned concept. After all, they lived in a world where women donned dresses made out of safety pins for public awards ceremonies.

But Vanessa had grown up with old-school values, do's and don'ts that were set in stone. And the more time she spent around Crash, the more those values were threatened. He was plowing through her list of don'ts at a frightening speed.

She forced herself to open her eyes. They had no future together, and she was allowing her whole character to be remolded for scraps of passing pleasure. That wasn't acceptable. For when Crash was gone, she'd have to live with herself, and she couldn't live with a self she didn't recognize and didn't like.

Crash wrapped his fingers around the delicate porcelain coffee cup Vanessa had given him. Like her, a few minutes ago it had been hot and steamy with promise. Like her, its warmth was fading fast.

He could see the changes in her face so easily. Half an hour ago her skin had been flushed, her eyes full of warm cinnamon and desire. The desire had faded to contentment, and then to doubt. Shadows of worry crept in along with the doubt, then her cheeks became tinged with shame. Why did their encounters, for her, always end in shame?

He traced her jaw with the pad of his index finger. "You're having regrets. Why?"

She sighed. "Because every time I try to keep you at arm's length, you duck under my arm."

"So why don't you stop trying to push me away?"

"Crash, you know why. This isn't right."

"It sure feels right to me."

"You know what I mean. I can't sleep with a student. It contradicts everything I believe in."

Though he understood where she was coming from, it annoyed him no end that once again, she was pushing him away. "What, you don't believe in great sex?"

"Crash, I've never had sex like this. I didn't know it existed, outside of novels and films."

He was male enough to preen. "That's me, world-class lover."

"The thing is, it's probably so mind-blowing only because it's forbidden."

Ouch. "Hey, don't mind that squishing sound under the heel of your boot. It was only my ego."

"Your ego is far too large to fit under my bootheel. I'm not falling for that."

"Okay, let's go back to this idea of the forbidden. What you're saying is that you wouldn't have looked twice at me if I hadn't been in your class?"

"Noooooo," admitted Vanessa. "I would have looked twice. But *you* wouldn't have looked at *me*, under other circumstances."

"Not true," said Crash.

"Admit it: As your prim, proper professor, I was a challenge, one you couldn't pass up."

"What are you trying to say, Vanessa? That you're not beautiful? Because that's a lie."

"I'm saying that you wanted what you couldn't have. Just as I wanted what I couldn't have. It's human nature. But the semester's almost over now, and the thrill of the forbidden, the thrill of the chase, will be gone. What's the point of waiting for that slow, miserable end?"

He stared at her. "You're absolutely brutal, do you know that?"

"*What?* I'm—I'm trying to make this easier for you. We both know you're going to walk away from this town once the class is over and you've fulfilled your obligation to your grandmother."

"You're not trying to make things easier. You're just assuming that I don't have a heart, Vanessa.

You're insinuating that only my *dick* is involved here. And I don't particularly take that as a compliment."

She opened and shut her mouth.

"The signals you're sending me are mixed as hell. I come over here and you jump me, so I oblige. We both enjoy it. And then afterward you treat me as if I'm some kind of leper. What is it that you want from me?"

She looked at him with wide, horrified eyes, still silent.

"What is it that you want?" he repeated. "I . . . care about you, okay? I'm not just some horn-dog trying to score on his professor for the thrill. I resent the hell out of your saying that. But you obviously have issues with our being intimate while the semester is still under way. So let's put things on hold until January."

When she remained silent, he didn't know what to make of it. "Unless you're done with me and my stud service? Would you like me to just disappear?"

"No," she whispered. "I don't want you to disappear." And after a moment, "I . . . care about you, too."

The things she refused to say were driving him crazy. There she huddled, the flannel sheet drawn up over the tops of her breasts, looking forlorn. And she wouldn't say why.

Part of him wanted to strip the sheet from her and make love to her until she called his name over and over. He could lose himself in her creamy flesh forever.

The other part of him was mad as hell. Frustration surged through him.

"Vanessa, talk to me, damn it! This isn't about me being your student. You've used that over and over again as an excuse not to get involved with me, and I'm sick of hearing it."

"It's not an excuse!" she flared.

"It absolutely is. What are you afraid of? Tell me. Just *say* it!" He loomed over her.

She flung herself off the bed and stood before him, naked and trembling, her hands on her hips. "Fine. You want the truth? My father made *one exception* to his ironclad rule of not getting involved with his students."

He closed his eyes, suddenly knowing what she'd say next.

"He fell in love with my mother, Crash. His student. My young, flighty, flower-child mother, who got pregnant by mistake. Then she couldn't wait to dump us both and run off to Brazil *to live life*." She pounded the wall with a fist. "I'm all for living life, Dunmoor, but not at somebody else's expense. *I'm not like you*. I can't just sleep with someone for the hell of it and then move on—to another state or business or lover. *Sex isn't a sport to me*."

Her words were a vicious slap: They stung and then burned. He set his jaw. "You think that's all it is to me?"

"Yes! Look at your patterns. You told me yourself about all the different women in your life, the beach babes and snow bunnies—"

"Jesus, Vanessa, I was in my early twenties! Give me some credit for growing up!"

"—how you're moving down to Florida next, how you're not the type for marriage—"

"Is that what all this is about?"

"—so I'm just trying to end it between us *now*, while it's still *fun* for you."

Furious, he thundered, "You want me to propose?"

"No!" she shouted. "We don't know each other well enough to get married!"

"Exactly, damn it! And we never will, if you end the relationship now. You're afraid . . . afraid of the sex, which makes you lose control. It makes you vulnerable—"

"It makes me *cheap*!" she cried. "It makes me *like her*."

The anguish in her voice chased away his own anger, and Crash strode to her and took her by the shoulders. "No, honey. It doesn't. This has to do with you and me, and it's *making love*. It's not a sport. It's not a moral compass. Vanessa, your mother *left* you. It doesn't matter that she left with a man. What hurt so much was that basic act of leaving."

She was silent, apparently absorbing his words. She didn't say that she was afraid of him leaving, too—and he didn't promise not to. How could he? He *was* a drifter. How could he break the patterns of the last twelve years? He ran his fingers through his hair, shoving it out of his eyes. Beside him, Vanessa did the same.

It was a relief when the phone rang. She pounced on it.

"Hi, Miss Eugenie . . . No, it's not too early. I've been up. Yes, absolutely I still want to see the portraits. Crash? Yes, I'll . . . get in touch with him. Tomorrow, then. Ten's fine by me. Thank you."

She hung up the phone and turned to him. "Your grandmother wants us to come and see some portraits by your grandfather. They're paintings that were never shown to the public, never sold. I've only seen a couple myself, and those were in a private collection."

"Portraits? In the traditional sense?" He couldn't disguise his surprise. "Old Tom didn't do portraits."

"Apparently he did some toward the end of his life," she said quietly. "I only found out about the existence of the others recently. They were mentioned in a couple of letters your grandfather exchanged with his dealer. The dealer wanted them, but Tom wouldn't sell. He eventually let the two I've seen go for financial reasons, but he hung on to the rest."

Crash shrugged. More secrets, more barriers to the old man's personality. Who knew—who'd ever known, what had gone on behind that craggy face of his?

Thomas Dunmoor had lived to paint. He'd observed and drawn life, not lived it. That was the trouble with these intellectual and artsy types. They always looked inward, or towards the goddamned tablet they wrote on or the board they painted on. Never did they look out, to the horizon. Or up, beyond the clouds. Or down, below the water.

He saw Steven's face, grinning uncertainly before he'd tipped backward into the water from the boat that day. Thumbs-up.

Yeah, thumbs-up, buddy. Oh, goddamn it. Why did I ever take you on that trip?

Because he'd wanted to connect with him, wanted to share with him, wanted to bond with him.

And perhaps he'd wanted to discover what it was that was so special about Steven—what made him worthier of their grandfather's love than he had been himself.

Suddenly Crash hurt, and he closed his eyes. Pain swept through his veins and crested in his heart, before rushing back out again by way of his arteries. The hurt pounded in his head and thrummed in his psyche. He willed it away again, tried to force it into whatever void it had lurked in for the past twelve years, but it was too strong.

"Crash?" Vanessa's voice held concern. "Are you okay? What's wrong? I . . . I'm sorry—"

"Nothing." He opened his eyes and tried to shake the feelings away. "Nothing's wrong." *Everything's wrong. Everything's been wrong since I came back to this cursed state.* "And never be sorry for saying what you feel."

He reached for his pants and pulled them on. Zip, snap, the jingle of his belt buckle: The small, normal sounds helped to anchor him in the present again. The fabric of his sweatshirt soothed him, too, and the unexpected assault of pain began to fade.

By the time he got his boots on and laced, he had everything under control. Everything except his feelings for the woman he'd just made love to, the woman who'd accused him of having sex for sport.

Vanessa had wrapped herself neck to toe in a blue terry robe and stood peering at him with her hands in her pockets. That particular shade of blue—a designer would have a name for it, some silly word like cornflower—set off her hair and eyes to perfection.

She was all cinnamon, nutmeg, and ginger, a delicious woman-cookie that he didn't know what the hell to do about.

"Crash," she said again, "I'm sorry. Not for being honest, but for being unfair. I'm angry at my mother, not at you."

He nodded, trying to figure out why he wasn't furious at Vanessa, why he was so attracted to her.

She was one of those same intellectual/artistic types who had shut him out during his formative years. Like old Tom, like Steven. But somehow she was also a bridge to them, an interpreter.

Ironic that he should trigger Vanessa's feelings about her mother: the wanderer, the sexual being, the one who had abandoned her.

It was as if they both tormented and yet completed each other. The problem was that Crash himself didn't welcome any more torment. And going to see a series of his grandfather's portraits, especially with Vanessa, added up to full-blown torture. He knew the paintings would be of his brother Steven, and he wasn't sure if he could take that. The last thing he wanted was to go emotionally nuts in front of Vanessa.

"Crash?" she said.

"Yeah."

"I know you're not sport-screwing me, okay? I do know that. But please understand that especially with the pressure from Conch right now, we can't be with each other until the semester's over. Promise?"

"Tomorrow's portrait viewing excepted," he said, with a wry twist of his lips.

"Right. So I'll see you in the morning—I'll pick you up and we'll go together."

"Yeah." *Maybe I'll have my feelings all figured out by then.*

Chapter Twenty-nine

HE DIDN'T HAVE them figured out, not even after another night spent pillow-punching and thrashing and cursing at the moon. The giant orb smiled knowingly down at him, as baffling as the *Mona Lisa*.

The moon was peculiarly female, magical in its soft glow, and it illuminated nothing but shadows and mysteries. The moon had followed him all over the world, like gravity. Like guilt. In his attempts to get away from her, he had simply come full circle.

He'd come back to Massachusetts without really knowing why. There'd been land for sale, an area suitable for a drop zone. There'd been the knowledge that his grandmother was close by, though at the time he'd had no intention of going to see her. Then Vanessa had entered the picture and changed his mind.

He was a strong man, a determined man, but he was beginning to recognize that there were forces in the world beyond his control. Coincidences and serendipities that didn't make sense, yet made perfect sense.

Crash wasn't a big fan of them. He'd prefer life to be logical and linear. He wanted it to make sense—which was laughable, really.

By morning, he'd decided that life, like the damned moon, was female. And he didn't know what to do with life right now, any more than he knew what to do with Vanessa.

But he did know that he wasn't going to stretch his emotions on the rack by looking at a bunch of portraits of Steven. He dialed Vanessa's number to tell her he wasn't coming, but the phone rang endlessly until her machine picked up. He cursed, tossing his own phone back into its cradle.

"What do you mean, go alone?" Vanessa asked. She'd come to pick him up.

She looked almost as good in blue jeans as she did naked. Some of her coppery hair was pulled back loosely in a clip, but most of it trailed down her back and over the lapels of the deep green blazer she wore over her sweater. She'd exchanged her chicken slippers for brown leather boots, and he found that he missed the silly yellow things. They lent her an endearing goofiness.

"Your grandmother wants you to be there. She wants you to see the paintings."

Crash's hair was disheveled, and his broad shoulders hunched. He'd stuffed his hands into his pockets, keeping them to himself. "I'm not up for it, okay? She'll have to understand."

Vanessa searched his face, but it was stony. That, in the end, became her clue. "Crash, why are you avoiding this? What is it that you don't want to confront?"

"Nothing," he muttered.

She took a step forward.

He took a step back.

She took another step, and poked him in the chest. "Liar."

He gently grasped her wrist and curled her finger back into her palm, but still he said nothing.

"Hey, Dunmoor. You're not playing fair. Remember yesterday? I'm going to use your own words against you: Talk to me."

He rolled his head around his shoulders and closed his eyes. "Sit down."

In terms of furniture, there weren't many choices. Vanessa headed for the single narrow bed and sank down on the edge of it.

Crash followed her, sitting on the other end. "I told you I had a brother."

"Steven," she nodded.

"I mentioned that he died in an accident, right?"

"Yes."

"A diving accident. What I didn't tell you is that I was there. I watched my brother take his last breath, do you understand? And I watched him die knowing that I was responsible for him being underwater in the first place."

"Oh, Crash," Vanessa whispered.

His face had turned ashen, his cheekbones jutting prominently from his Nordic face.

"How can you blame yourself? It was an accident."

"Steven was an introvert, an artist. If I hadn't talked him into it, he'd never have gone. I took him out of his environment and put him into mine. I might as well have drowned him in a bucket."

"Crash! How can you say such a thing? Listen to me: Steven was a grown man, and he made his own decision to dive with you. You didn't drag him into the water on a choke chain."

"You don't understand," said Crash.

"What? What don't I understand? You're blaming yourself for something that wasn't your fault."

"It was, Vanessa. I'm—oh, God." He covered his eyes with his hands, hiding the deep sea green from her gaze. An ocean of salt water lived in those eyes, a vast body of tossing, surging emotion and guilt.

"God forgive me, I was jealous," Crash said, his voice rough. "I wanted to pull him into an environment where he wasn't better, more talented than me. Growing up with Grandpa Tom and Steven and not being able to draw a stick dog—it was torture. Even Grandma Eugenie was creative in her way—she was a decent potter. I created nothing but havoc in the household. I was the young savage, the throwback."

Vanessa slid next to him on the bed and tugged at his hands, slowly prying them away from his eyes. "That still doesn't make you responsible for Steven's death."

"But I am, Vanessa. I pulled him into an environment where he wasn't competent. And what's worse, I laughed at him, just as he'd laughed at my stick figures and splotches of paint."

"So you're human." Vanessa squeezed his hands in her own. "You had some emotions that weren't completely noble and righteous. Big deal."

"Oh, it's a big deal, all right." Crash's lips flattened. "I turned around briefly, to take a photograph, and my foot got caught in some fishing line. Once I'd cut myself free and I looked around for Steven, he was gone. He'd swum into that goddamned wreck without me. He knew better, but I'd given him the incentive to prove himself."

Crash closed his eyes and pulled his hands from hers. "Steven died because of me."

He opened his eyes again, staring straight at her. "And Grandpa Tom never forgave me. 'Reckless,' he said. I'd gambled with Steven's life."

Vanessa reached for his fingers again, but he wrapped his arms around himself and shoved his hands under his armpits. It was classic body language.

"Listen to me, Crash." She got up and sat on his knees uninvited, straddling him. She took his chin in one hand and forced him to look into her eyes. "I don't care what you said to your brother. *It was an accident*. Nothing that came out of your mouth caused it to happen. Your words weren't powerful enough to kill Steven."

Crash's lips twisted.

"Are you hearing me? Is this getting through? You're one hell of a man, Crash Dunmoor, but you're not God. And you're taking God's responsibility onto your very human shoulders. *It doesn't belong there*."

He stared at her silently. Somewhere in the far reaches of his ocean green eyes, a wave crested, fell, and became a solitary tear. Crash squeezed his eyes shut against it, tried to keep it in with all his might, and it undid her.

"Your grandfather was wrong," she whispered. "He should never have said those words to you. He was wrong. And while it may be too late to receive his forgiveness, it's not too late for you to forgive yourself." She took his face between her palms, cupping his dear, stubborn jaw, and kissed him gently on the forehead before slipping off his knees. She held out her hand. "Come on, Crash. We're going to be late."

He stood up. "Vanessa, thank you. Thank you—but I'm still not going. Those portraits—they're going to be of Steven, and I just can't look at them right now."

"Then when?"

He passed a hand over his face. "I don't know. Maybe never. I haven't seen any pictures of my brother for twelve years."

"It actually helps, Crash." She said the words quietly, but his head jerked back as if she'd tried to slap him.

"How would you know that?"

"I know. I know because . . . my mother tried to get in touch with us many years ago. She sent a letter, and some photographs. My aunts hid the packet from me, and I didn't find it again until I was home from college one summer and helped them clean out my father's basement. Crash, I wasn't sure I wanted to open it. It took me a month."

His eyes were riveted to her face, unblinking. "And then?"

"I did. I opened that monumental, mysterious envelope that had the power to change my life . . .

and it didn't. I saw a perfectly ordinary woman whom I didn't recognize and for whom I didn't feel much but anger. She had my coloring. She had an average smile and a middle-aged body and a life apart from me, somewhere else." Vanessa shook her head.

"Did you try to get in touch with her?"

She shrugged, her mouth twisting. "Why? Her letter wasn't passionate, or apologetic, or even frantic for information about me. She tried once to contact us. That's it. Then, duty done, I suppose she went back to her own life."

Crash went to her and put his arms around her. "I'm sorry."

She hugged him, inhaling the scents of his warm skin and the detergent in which his shirt had been laundered . . . and . . . did loneliness have a smell?

"Don't be sorry," she said. "I wasn't. It surprised me. I expected an avalanche of feeling, something melodramatic and earthshaking. Instead, all I felt was the urge to put the photos and the letter away and go on with my life. The whole thing was such a letdown." She pulled away from Crash and looked up at him. "Don't you see? Just get it over with."

He sighed and looked away. When he met her gaze again, he finally nodded. "Okay. Let's go. Do you mind separate vehicles, though? I need to head out to the airfield afterward."

"Sure," she told him. "I'm getting good at winding around this cursed mountain by myself."

He arrived at the hospital first, to find Grandma Eugenie listening to some lively big band tunes on her portable sound system. A large black portfolio stood propped against the foot of her bed.

Eugenie's eyes were closed, and though she lay against her pillows, she moved her head in time to the music, snapping her fingers and tapping a toe against her covers. She looked so frail, and so impatient with her own body, that tenderness caught in his throat, almost choking him.

"Grandma," he said, moving to her bedside, "would you like to dance?"

Her eyes flew open, and she smiled. "Why, yes. Yes, I would."

He helped her out from under the blankets, smoothing a stray lock of hair out of her face as she eased her feet into her blue velour slippers. Then she stood up shakily, bracing herself against him.

He slipped an arm around her waist, and took her hand in his. Together, they began to move to the tempo of the music. Her breathing was shallow, her steps strained, but the joy in her eyes was almost childlike.

A memory tickled the edge of his consciousness, and then tumbled in: old Tom whirling Eugenie around her bright yellow kitchen to this same music. She'd giggled like a girl, and brown sauce from the wooden spoon she held had dripped onto his grandfather's plaid shirt.

Crash looked down at her white curls and delicate shoulders, at the bright, brave lipstick she insisted on wearing. The flesh under her jaw fought gravity as hard as he'd ever fought it. She clung to her mischief as she clung to life. And he'd clung to his isolation and hurt.

He tightened his arms around her, and bent to lay his cheek on her head. "I love you, Grandma."

"Oh, Christopher. I love you, too."

A whisper of clothing from the doorway had him lifting his head. "Vanessa? Is that you?"

"Yes," was the muffled response. Then there was a strange, feminine honk—had she blown her nose?

The last strains of music faded, and he dipped Grandma Eugenie gently, to her great delight. "Thank you, sweet boy," she said.

"You're welcome." He helped her back into bed, sliding her feet out of her slippers and tucking her legs back under the covers. When he looked up, Vanessa stood in the doorway.

"Hi," she said, her eyes darting away from his. She walked forward and kissed Grandma Eugenie on the cheek. "How are you doing?"

"Nobody on staff of this godforsaken place will give me any wine," the old lady complained. "I have to rely on occasional senility for a good buzz."

"That's terrible," Vanessa told her.

"How'd you like to smuggle me in some sherry?"

"Not a chance."

"Huh. Some comfort you are." But Eugenie's lips twitched. She shifted restlessly in the bed. "Well, go on, then. The portfolio's right there."

Vanessa looked to Crash. He shrugged and walked to it, unzipped it. The thing contained at least thirty canvases of varying size, none of them on stretchers.

He stared down at them, almost unwilling to touch the paintings. Seeing them in slides, projected across a room, had given him some necessary distance.

With a deep breath, he banished his reluctance and pulled them out in a pile.

"Put them there," Eugenie said, pointing to the end of her bed. She shifted her feet over to one side.

The first canvas was a self-portrait, which Thomas had executed without vanity, without mercy. Crash clenched his jaw as he looked down at the old man's face, wrapped in a mantle of sagging flesh and sorrow. Old Tom's eyes brimmed with blue trouble, bloodshot and fogged by weariness. He stared straight from the picture plane with no pretenses, and no particular liking for what he saw.

Crash blinked rapidly and had to remind himself that his grandfather had been looking into a mirror, and not at him. This wasn't a photograph.

He moved on to the next one. Two young boys wrestled in a patch of grass. They were grimy and mud-smeared, hair tousled, each determined to best the other and make him eat dirt. This painting was done with a good deal more affection: lines were softer, colors less harsh. A golden glow bathed the scene in light, whereas a black background threatened to obscure the self-portrait.

"You and Steven?" Vanessa asked. He nodded.

Crash stared at the painting for a couple of minutes, surprised by the affection inherent in this canvas. Finally, he moved on to the next one.

It could only be described as bizarre. The old man, barefoot and dressed in nothing but a pair of old trousers, must have lain on a glass tabletop over a camera, and then done the painting from the resulting photograph.

His chest and arms and the side of his face were pressed against the glass, as if he were trying to swim past it. The effect was disturbing, and Crash averted his eyes, thinking of how his brother had died. Steven had been trapped, unable to swim past the barrier holding him under the water.

But something forced him to look back at the canvas, and it was then that he saw the title old Tom had scrawled in the corner: *Apology*.

Vanessa took the painting from the stack and scrutinized it, while he went on to the fourth and fifth. In one, a dark-haired boy sprawled across a hardwood floor, drawing. In the other, Tom had captured a blond, towheaded boy midleap, as he dived awkwardly off a boulder into a lake.

"It's you," Vanessa said.

Crash nodded. He remembered that boulder. "That was my favorite place to sit and fish. I dug a hollow under it to store some of my favorite things: cool rocks, an old Indian arrowhead, a collection of bottle caps."

What surprised him was that his grandfather had known he used to go there. How had he known?

The next few paintings were clearly Steven at different ages: Steven reading, Steven asleep, Steven gazing out a window.

His gut clenched, and in spite of the nasty little kernel of jealousy, he wished with all his heart that his brother were present right now, that he'd never tried to draw him out of his studious, artistic shell and into the physical world.

Had he really wanted to share and bond with him, or show him who was boss in the outside world?

The pain shot through his veins again, driven by a mixture of guilt, shame, and regret. He'd been a selfish, egotistical bastard, competing for their grandfather's love.

And for what? Bitter, mirthless laughter echoed in his head. Here was the proof: For every one painting of him, or of the boys together, there were three or four of Steven alone.

For every hockey or lacrosse or baseball trophy he'd brought home proudly, two or three of Steven's drawings or sculptures had been framed or displayed in the house.

And now that poor Steven was gone, he'd achieved spiritual sainthood, while Crash still floundered and competed in the physical world.

Goddamn it, the two of them, old Tom and Steven, were probably up there in some heavenly studio painting away while he was still trying to reconcile all his emotions.

Crash felt like an asshole. Thirty-six years old and still looking for approval from a dead man? Pathetic, absolutely pathetic.

He straightened and turned away from the canvases. "I can't look at these any longer. There's no point." It was time for him to move on. Time to leave this state, this area to which he should never have returned. The cold was setting in, anyhow. He'd follow the rest of the guys down to Florida and sell off this Massachusetts site.

"There *is* a bloody point, Christopher," said Grandma Eugenie. "Get your stubborn backside over here this instant." Her voice was irascible, all sweetness gone.

He stiffened.

"Don't you raise that chin at me, young man. I wiped applesauce and macaroni and creamed spinach off that chin. I bought zit cream for it. So if you think it intimidates me now, you're ever so wrong."

He stole a glance at Vanessa, who pressed her lips together and averted her face. He looked back at Eugenie, whose curls quivered with temper.

Crash folded his arms. He was sick of being manipulated by these two women. Now one of them was speaking to him as if he were three, while the other *laughed*. Damn it, she could try to disguise it, but she was laughing!

"You're just like Tom," his grandmother said.

"What?"

"Smart as hell, determined, and successful at whatever you choose—with one major exception."

He was starting to get really pissed now.

"Both of you: *thick* when it comes to people you love."

"Now wait just a minute—"

"You're like a dog, barking in the mirror at his own reflection . . ."

"A *dog*—would you care to explain that—"

". . . and so was he. At war with your own selves, you idiots!"

"Idiots?"

"Get over here, Christopher, before I leap out of this bed and snatch you by the ear. You will look at these damned portraits, all of them, if I have to hold you at gunpoint." She was working herself into a tizzy, and he was afraid she'd have a stroke if he didn't acquiesce.

"Calm down, Grandma." He walked once more to the end of her bed.

"I will not calm down until we've solved this for once and for all. You men think you rule the world, and yet you have the emotional intelligence of dirt."

Vanessa pointed silently to the next painting, and he took it in reluctantly. A blond boy stood solitary in the wilderness, slouched against the trunk of a tree.

In several others, the boy was pictured with a volleyball, with a hockey stick, with a lacrosse stick. In each case, the intensity of the action was unnerving. The boy's loneliness was clear, but somehow his concentration defeated it. The loneliness was the ball, and the ball was being smacked, hit, tossed away.

These paintings showed little of the boy's face—they were all shoulders, skinny arms, tube socks, and cleats. They shook Crash, simply because he knew the boy was him, and him alone. But it was the next five that floored him.

Old Tom had focused on his face. His own eyes stared back at him from the canvas, blazing with youthful defiance, framed by unruly spikes of yellow hair. His chin jutted awkwardly, admitting none of the vulnerability that could be discerned in his nose, which was bandaged from the time he'd broken it on the boom of a catamaran.

He handed the canvas to Vanessa and focused his eyes once again on his own, but he was older now, teenaged. He sat on the hood of Grandpa's old Buick. Crash shook his head as he thought of the ugly scene that ensued when he'd proudly showed old Tom the mail order "lightning streak" stickers he'd adhered to the sides of the car.

To Crash, they'd been the ultimate in coolness. Tom had bellowed that a Vegas pimp wouldn't be caught driving the thing.

He moved on. Now Grandpa had depicted him in profile, wiring a new stereo speaker to the sound system. He'd blown the old one while trying to impress Becky Latham, a girl from school. This brought a slow grin to his lips. He'd gotten into more than his fair share of trouble, hadn't he?

Crash stared at himself sleeping on the worn old couch in front of the parlor fireplace. He was at peace, mouth slightly open, no defiance or challenge in his expression. His blond lashes brushed his cheeks.

The last canvas presented the back view of an older man looking out to sea. Far in the distance, a small blond-headed figure sailed toward a troubled horizon, not looking back. The old man in the foreground slumped, hands shoved deep into his pockets, unable to wave good-bye.

The picture was signed and dated eleven days before his grandfather's death. Crash gave it to Vanessa and straightened for the second time, glancing at Eugenie, then moving to the window, where he stared out at the hospital's parking garage, layer upon layer of concrete and cement.

"He loved you, Christopher. He observed you, noticed you more than you think. He just didn't know how to tell you." Eugenie's voice had softened, lost its edge. "You men." She sighed. "You're so helpless in your bullheadedness. So dense behind your ever-smart remarks. You can figure out how to destroy or save the world, but you can't figure out how to talk to each other. You'll compete and butt heads until you fall stiff with exhaustion to the ground, but you can't admit to each other that you might be wrong, or take back words you've said in anger."

"You're generalizing, Grandma," Crash said, for the sake of argument.

"Ha. I'm generalizing from experience. And my experience has been with you boys and that old codger I married."

Crash continued to look out the window, unable to meet either her gaze or Vanessa's. He felt . . . odd. As if he stood poised in front of two unguarded goal posts without a ball, and yet he'd pushed and fouled and fought desperately to get there. He was padded and helmeted and ready with a snarl—but he had no way to score.

"Dig up the painting *Apology*, would you, dear?" Eugenie spoke to Vanessa. "There. Now flip it over. Christopher, look at it."

He turned reluctantly from the window and its less-than-spectacular view of the parking garage. He took the few steps back to the canvas, which Vanessa had reversed and laid on top of the pile. Hands in his pockets, he stared down at it.

Old Tom had scrawled, "For Chris. Much love, Grandpa."

He stared at the words until they blurred and faded and then came into focus again. And still he stared. He looked at the words until a teardrop, then two and three, fell on top of them. He thought they must be his, and it seemed right and fitting.

Then Vanessa passed her knuckles under her eyes, and he realized with a start that the tears were hers.

"Hey," he said. "Hey, hey, hey." Stupid, inadequate words. "Don't do that, sweetheart. You don't need to do that. Not for me."

She sniffed, pushed her hair out of her face impatiently, and dug into her shoulder bag for a tissue.

He wanted to take her in his arms, but Grandma was perched there in her bed like an inquisitive crow, and he had no intention of throwing her any juicy worms to enjoy. Until he figured out what his feelings for Vanessa were, he'd rather his grandmother remained in the dark. Though, come to think of it, he didn't care for that little lipsticked smirk of hers.

And something else bothered him. "Why didn't you just show these to me months ago, Grandma? Why force me to take Vanessa's seminar?"

"Because you needed to study the whole body of work, in order to understand how atypical these last paintings were. Don't you see? Otherwise, you would have looked at these and shrugged. You would have asked, 'so what?'"

He nodded.

Beside them, Vanessa finally spoke up. "But why, Miss Eugenie, did you keep them from *me*, knowing I was trying to write a definitive, complete book on your husband's work?"

The old lady sighed. "Oh, Vanessa dear, I'm sorry. I wanted to keep the whole tragic story hidden from the public. Then when Crash turned up, I was forced to change my mind. I needed your help."

Vanessa took his grandmother's hand in one of hers, still clutching the wadded tissue in the other. "I'd like to look at these again, if you don't mind. But for now, I'll leave you two to talk."

Eugenie nodded. "You can have all the time

you need to study them. Thank you for understanding, my dear. And thank you for coming."

Crash watched her lithe, jeans-clad figure walk
to the door, and wanted to take her hand and stop
her. Somehow, she belonged here in this room
with him and Eugenie. Her hair streamed down
her back like some bright, coppery emotion, glinting nameless in the light. It was unbound and
generous, straight and true. He wanted to gather
it into his hands and kiss her senseless, but she'd
asked him to back off. For her sake, and for his, he
had to honor that request.

Chapter Thirty

A MONTH LATER, the brilliant autumn sky had turned moody and gray. As Vanessa drove home from the college one afternoon, irritable clouds began to spit nasty little shards of ice that shattered, but clung to her windshield.

Winter was coming to claim the landscape, and she thought of the ancient Greek myth of Persephone. Hades had struck the earth open and claimed her, resulting in the winter of her mother's sorrow.

Hades had gotten hold of Vanessa's spirits, too, and was sitting on them like a fat toad. The only shaft of light she could acknowledge from under this amphibian load of depression was that the semester was almost over. She and Crash would no longer see each other once a week, and that was an excellent thing. Wasn't it?

He'd said that they would reevaluate their relationship in January, but she knew what that meant. He'd be moving on. He might care for her, but he didn't love her, and simple caring wouldn't change a man with that kind of history.

He was quiet around her these days, intensely introspective. She rather missed the old Crash: mocking, irreverent, hell-bent on making her uncomfortable. But he'd changed somehow, and she thought it had everything to do with his stunned discovery that his grandfather had indeed loved him, and had apologized in the only way he knew how.

Miss Eugenie, too, seemed less restless now that she'd discharged a duty she felt she owed to both Crash and her late husband.

Whatever the outcome of this bizarre legal agreement, at least Crash now knew his grandfather's work. She wondered what his final paper would be like. It was stowed in her shoulder bag, along with the rest of the students' papers.

Vanessa navigated the Cruiser through the ever-worsening weather, and breathed a sigh of relief when she turned into her own snug little driveway.

She'd make a cup of hot chocolate and light a fire. She'd grade her papers, then call Shelly.

Three hours later, Vanessa turned over the last page of Crash Dunmoor's final paper and blinked back tears. They were tears of pride and joy, and at the same time tears of loss.

He had written a brilliant paper. Brilliant and evocative, and crafted with a depth of understanding that could only have come from true engagement with subject matter he had wrestled with to the point of exhaustion.

He'd broken through emotional barriers that he'd refused even to recognize at the beginning of her class. And he'd come to an empathetic understanding of the body of Thomas Dunmoor's work.

It was the empathy that made her cry. Men's men like Crash didn't *do* empathy. They did push-ups.

But he'd lowered that fighting jaw of his, reeled it all the way in, and lowered it to introspection. To self-analysis. And then he'd put himself into his grandfather's shoes. He'd walked in those shoes for all twenty pages of his paper, and he'd only stepped out of them when he'd achieved comprehension and even a certain amount of admiration.

"A," she printed at the top. "Congratulations. This is one of the finest papers I've ever read. Vanessa L. Tower."

She thought of Creepy Creighton's face when he saw her grade sheet, and retraced the lines of the "A." She didn't care what he said or did. She wasn't going to grade according to blackmail.

She finished her paperwork for the semester

and recorded all the grades in a personal note-book. It had gotten dark while she worked, and she went to turn on the porch light.

As she passed the darkened dining room win-dows, a familiar figure caught her eye: Deirdre Weinberg was leaving the house across the street. A girl standing inside the doorway waved good-bye. The secret of Conch's snitch was revealed.

Anger boiled in her belly, and she immediately thought of Deirdre's B, the last grade she'd recorded. She was only human, and it would be fairly easy to justify knocking it down a few points. It was only what the little troublemaker deserved.

But marking her down wasn't any better or more honest than marking Crash down. She was paid to evaluate Deirdre as a student, not as a hu-man being. Vanessa turned on the porch light and resolutely turned her back on the house across the street.

Her reward was an unholy, gleeful idea. In mid-December, what else did caring neighbors do for one another but bake cookies?

Since her baking skills left something to be de-sired, Vanessa usually did people a favor and or-dered cakes, pies, or cookies from Shelly. Next morning, however, she turned on her oven with a grin.

While she didn't deliberately try to sabotage the recipe, she also knew that her oven heated unevenly and generally functioned at a good twenty-five degrees higher than it was supposed to.

The resulting sugar cookies were a tiny bit black around the edges, and looked as if they'd just come back from a trip to the Caribbean. She lined a pretty little basket with a napkin, dumped them into it, and walked casually across the street.

The girl who opened the door at her knock assumed a peculiar expression, as if she'd just been sniffing bug spray. "Er . . . hi?"

"Hello!" Vanessa said warmly. "I just wanted to wish you girls a happy holiday." She extended the basket.

The girl blushed to the roots of her hair.

"I'm Vanessa Tower, and I live across the street. You're all students at Seymour College, aren't you? I teach there."

"Yes," the girl managed. "Uh, thank you."

"You're a friend of Deirdre Weinberg's, I believe? Please do tell her I said hello." With a sweet smile and a wiggle of her fingers, Vanessa crossed the street without looking back. *Ha*, she thought with satisfaction. *Now Deirdre will at least sweat bullets until she gets her grade.*

Vanessa got into her car and drove to the college, where she parked and walked to the Fine Arts Building. She entered the familiar smoked-glass doors and traversed the long ugly mint green hallway. The chair's office was at the far end, and her heels made little *clip clops* of echoing doom as she made her way to it.

The grade sheet for her seminar practically smoked a hole in her shoulder bag. She held her head high, since it was shortly to be chopped off—professionally speaking.

She set one foot and then the other shakily into Creepy Creighton's receiving area and managed a taut smile for his assistant.

"Dr. Tower," said the woman, "how are you?"

"I'm fine, Tina, thank you." *Just thinking about a new career as a sanitation worker, or a poodle-groomer.* "Here's my grade sheet for the semester."

Creepy Creighton raised his head from his desk behind Tina and gave her a long, measuring stare. She returned it, hostile and unblinking. He looked back down at his papers.

Vanessa turned on her heel and exited the office.

It didn't take long for the shit to hit the fan. Within two days, Vanessa received a certified letter at her home.

She'd turned on the television so that she wouldn't feel so alone, and so that something would distract her from thinking of Crash. He was history, just like her career. He would move on to another mountain, another casual fling with another woman.

One eye on a mindless Christmas cartoon, she

opened the letter with numb resignation. It was brief and to the point. Allegations had been filed against her in the president's office, charging her with conducting an improper relationship with a student and rewarding that student with a higher grade than he had actually earned. She was asked to explain her actions to the president and a select committee at a specific date and time: namely, on Friday, at ten o'clock. Today was Wednesday afternoon.

On the television, a tubby Santa zoomed down a snowy hill behind eight reindeer.

Vanessa smiled grimly. Dr. Conch, unable to blackmail her, was now challenging the grade and insinuating she'd given Crash an A for dubious services rendered.

"Ho, ho, ho," said the television Santa, waving at her.

'Ho, 'Ho, 'Ho, indeed. She got up and went into the bathroom, staring into the medicine cabinet mirror. No tortured, dyed, deep-fried hair. No tarantula eyelashes. No scarlet harlot's pout.

It was just her, staring glumly at her wire-framed glasses, freckles, and pasty white skin. Yet the president and his committee would believe she was a whore because she couldn't in all honesty deny that she'd had a sexual relationship with Crash Dunmoor.

On screen, Santa and his reindeer dashed

through a quaint little village, tossing red and green packages to bright-eyed little cartoon children.

Yeah, well. She'd oohed and ahhed over Crash's package, hadn't she? And now she was going to pay the price. She'd have coal in her bank account for the New Year.

Vanessa decided that the only intelligent thing she could do at this point was to get drunk. She picked up the phone and dialed Shelly's number.

Chapter Thirty-one

"I *TOLD YOU* that you should have gotten a vibrator," said Shelly, shaking her head.

Vanessa peered solemnly at her friend through the top of her fourth glass of wine. Shelly had two noses, or—whoops, a nose and a half. She wished that sucker would stay still.

Then it became clear to her: actually, it was Shelly's jaw that was moving, but her nose—what a cute nose, really—was trying to keep up. Competition was the nature of things, and that was why you had people out there like Creepy Creighton, cheating to get ahead.

Now, Shelly's nose wasn't cheating, egzackly. But it was competing, moving so fast in order to keep up with Shelly's smart mouth. Hey, Vanessa was beginning to understand Picasso's later work in a truly meaningful way. An eye here, a breast there, an arm on top of a head? It made perfect sense: They were all in competition for the human eye and wanted to be noticed first.

Well, look at that. She was a philosopher. *In vino*, Verdi. Er, *veritas*.

In vino, Viking. Now, Crash, he only had one nose. It might be crooked, but at least it didn't move or blur or shape-shift.

"The beauty of a vibrator," Shelly was saying, "is that you can't fall in love with it."

Huh? *In vino*, vibrator? No, no, no, that definitely didn't sound right. The Romans would object. Vanessa had another sip of wine.

"Sweetie, I'm thinking you might want to switch to water."

"Water," announced Vanessa, "ish the source of life."

"Um, yes it is. You're absolutely right about that. Now drink some." Her friend set a tall glass in front of her.

Vanessa shook her head. "Red, red wiiiiiine," she sang, while Shelly squinted and acquired yet another nose.

". . . can't 'member the next liiiine."

"Oh, God. At least you're a happy drunk, if not a tuneful one."

"I'm not intossicated in the least. I want you to undershtand that. I'm just in love with the wrong guy, and I'm gonna get canned, and it all calls for a sort of reverse celebration, before I have to go to Poodle Manicures 101 to shtart my new career. Got it?"

"Yup," said Shelly. "Now, come on back to my place. We can continue the discussion there."

"Or do you think I'd make a good garbage collector? I bet iss a good workout, hopping on and off the back of a truck like that. And no panty hose requirement . . ."

"Good point. Let's talk about it in the car, okay?"

"Okay."

Vanessa woke with a backhoe digging at her skull. A very large, loud backhoe with huge metal teeth that were gouging holes in her cranium.

A white object emitting steam blurred in front of her nose, and she slowly registered that it was a mug of coffee, extending from Shelly's friendly paw.

"Uuuuunnnnnhhhhh," Nessa whined.

"I know: you'll never drink again. Now sit up and take the mug."

"Ohhhhmmmmmmm."

"Up," Shelly repeated. "Semivertical. Now."

With another pathetic animal noise, Nessa struggled into a sitting position and reached a trembling hand for the coffee. "What did you do to me? I feel like I ate Drano."

"Honey, I didn't do anything. That nice Drano

feeling stems from the fact that you found beer in my refrigerator last night when I got you home."

"Beer? I hate beer."

"Not last night you didn't. Then you made a plate of nachos that defy the normal laws of gastronomy . . ."

"Huh? I don't cook!"

"And that's a damned good thing," Shelly said with feeling. "Because you don't want to know what you put on those poor innocent chips. They were wilted with outrage before you stuck them in the microwave."

"Wh—what did I put on them?"

"Let's see. Ketchup, pickles, thousand island dressing, sour cream, and jalapeños. I think a little horseradish, too. And garbanzo beans, because I didn't have any other kind."

"*Garbanzos?* Shelly, you're supposed to be my friend. Why didn't you stop me?"

"Oh, I tried. You've obviously never encountered yourself drunk."

"But I never drink to excess!" wailed Vanessa. "What is wrong with me?"

Shelly folded her arms. "You're in love."

"Oh, yeah. I forgot about that. It really does weird things to a person."

"Uh-huh. Vanessa, have you even told this Crash character that you're in love with him?"

She spit coffee on herself. "No. And I won't, either. He's not the settling-down sort. He rambles, he hang glides, he jumps out of planes. He goes where the action is."

"I thought you'd been giving him a lot of action."

"That's not funny."

Shelly smothered her grin and shrugged. "Sorry."

Vanessa managed to get her next gulp of coffee down her throat instead of her shirt. "Because I love him, I'd never ask him to change his life. It wouldn't work."

"Hmmmm," said Shelly. "So what are you going to do about tomorrow?"

"I'm going to put on my best suit, and I'm going to march in there with a copy of that paper as evidence that Crash earned his A fair and square. I'm not going to lie, but I *am* going to do my damnedest to take Creepy Creighton Conch down with me for blackmail."

"You go, girl."

"Oh, I'll be going. Straight to the unemployment office . . ."

Chapter Thirty-two

CRASH STOOD in the plane in full gear, ready to make a jump. A spectacular sunlit morning spread out before him, all crisp air and blue sky. Gravity itself seemed to have evaporated with the morning dew, and almost all of his guilt, too.

While he would always regret taking Steven on that fateful dive trip, and forever wish that he had followed him sooner into the old wreck, he felt a lightness in his heart that hadn't been there for years.

He should be packing, not perching on a mountain. He'd made tentative arrangements to head down to Florida, but he was reluctant to finalize things. Grandma Eugenie was sick, after all, and he should stick around to make sure she had proper care. She wasn't getting any younger, and though he didn't like to think about it, the next few months might be the last opportunity they had to spend time together.

Crash tried to avoid thinking about Vanessa, for the most part. Her smile crept into his consciousness, and he often woke up racked with fantasies about her. He could contact her again in January, mere weeks from now.

Yet the idea scared him. His feelings for Vanessa were unlike any he'd had before. They were serious feelings, and he wasn't sure he was ready to settle down. Wasn't it more fair of him to stay away? Allow her the opportunity to meet someone else, a man with whom she had more in common? Wouldn't she be happier with a more stable type, someone with whom she could share scholarly tomes? Someone who wouldn't have this constant need to travel . . .

The thought made him miserable, but it was better than having *her* made miserable.

Crash stared out again into the sunlit blue as the pilot circled the drop zone. Freezing wind roared in his face, but he enjoyed the cold. The thought of Florida and the brilliant sameness of the winter there for once held no appeal. A rented condo infested by someone else's beach décor—ugh.

He thought suddenly of Grandma Eugenie's mellow old Victorian, which undoubtedly needed work. He imagined the kitchen sterile and unused, the fireplaces cold and dark, the front porch needing a paint job. It was wrong for the beautiful old place not to have life in it.

What, are you thinking of moving in there? Yeah, right.

Crash gave a dry, humorless chuckle. Try as he might, though, he couldn't think of a single place he'd rather be than right here in Massachusetts. And he'd been all over the world, from China and Japan to Europe to Australia. What was wrong with him?

Maybe he was getting old. And with that thought, Crash jumped.

Familiar adrenaline surged through his veins, proving that his blood wasn't turning to pudding. And then it vanished just as quickly as it had appeared. He yanked the rip cord, pulling his chute.

Maybe he was growing up. He floated groundward, watching as trees, rocks, bushes came slowly into focus. Or maybe . . .

Maybe he'd fallen in love.

His head jerked back, and his eyes widened. He was in love with Vanessa. The implications were enormous, earth-shattering.

Her sweet, earnest freckled face appeared before him, and he knew he wanted to wake up to that sight each and every morning for the rest of his life. Not only did he love her, but he wanted to marry her. Have children with her.

Crash's eyes glazed over with shock, with joy,

with amazement—and then he hit the ground. Hard and unexpectedly, without his legs bent. It wasn't the earth that shattered, but his knee.

Shelly dropped a queasy, green Vanessa off on Maple Street and made her way to the coffee shop. She felt the familiar surge of pride as the neat, colorful premises of Joe to Go came into view. Soon her little café would have a twin, if Starchie and his plans actually materialized. And then a triplet.

She still found it hard to believe that Giff Smiley was for real. But—speak of the devil, there he was, sitting in that cool old Mercedes-Benz roadster of his in the parking lot behind the building. He'd leaned the driver's seat back, and appeared to be snoozing under a pair of sunglasses that cost more than her heating bill. His dark hair gleamed mahogany in the sunlight, and he looked every inch a lazy aristocrat.

She pulled her ancient Camry into the next parking slot, cut the engine, and got out. She leaned on her roof and removed her own sunglasses, which had cost $12.99 at the local pharmacy. "Hey," she called to Giff, "no vagrants allowed. This is a high-rent area."

He didn't move, just rolled his face toward her with a grin. "Good morning."

"And that jalopy of yours is gonna have to be towed."

Giff stretched his arms like a cat in a window. "My jalopy is a classic, a collector's item."

"Huh," said Shelly, watching his long body unfold from the car. "Maybe once we sign the paperwork, you'll be able to afford a new car."

Giff walked over to her and looked at her over the top of his glasses. He really *was* kind of . . . sexy.

Right, Shel. You think a guy who wears starched jeans is hot? Go give yourself a swirlie in the john and wake up.

"So your lawyer signed off on everything?" he asked.

"Yeah. After I checked your references, who all had a good laugh that I was calling. Honestly, Giff, you could have warned me."

"About what?" They started to walk toward the building's entrance.

"The freaking *Mayflower*? Et cetera, et cetera, et cetera."

"Oh, no. They didn't go into all that, did they?"

"Sure they did. 'And what did you say your name was, dear?'" she mimicked.

Giff laughed. "Oh, that would have been Magda Kent."

"Bingo." She wasn't going to repeat what his last reference had said. *Virgin*?

He removed his sunglasses as they entered the shop, and she stole a look at his eyes.

"Not even," she muttered, stuffing her keys into her coat pocket.

"I beg your pardon? Not even what, Shelly?" Giff asked. "If we're going to be business partners, we may as well speak freely."

Oh, yeah? She felt her cheeks warming, which was a shock. She was sure she hadn't blushed since the age of ten. "Uhhhh," she stalled, unable to think.

"Come on," he teased. "You can tell me."

"Oh, fine. You really want to know? Another one of your references said you're such a nice guy that you're probably still a virgin."

For a moment he was speechless. Then he threw back his head and howled with laughter. "Antonia Chatsworth," he gasped, when he could catch a breath. "And it's not true. Why, have you been wondering about that?"

Shelly really wanted to crawl into the Dumpster outside Joe to Go and never be seen again. Why, why, *why* had she opened her smart mouth? "No, of course not!"

He grinned. "I just declined to ah, do Antonia the honor. We've been friends since birth, and then our families tried to throw us together. It was too weird. She's like my sister."

"Uh, really. You don't have to explain," she muttered.

"No, it's fine." His eyes danced. "I'm the one who told you to call her."

"I'm s-sorry. My mouth gets possessed by the devil sometimes . . ."

"Lucky devil," Giff murmured, his gaze on her lips.

"Excuse me?"

"Oh, I think you heard me."

Her lungs seemed to collapse, and she forced them to expand again. "Giff, I have to ask you a question, and I have to ask it before we sign any papers."

"Sure." He leaned lazily against the wall. "Go ahead."

That's easy for you to say. She swallowed. "You sent me flowers."

"I know, filthy bastard that I am. Appalling. I'll never do it again."

She laughed weakly. "Um. The thing is, I'm not sure you're viewing this arrangement between us as purely a business opportunity, and if that's true, then is it really a good idea for us to, uh, work together?"

"Darling Shelly, are you accusing me of being devious?"

She licked her dry lips and nodded almost imperceptibly.

"Good call. You're absolutely right." Giff beamed at her.

"What? You're admitting it?"

"Of course. Would you rather that I lied to you?"

Shelly blinked. "No, I guess not. But don't you see that we shouldn't go into business together? It's bound to get awkward."

"Why?"

"What do you mean, why? It *will*."

"Shelly. You're automatically assuming that things won't work between us, which is really very cynical of you. No doubt you've had a bad past experience, and one day you'll tell me all about it. But for right now," he stepped close to her and looked into her eyes, "for right now, will you be just a little tiny bit optimistic? Hmmmm?"

Optimistic? About a romance between her, the original Blue Collar Babe, and the Man from the *Mayflower*? "Giff, you're obviously some kind of Boston Bigwig," she said. "I'm nobody. My dad is a plumber, my mom's a dental hygenist . . ."

"Shhhh. My great grandfather was a bricklayer. Shelly, I'm just a regular guy. Give me a chance, will you? I'm more than just a dopey name."

She couldn't help laughing at that. "I've never met anyone like you before," she whispered.

"And you never will again," said Giff. "So take me now, baby!" He traced her cheek with a gentle finger. "I want very badly to kiss you. But for some reason . . . I think I should wait until you kiss me. Would you like to?"

She stared up into his face, absorbing every

word he didn't say. His eyes told her. Chocolate brown eyes that told her he was kind, and patient, and that he would befriend and cherish her no matter what happened. Giff's eyes promised that he would never violate any part of her, neither body nor spirit.

Shelly inhaled the scent of him: expensive soap, warm male skin, and the inevitable starch. It was a calming, soothing scent, one that made her want to slip her hands inside his shirt and lay her cheek against his bare skin. And oddly enough, it was a scent that awakened long-dormant desire within her. Yes . . . it was desire that stretched, yawned, and slowly uncurled. Did she dare stroke it and feed it?

She touched his jaw tentatively, running her fingers over the tiny bristles emerging from his skin. She slipped an arm about his waist, and stood on tiptoe. He bent to meet her, but didn't make any other move.

Her breath caught in her throat, and slowly she touched her lips to his. Giff's arms wrapped around her, and only then did he take command of the kiss, exploring and tasting her, gently nibbling, and finally consuming her with very un–Brooks Brothers abandon.

The instant she put her hands on his chest and pushed, however, he pulled away. Giff Smiley was nothing if not a gentleman.

It was then that her doubts about the situation faded away.

He smiled at her. "So, did you want to sign that paperwork?"

She smiled back. "Yeah," she said. "I do." She looked at her watch. Seven A.M. "I'm sorry, but I'm pressed for time. Can we hurry?"

She didn't dare show up at Crash Dunmoor's cabin until at least eight, but she'd damn well accost him then, before he got away for the day. She wasn't going to let Vanessa face the music alone.

"Why are you in a hurry?" Giff asked, producing the papers from a Ghurka bag that cost more than her mortgage payment.

"I have to go see a man about a mule. A really stubborn one."

Crash was awake, but barely, when a firm knock came at the cabin's door. He scratched his chest, squinted, and cursed viciously at the pain in his leg. Only *he* could have fallen in love from twelve thousand miles in the air and busted his knee on the way.

Finally, he decided that he'd better answer the damned door. Shrugging a sweatshirt over his head, he hopped over and stuck his face out.

The woman on the other side of the door was a knockout, but she wore too much makeup. Women in red lipstick weren't his style. Vanessa, for example, never wore red lipstick . . .

"Hi, Crash. I'm Shelly Zimmer. I'd like to come in."

How did she know his name? And didn't normal people wait to be invited inside a home?

"I'm a friend of Vanessa's."

Crash opened the door fully and gestured her inside.

"She's in trouble, and it's because of you, and the least you can do for the poor woman is to help her out."

"What do you mean, she's in trouble?" He was instantly awake and alert.

The little pistol marched into the cabin and sat in the only available chair, the one with two legs and a runner.

"Please sit down," he murmured. "Would you like som—"

"Do you have any strong black coffee?"

"Coming right up. Now what's this about Vanessa being in trouble?"

"Oh, not physical," said Shelly. She finally seemed to notice the cast on him.

He hopped to get the coffee, not waiting for her to comment.

She jumped up. "I'll get it. What happened to your leg?"

Crash waved her away. "Enlightenment at the wrong moment."

"Uh-huh. Well, whatever."

"So go on."

"That cretin of a chair tried to blackmail Vanessa, and when that didn't work, and she gave you an A—"

"She gave me an A? Very discerning of her."

Pistol Shelly glared at him. "Would you let me finish?"

Crash raised his brows. He didn't think there was anything short of murder that would stop her.

"To make a long story short, the chair found out somehow that you two have been bumping uglies, and . . ."

Bumping uglies? Now that was a vile way to put it.

". . . he's turned her in to the president's office, suggesting that she gave you the A for services rendered. So tomorrow she has to go in front of some committee and defend her actions. I think you should be there."

Crash hopped back over and handed her a cup of black coffee. "I think so, too," he said.

"Oh." Shelly blinked, looking almost disappointed that she wasn't going to have to bully him into going. "She's probably going to get fired for becoming involved with a student, and I know she won't lie about it."

"She won't lie about it," he said, "but I'll make sure that she doesn't get fired."

Shelly eyed him with cynicism. "Oh? And how are you going to do that?"

Crash returned her gaze with what he knew

was an obnoxious smirk. "That's none of your business, sweet pea."

She bristled, and her eyes narrowed. "I know that technically none of this is my business, but Vanessa is a dear friend, and I don't want to see her get hurt."

"Believe it or not, Vanessa's happiness is my highest priority."

She looked at him as if he had three heads. "Oh, really."

"Yes. Now why don't you tell me how you know so much about what I had mistakenly thought was my private life?"

Shelly sighed. "Well, Vanessa had a little too much to drink last night. A lot too much, actually."

"Our prim professor? What was her poison?"

"First it was wine. Then it was beer, followed by a plate of noxious nachos . . ."

Chapter Thirty-three

VANESSA HAD blessedly recovered from her majestic hangover. Green and shivering, she'd watched bad television until her abused body ended its revolt.

Now she lay awake in the small hours of the morning, dreading the upcoming meeting.

Ha, it wasn't a meeting. It was going to be a bloodbath. She wished she had a phalanx of attorneys to take with her, and briefly thought about calling Miss Eugenie.

She quickly dismissed the idea. It would be humiliating enough to disclose her relationship with Crash to the college president and his committee. No way was she going to reveal it to Eugenie Dunmoor as well. Fuhged-daboudit, as Shelly would say.

After fruitlessly trying to fall back asleep, she

got up, took a shower, and toweled off. She stood naked in front of the mirror for a moment, looking at her body. It was an average body, not too fat, not too thin. It hadn't changed since Crash had, er, driven it to peak performance. And neither had her mind. She hadn't degenerated into a fallen woman, a Vessel of Shame.

Why had she ever thought sex could turn her into her mother?

She might be in hot water right now, and she'd made the mistake of sleeping with a student, but she hadn't left a grieving husband and a two-year-old child simply because she'd gotten bored and encountered a tastier man-morsel.

The more she thought about it, her mother's behavior wasn't really a question of sexuality. It was a question of character.

Most women would have put husband and child over self-gratification. Her mother wasn't most women. It wasn't lust that had driven her away, it was some kind of hollowness within her, some kind of search for a more perfect life. She and her father hadn't been inadequate—her mother had. Maybe it was at long last time to stop being a good girl—and become a happy, healthy woman.

Vanessa dressed conservatively, in a navy gabardine suit and stockings. She twisted her hair up and pinned it firmly to her head. She placed pearl earrings into her lobes, adjusted her glasses, and eyed the ugly, serviceable shoes she usually wore with this suit.

No, she decided after a moment. She was not going to defend her judgment or her virtue in yukky loafers. This meeting called for killer heels—the sleek, toe-pinching variety.

She rooted in the back of the closet for them, noting with satisfaction as she slipped them on that they could function as the perfect weapon. If she lost her temper, she could employ the slim, wicked heels to stab Creepy Creighton in the heart.

Pushing the bloodthirsty thought to the back of her mind, she went to her desk and retrieved all her notes and records of the seminar. She also armed herself with copies of Crash's paper, her grading criteria, and the documents signed in front of Miss Eugenie's lawyers.

At nine forty-five, she left her house and drove to the college, parking in front of the president's offices. They were housed in a gray Romanesque building that probably featured a medieval torture chamber in the basement. Vanessa half listened for the scraping of chains as she announced herself to the receptionist.

No moans or shrieks echoed from the bowels of the place as she cooled her heels in a hideously uncomfortable chair, but then any miscreant professors were probably gagged before inquisition and purification by pain.

At last the heavy polished door of the president's office opened, and he gestured for her to enter. He was a tall, broad-shouldered gentleman with a grave expression and no-nonsense eyes. He didn't look like a nasty political good ol' boy. Maybe she stood a chance.

Doubtful. Who was she kidding? Even Stalin had looked like somebody's grandpa.

Vanessa walked to the door, shook his hand, then froze as she saw Creepy Creighton already ensconced in a leather armchair, a cup of coffee in his hand. Wonderful. So he'd been having a nice cozy chat with *El Presidente* before she even got here. Her nostrils flared in anger.

He regarded her blandly from behind his officious navy blue glasses. "Good morning, Vanessa."

"Dr. Tower," she corrected. She would insist on at least the appearance of respect from him.

The president shut the door behind him after she'd politely turned down his offer of coffee. He took a seat behind a massive ornamental desk, and she took the chair opposite Conch's.

"Dr. Tower, as you know, your department head has brought some serious allegations against you."

She nodded, forcing herself to remain calm. At least this meeting only involved the three of them, which indicated that the president wished to keep things hush-hush.

"I'm going to ask for your full cooperation in this

matter. You'll be given the opportunity to voice any objections or give any explanations you deem necessary, but I do ask that you tell the truth. Only if I feel that a full-scale investigation is warranted will the information presented leave this room.

"Dr. Conch alleges that you have had . . . improper relations . . . with a male student who was enrolled in your seminar under unusual circumstances. He also alleges that due to the situation, your judgment about the student's grade is questionable at best. Because a large bequest to the college art museum hinges upon the grade, these allegations are even more serious. How do you respond?"

"Mrs. Thomas Dunmoor placed her trust in me," said Vanessa quietly, "to be objective when it came to her grandson's grade. I have not betrayed that trust—"

Creighton Conch snorted. "She put that trust in you *before* you slept with her grandson."

"Conch," the president said, in warning tones.

"Perhaps you should ask the chair where he comes by his information about my private life."

"Well?"

Creepy Creighton pinkened slightly. "I was informed by another student."

"And that student had irrefutable photographic evidence?" Vanessa prodded.

"Not exactly," said Conch. "But she happened to notice—"

"So essentially you're making these allegations based on hearsay." Vanessa stared him down. Legally, she probably had him there.

"It's not hearsay, and you know it."

The president steepled his fingers on top of the desk. "Dr. Tower, are the allegations true? Did you have an affair with the student in question, Christopher Dunmoor?"

She clenched her hands into fists. She could lie. Lie, and save her dignity and probably her career. They couldn't prove anything without photographic evidence, which they clearly didn't have. She took a deep breath and opened her mouth, but her damned integrity flew out before the lie did. "Yes. I had an affair with Christopher Dunmoor."

An expression of malicious delight crossed Conch's face, along with a glance at her that clearly said he thought she was a moron for telling the truth.

"I'm very sorry to hear that, Dr. Tower," said Seymour's president.

"However," she added, "that affair is finished."

The president shuffled some papers on his desk.

"And I have an allegation of my own, which may cast some light on Dr. Conch's motives for being here today."

Though the president's expression communicated that he thought she was lower than rodent dung, he said only, "Go on."

"Dr. Conch, who was very enthusiastic about the prospect of acquiring the Thomas Dunmoor legacy for the college, came to see me at the start of the semester. He told me that he knew he could 'count on' me not to give Christopher Dunmoor any higher grade than a B."

"That's a preposterous lie!" erupted Conch.

"Quiet," said the president.

"I interpreted this as unfair pressure, and frankly as dirty tactics, but I made the decision to ignore Dr. Conch's statement."

"Around the middle of the semester," she continued, glancing at her notes, "on October 28, to be precise, Dr. Conch came to my office and attempted to blackmail me—"

"A complete fabrication! How dare you—"

"—saying that he knew of the personal relationship between Christopher Dunmoor and me. If I didn't wish that relationship to be exposed, I would give Christopher Dunmoor a B, no matter what his academic performance, so that the college would inherit the Dunmoor collection. I became angry and asked Dr. Conch to leave my office immediately."

"Ridiculous! She's just—"

"Dr. Conch, let her speak."

"Christopher Dunmoor turned in his final paper on the due date, and I read it very carefully. I find it to be excellent work, some of the finest I've ever come across from an undergraduate student. My judgment in this area is not prejudiced or impaired in any way. I stand by the A that I gave this paper and the A I gave him for the semester. You are free to look at his other grades, reaverage them, or read the paper, of which I have brought a copy."

The president cleared his throat. "I had already requested a copy of the paper from your chairman, and I've actually taken the liberty of having it read by two art historians at other colleges. They agree with your grade."

"What!" hollered Conch.

"Dr. Conch, please refrain from comment until I ask for it." The president pushed his glasses up his nose. "The counterallegations that Dr. Tower has made are also very serious, and if they are true, you should be ashamed of yourself. Are they true?"

"Of course not! Dr. Tower is only attempting petty vengeance."

Vanessa looked longingly at one of her wicked heels, but stayed seated and shod.

"I find myself in a dilemma," said the president. "Both sets of allegations are largely based upon one person's word against another's. However, Dr. Tower, you have chosen to admit having an affair with a student, and very clear rules exist in the event of that situation. Clear rules and clear consequences."

A tense silence ensued.

"I regret that I'm going to have to ask for your resignation, Dr. Tower."

Though she knew it was coming, the words knocked the breath out of her, and she sat stunned for a moment.

Then the door flew open behind her. "I suggest that you retract those words," said Crash Dunmoor.

"I beg your pardon!" said the president.

"What are *you* doing here?" said Creepy Creighton.

"Your leg! What did you do to your leg?" asked Vanessa.

Crash leaned on his crutches and glared at all three of them. "This meeting involves me personally, and I'd like to know why I wasn't invited because I have a lot to say."

"You're not an employee of the college," said the president.

"This is a private conference," said Creepy Creighton.

"Oh, Crash, please go away. You're only making it worse for me," Vanessa moaned.

"Who *are* you?" asked the president.

Crash caught the edge of the door with the rubber tip of one crutch and swung it closed in the wide-eyed receptionist's face. "I'm Christopher Dunmoor," he said. "I'm also mad as hell, and I'm going to marry this woman, if she'll have me." He jabbed his other crutch in Vanessa's direction.

They all goggled at him.

"I'm not sure what is going on here," he continued, "except that I earned an A from Dr. Tower, here, which ensures—"

"That's up for debate!" Conch declared.

Crash threw him a contemptuous glance. "Conch? Is that your name?"

Creepy Creighton nodded.

"Conch, if you don't want a crutch through your windpipe, then shut up." Crash bared his teeth at him. "As I was saying, I earned an A from Dr. Tower, which means that my grandfather's paintings will come to me via my grandmother's bequest. However"—he smiled sweetly at the president—"I don't have the facilities to properly house 2.6 million dollars' worth of valuable art. What better institution to care for them, then, than the college that employs my future wife?"

"Now wait just a minute, Dunmoor!" Vanessa felt a mixture of shock, rage, and gratitude.

"If she'll have me," Crash added quickly, bestowing upon her a "just-shut-up-and-we'll-talk-about-it-later" look.

The president looked thoughtful.

Conch looked venomous.

Crash looked pleased with himself.

Vanessa decided she hated all men, most of all Crash Dunmoor.

"Will you have me, sweetheart?" he asked her.

"I will begin," she said, "by having your head on a platter."

"She'll have me!" he said joyously to the room at large. "Now, Mr. President, you understand that my future wife doesn't normally sleep with her students. But I was"—he hung his head modestly—"irresistible."

Vanessa choked.

"It was true love, you understand."

"Absolutely." The president nodded. He was no fool.

"Now, Seymour College is the perfect spot to house my grandfather's work. I really believe that. But I also believe that my future wife, as an expert in the field, should perhaps be endowed with an independent chair for research. What do you think about that?"

"I think that's an excellent idea," said the president in hearty tones.

"And as such, she could still teach if she likes, but would have a flexible schedule and not be answerable to certain vermin in regrettable positions of power?"

"I understand what you mean."

"Oh, good," said Crash, looking delighted. "One other thing: My future wife would require tenure."

"That's viable, too, upon publication of her second book."

"Well, then, if you'll just put all that in writing, I think you have yourself a 2.6-million-dollar deal."

Under Vanessa's outraged gaze, the two men shook hands on it.

"Excuse me, gentlemen," she broke in, "but this happens to be *my* career you two are planning out."

They froze and turned sheepishly toward her.

"Do you, ah, have a problem with what we've discussed?" inquired the president.

"Yes: the fact that I haven't been consulted."

"You don't want the chair?" Crash asked. "Or the tenure?"

"Let me point out that I have *earned* the tenure, through excellent teaching, years of service projects, and writing two books—not to mention numerous articles." She folded her arms across her chest. "While I won't turn down being nominated for a chair, I'd prefer that the nomination go through a committee of my peers and be voted upon."

The president nodded.

She turned to Crash. "And let's get something else straight: I enjoy teaching my classes, and I don't need a man to lighten my load, okay?"

He hung his head. "Sorry."

"As for the vermin in that regrettable position of power . . . perhaps he will simply agree not to harass me in the future."

"I'm sure that can be arranged," agreed the president.

A squawk from the other chair reminded him of Creepy Creighton's presence. He turned his head, and looked down his nose at the man. "Get out of my office, Conch."

Chapter Thirty-four

"HOW DARE YOU?" Vanessa shouted, stabbing her index finger into Crash's chest.

They stood under the portico of the president's building, and he kept grinning like a loon.

"You, you, you *cannot* storm into a private meeting and then blackmail top officials into—"

"Bribe," interrupted Crash. "This was definitely bribery."

"Whatever! You can't sit there and plan out my future like I'm a, a, a chess piece! Who the hell do you think you are?"

"We had this conversation once," he told her. "On the roof of my cabin."

"Shut up, Crash! You're incorrigible. What gives you the right to barge in there and pretend you're going to marry me—"

"Whoa, whoa, whoa!"

"What happens when they find out that no such thing as a wedding is taking place? Huh? Have you thought about that?"

"Well, if you'd prefer just a civil ceremony, I guess that's okay."

"Crash, be serious."

"I've never been more so. I love you, Vanessa. I love you more than life itself. I broke my leg the other day, figuring it all out."

She stared at him, and her lip trembled. "You love me?"

"I love you. Do you love me?"

She stood stunned for a moment. "Yes," she said. "No. No, I'm too mad at you right now to love you. How can I love somebody I want to smack?"

"Vanessa, sweetheart. Do you think you could love me after you beat me into a pulp?"

She nodded.

Crash tossed one crutch to the ground and used the other to awkwardly get down on his good knee.

"Then will you marry a pulpy, bruised man with a broken leg?"

"Yes," she whispered.

He kissed her, deep and hard, and she kissed him back, her anger melting helplessly against his mouth. She couldn't quite believe it: The man she'd had to drag down a mountain, the man whom she'd dubbed "the Louse" upon first sight, was going to be her husband.

She looked up at him, at the stubborn, masculine planes of his face, his green eyes and the impossibly wild tangle of hair. Crash Dunmoor, the legend of her fall.

To marry him in a courthouse would never do. If ever a man required an *uncivil* ceremony, he did.

"Crash?" she said.

"Hmmm."

"When your leg heals, I want you to reread every sky-diving manual in the universe. And then—oh, God, I'm crazy—then, I want to say our vows in a plane over your drop zone. And do a tandem jump when we repeat a mutual 'I do.'"

"But that's dangerous," said Crash. "And besides, the skirt of your bridal gown might fly up over your head, revealing your naughty undies."

"I'd be wearing a bridal flight suit. And how do you know I have on naughty undies?" Vanessa blushed.

"No visible panty lines," said Crash. "So you're either commando, or you have on a thong. I doubt you'd go bare-assed to collect a pink slip."

"A thong it is. Emerald green silk. And I'm serious about the parachuting ceremony."

"Professor, you're getting awfully adventurous for a bookworm."

"It's fun," she confessed. "Of course, you got awfully studious for a wildman."

"And that wasn't half-bad either. Come 'ere, baby," Crash growled, pulling her into his arms for a kiss. "I really want to study that thong you're wearing . . ."

Epilogue

VANESSA GULPED as the plane climbed ever higher. Soon they'd be circling the drop zone and she and Crash would exchange their wedding vows. She told herself that terror was a highly appropriate emotion. Wasn't every bride nervous on her wedding day? And if Crash was willing to risk his newly-mended knee again, she could risk hers.

Aunt Tabitha and Aunt Gertie had refused to go up with them, preferring instead to organize the reception back at Miss Eugenie's old Victorian house. The cancer was in remission, and she was glad to be home. Vanessa and Crash would live on the second floor, keeping an eye on the old lady and her cat, Lancelot.

Her father sat in the back of the plane with his very attractive new lady, Jeanine. His face, behind the beard, gleamed ruddy with excitement and pride.

As the plane banked to the left, Crash took her hand and gestured that they needed to get ready.

"That's my girl!" shouted Papa over the noise of the engines.

She shot him a sickly grin.

Crash squeezed her hand. "I love you."

She nodded. "I love you, too. But oh, God! Why did I ever suggest this?"

Miss Eugenie's minister looked as if he heartily agreed with this question, but he prepared to belt out the fastest, most unconventional nuptial service ever.

Crash hooked his harness to hers in preparation for the jump. "Don't worry," he said. "I've got you, babe."

Chestnuts are roasting by the fire this holiday season,
so curl up with the best in romance from Avon Books

THE IRRESISTIBLE MACRAE by Karen Ranney
An Avon Romantic Treasure

Riona McKinsey is captivated by dashing stranger James MacRae, whose kisses ignite a burning passion deep within her heart. But the dutiful daughter is promised in marriage to another man—and responsibility comes before love. Or does it?

RISKY BUSINESS by Suzanne MacPherson
An Avon Contemporary Romance

When beautiful but klutzy model Marla Meyers takes one spill too many, it becomes Tom Riley's job to keep an eye on her. Yet as passion flares between them, who is going to protect Marla from a sexy heartbreaker like Tom?

THE MACKENZIES: COLE by Ana Leigh
An Avon Romance

The last time Cole MacKenzie saw Maggie O'Shea, she was a scruffy kid with dirt on her cheeks. Now the tomboy is all grown up, but she hasn't outgrown her teenage crush. And she's about to prove to this cowboy how much of a woman she's become.

HER SCANDALOUS INTENTIONS by Sari Robins
An Avon Romance

The dashing Duke of Girard believes Charlotte Hastings holds the key to ensnaring a traitorous villain . . . so he kidnaps the spirited miss and claims her as his betrothed! Charlotte is willing to maintain this ruse, but succumbing to her "fiancé's" sinful charms is another matter.

REL 1102

Don't Miss Any of the Fun and Sexy Novels from Avon Trade Paperback

The Dominant Blonde
by Alisa Kwitney
0-06-008329-8 • $13.95 US • $22.00 Can
"Clever, smart, and sexy. Fast and funny."
Rachel Gibson, author of *Lola Carlyle Reveals All*

Filthy Rich
by Dorothy Samuels
0-06-008638-6 • $13.95 US • $22.95 Can
"Frothy and good-natured . . .
it's part *Bridget Jones Diary*, part *Who Wants to Be a Millionaire*."
New York Times Book Review

Ain't Nobody's Business If I Do
by Valerie Wilson Wesley
0-06-051592-9 • $13.95 US • $20.95 Can
"Outstanding . . .[a] warm, witty comedy of midlife manners."
Boston Herald

The Boy Next Door
by Meggin Cabot
0-06-009619-5 • $13.95 US • $20.95 Can

A Promising Man (and About Time, Too)
by Elizabeth Young
0-06-050784-5 • $13.95 US

And Coming Soon

A Pair Like No Otha'
by Hunter Hayes
0-380-81485-4 • $13.95 US • $20.95 Can